HOLLYWOOD CAR WASH

HOLLYWOOD CAR WASH

❁

A Novel

Lori Culwell

ASJA Press
New York Lincoln Shanghai

Hollywood Car Wash

ASJA Press
an imprint of iUniverse, Inc.

iUniverse books may be ordered through booksellers or by contacting:

iUniverse
2021 Pine Lake Road, Suite 100
Lincoln, NE 68512
www.iuniverse.com
1-800-Authors (1-800-288-4677)

This is a work of fiction. All of the characters, names, incidents, organizations, and dialogue in this novel are either the products of the author's imagination or are used fictitiously.

ISBN: 978-0-595-44116-7

Printed in the United States of America

Prologue

❁

It's not like Sondra Smith and I were ever best friends. I'd arrived at her office several hours after my first table read, which was exactly three days after my first trip to Los Angeles. I was already having a big week.

"Ms. Smith?" I said timidly, poking my head into her office. "I'm Amy Spencer? Here for our marketing meeting?" Sondra was a mid-forties power woman with alabaster skin, spiky red hair, and a ton of makeup that looked like it took hours to apply. She even looked intimidating sitting down, which was why I was compelled to end every sentence in a question. "Yes, hello, nice to see you," she said, sounding less than enthused. "Have a seat. We have a lot of work to do."

I plopped myself in the giant leather chair next to her desk. She looked at me for a long moment, sighed, and began.

"Listen," she said. "I don't want to make you uncomfortable, but you're going to need to tell me anything and everything about yourself, so I can design an appropriate outreach strategy to the media. Once the show launches, we're basically going to make you into a brand. We want to put you in the position to be the next Hilary Duff or Lindsay Lohan, you know? They both got their start in television."

With that, she reached into a sleek black leather portfolio, pulling out a pad of white paper and a typed list. "We're just going to go over a few basics about your life, so I can decide which angle is best for you. Do you have anything major in your past that we should know about? Siblings in trouble with the law? Any uncles in jail in Tijuana?" She attempted to lighten the mood with a short laugh, but it came out a little like a grunt.

I drew in a breath. I **had** checked the "deceased" box under Father on the paperwork from the network, but I didn't know if that information had made its way to Sondra.

"My dad ... died." I said slowly.

"Of what?" she said, then quickly, "I'm so sorry." Then again. "Of what?"

"He ... had a heart attack," I said. "It was two years ago."

Sondra's face remained expressionless, and she barely looked up. "Were there drugs involved, or any other kinds of issues? Is there anything else that's going to come up later about this?" She grimaced, scribbling feverishly on her pad.

Anything else that's going to come up about this? Did she mean my feelings? "No ... it was a heart defect," I said. Why were we still talking about this? Did she also want to know about the coma, and the ICU, and the mountain of hospital bills that didn't stop coming even after he died? I felt my face getting hot.

"No, he had a congenital defect," I said. "He was forty-six, and he had a heart attack." I willed myself not to cry. She pretended not to notice.

"I'm not trying to sound harsh, but I don't want the **Enquirer** going to your hometown, digging up some dirt about how your dad was really a crazy drug addict who had just been released from prison and was doing speedballs in front of your local strip bar, and that's what caused his death ... do you know what I mean?"

I resisted the urge to jump across the desk and strangle her. "He had a heart attack on the way home from work," I said. Then, more assertively: "That was it. Can we talk about something else?" My face ached from fighting back tears. "Let's move on."

She paused for a moment, and I wondered if she was going to push it even further. "What about you? Do you have any medical issues?" she said. "Anything that we might have to spin later, like Marcia Cross with her migraines, or Camryn Manheim with her Rheumatoid Arthritis, or Linda Hamilton, with her bipolar disorder?"

I let out the breath I'd been holding, thankful that she'd moved on from the subject of my dad while at the same time impressed with her near-encyclopedic knowledge. "No, none of that stuff. I'm fine, but I'll let you know if I start to feel sick," I joked.

Nothing. No reaction. Maybe she was frozen by Botox, and was laughing inside. She looked down at her list.

"OK, what about sex?"

"What about sex?" I said, mentally gearing up for another mini-drama.

"I mean, have you had it?" she said, looking up across the desk. "I'm just trying to suss out whether or not to work the whole 'Jessica Simpson/Britney Spears/ cast of *Seventh Heaven* I'm a virgin' angle, since your character on the show is supposed to be sixteen. It's a stance some of the girls want to take. We can try it, but it's a little hard to back down off of if someone comes out of the woodwork and said you had some wild spring break weekend with them, or anything like that."

I made a mental list. Virginity = lost to high school boyfriend during prom of junior year. Subsequent experiences = Charlie, co-star in freshman year production of *Hamlet* at Hudson. Henry = summer romance between freshman and sophomore years. So, three. Not bad, not terribly slutty, but definitely nowhere near Jessica Simpson territory.

"Yes, I've had it. Probably not with anyone who would talk to the *Enquirer*." I said finally, attempting to answer the question while giving her as little information as possible. Why was this her business?

"OK then … what about videotapes? Don't want those coming back later to haunt us."

"Oh my God!" I squealed. "I'm from Bay City, Michigan. We don't videotape ourselves having sex in Michigan, okay? These questions are crazy." Was this some kind of test?

"OK, OK … she said. "Listen, it's better for everyone if we're just open about everything from the beginning. Then we have a strategic plan ready to go for when it comes out. The one thing we cannot tolerate is being blindsided because you've kept something from us. The more information you give us, the more we can help you." She finished up with a little nod, as if to signify the end of this tender moment.

"What about beliefs? She continued. "Are you a strict vegetarian, or a vegan like Alicia Silverstone, or macrobiotic like Gwyneth Paltrow? Do you not wear shoes made of leather, like Moby? This is something we need to tell the stylist, who you'll definitely need to see sooner rather than later. Also, we might be able to work that angle in the media, like in the *Vegetarian Times*. Chris Martin was voted "World's Sexiest Vegetarian" by PETA, for instance. Just make sure if you're going to claim you're a vegan, you don't get photographed eating a hamburger. Those people are militant when you betray them."

"Nope … I love steak." I said.

She didn't look up from her list. "Religion? Are you a militant Baptist or something? Were you raised in a commune, are you a Christian Scientist, or do you have any relatives that are Jehovah's Witnesses? Religion itself is not necessarily a bad thing, but those groups are very likely to pop up out of nowhere at critical times in your career and 'claim' you." She seemed serious.

"It's fine," I said. "I was baptized Lutheran, but I haven't been to church in awhile."

Finally, she was done with her 'questions' list and seemed satisfied that I had no major skeletons in my closet.

"We'll need to meet again before the show premieres, but I think we're going to try to market you as an "overnight success Cinderella story," like Kimberly Williams when she was cast in *Father of the Bride* in the early nineties," she said. "Everybody loves a rags to riches story … one minute you're shucking corn in some field in Iowa and the next you're the star of a Hollywood TV show!"

I didn't bother mentioning that, in fact, I was from Michigan, and that I had never even been in a cornfield. Somehow, the real details of my life seemed less important by the moment.

SEASON ONE

CHAPTER 1

❀

Really, if it hadn't been for my perky college roommate and her obsession with Spinning class, none of this would have happened in the first place. In fact, I wouldn't have found out about the audition if it hadn't been for Carrie Ann and her annoying habit of getting up so early, which had led her to wake me up at 11:30 am on a Monday in February, three years earlier.

The door of our room closed with a loud *thud* and she flipped on the light, perhaps to spite me.

"Amy! Wake up! You're going to be late!" She said, perkily.

I groaned. How one could at once be an early riser and a theater person was beyond me. I could tell she'd already been out in the world doing productive things while I was still sleeping off an all-night student film shoot that had gone on well past four a.m., and I resisted the urge to smack her in her already showered and made-up glory. People should not be allowed to be chipper before noon, I thought. At least not people who live in the fine arts dorm.

She redeemed herself by producing coffee and a huge muffin from a bag. I decided to speak to her again.

"What are you talking about?" I said, glancing over at the clock. "It's Monday, right? I don't have to be anywhere until three thirty. I have voice class, then English."

"I know that," she said. She was breathless with excitement. "There's an audition on the bulletin board for a TV show! You have to go right now ... I signed you up for the first slot."

I laughed. "You signed me up for that bogus TV show thing? When I actually wake up, you are so dead." I attempted to cover up my head with a pillow to block the florescent dorm room light. A "modeling and acting school" had been posting the same fake TV show audition for months. I thought everyone in the department knew this.

She rolled her eyes. "It's not that one," she said insistently. "You have to go! You would be so perfect!" Carrie Ann perched herself on the edge of my bed. She and I had been roommates since freshman year—a situation that worked out, in part, because we were so different we had never competed for a role. At 5'1" with a head of curly red ringlets, Carrie Ann never met a musical she didn't like. I, on the other hand, was tall, had dark hair and pale skin, and fancied myself a cross between Parker Posey and Hope Davis in terms of being a serious indie film actress. We were the drama department's version of "The Odd Couple."

I sat up. "It's probably an audition for some Stuckey's commercial. Now seriously—go away."

Undeterred, she kept bouncing on my bed. "You *say* that, but if you really want to be in indie films, you have to be willing to do anything! I would take ANY part on Broadway, just to get myself there. I would sweep floors! Remember what Mark Twain said about being ready to be lucky. You have to be ready! Plenty of well-known indie actors have been on TV! Michelle Williams was in **Dawson's Creek**, Parker Posey was on **Boston Legal**, and even your beloved Philip Seymour Hoffman was once on **Law & Order**, if you'll recall." She seemed prepared to go on this way *ad infinitum*.

"OK, stop!" I said. "It was E.B. White who said that thing about being 'ready to be lucky,' not Mark Twain." I huffed myself out of bed and pulled on a sweatshirt, hoping maybe she'd be gone when I got back. I knew she was right; I was just tired and cranky.

I shivered in the still-cold winter air as I sprinted to the drama department from the dorm, stopping to check the bulletin board. Hanging from the middle of the board was a typewritten sign, with a signup sheet attached.

Audition
<Untitled Television Project>

Women age 18–20
Fresh-faced, Midwest types
Monday (yes, today!)
Auditions start at 12:00 pm SHARP
Bring any photos
Dialog provided

The audition notice had already attracted a lot of attention. Depressed-looking drama types had begun to crowd around the bulletin board.

"Is it a lead?"

"I don't know … it doesn't say."

"It's probably extra work … my cousin was an extra in *War of the Worlds*, and he had to stand in the freezing rain for seventeen hours. He said it sucked. There was almost a lawsuit and everything."

"Are you going to do it?"

"No, man … I'm staying true to my craft. Besides, they're not going to cast a real-looking person from Michigan for a Hollywood TV show. Never gonna happen."

I pushed through the crowd and into the main theater, where I'd starred in a production of *Miss Julie* the semester before, hoping to get in and out before anyone I knew spotted me there and mocked me.

As I walked down to the stage, I saw Jody Barker, one of my acting teachers, who was running the audition. "Hi Amy," she said, smiling and handing me a bunch of stapled-together papers. "Glad you're here. We're just going to ask you to do this dialog … I'll read along with you. Some brief background—this character's parents have been killed, she's just found out, and she's now going to have to go live with her gay uncle, whom she's never met before. This scene is at her parents' funeral, where she meets her uncle for the first time."

I drew in a sharp breath when I heard the word "funeral." This was definitely not something I wanted to be thinking about. I just woke up, I thought. I am not ready for this.

For a moment, I was frozen. Theater was usually where I stopped thinking about my dad. Besides, I wasn't at all sure I wanted to get out these emotions and use them for a TV show audition. Weren't some things supposed to be off limits?

"Amy, are you okay?" said Jody. "We need you to start."

Her voice snapped me back to reality. Maggie Gyllenhaal would never let something like this get to her. She'd use the emotion in her performance. I took a deep breath and looked down at the script.

As I read over the lines, I decided that instead of giving the typical "hysterical crying" audition they were probably expecting, I would go for the most realistic portrayal possible, even though a totally real performance was unlikely to even get me a callback. I fumed inside—TV people who wrote some melodramatic show wanted to see what it was like to get news like that, I thought, I would show them. Tragedy of that magnitude doesn't make you hysterical, in fact—it just crushes you, and ends up making you feel like there's a wall between you and the rest of the world. Perhaps they'd enjoy seeing that—I'm sure their show was all about the "black depression" phase of accepting a parent's death; that really sounded like good TV.

I thought back on what I was doing when I got the news about my dad, read the lines, and before I knew it, the audition was over and I was on the way to lunch. While I was eating, I actually laughed about how stupid it was to make a show with that premise, and how wrong they were going to get the portrayal of the character. I would never watch that show, I thought. Not in a million years.

❦   ❦   ❦

Two days later, I was sitting in Abnormal Psych class, willing myself to stay awake through a lecture on "*pica*, a mental disorder that causes sufferers to eat dirt and cigarette butts" when I heard my cellphone ring in my backpack. I lunged for it, scolding myself for leaving it on. Because it was faster to just answer the phone then try to turn it off, I tried to answer with my head inside my backpack.

"Hello?" I whispered frantically. "Hold on one second." My Abnormal Psych professor had promised an instant "F" to anyone who talked on a cellphone during his lectures; rumor had it that even the buzzing of a phone turned on vibrate would set him off. I ran up the stairs and out of the lecture hall.

"This is Shannon from the drama department," said the voice in the phone as I made it outside and closed the door. "Can you come into the office right now to meet with Dr. Simon?

"Of course," I said, intrigued. This was definitely preferable to the horrors of Abnormal Psych. Dr. Ellie Simon, dean of the drama department, was one of the coolest professors on campus. Twenty minutes later, I walked into the drama department office. "Hi Dr. Simon," I said, poking my head in the door. "You called?"

She looked up, taking off her funky black glasses to reveal kohl-rimmed eyes. Maybe she was my mom's age, but you could never tell. "Amy—come in. Sit down."

If Hudson University had a "rock star" equivalent, that would be Ellie Simon. A renegade actress/punk/writer/performance artist from New York, she had worked with the Wooster Group, the Ontological Theater, and La Mama, to name a few, and was supposed to be a personal friend of David Mamet's. She was one of the most popular professors in the drama department, and in my estimation, a one-woman antidote to my mother's theory that "no one can make a living in the arts." Her production of **Miss Julie** the semester before had made history in the drama department by selling out every night and getting a rave review by the local paper, which praised my "haunting ability to capture grief onstage." This performance had led to my being cast in the cool student film I'd just finished. I felt like I was on my way, and I owed it all to her.

"Is this about the honors program?" I said. "I'm almost done with my application." In reality, the application was sitting under a pile of laundry in my closet, and was on my "things to do" list, right under "do laundry."

She smiled. "Actually, this is about your audition on Monday. Last week, I got a phone call from Kim Wilson, one of my old friends from New York. She's a casting director in Los Angeles now. They need a good actress who looks like she's actually *from* the Midwest to star in a new show with a pretty progressive concept—like a **Six Feet Under** meets **Felicity** meets **Queer as Folk**. Actually, she's been working on the project for awhile … the actress who was starring in it just got fired. Kim couldn't find anybody else to replace her, so she called me. I sent the tapes yesterday, and Kim called this morning. They loved your audition, Amy. They want to fly you out to Los Angeles to meet with the producers of the show. You've made it to the last part of the audition process."

For once, I was actually speechless. "Is there some mistake?" I said, in disbelief. "I don't even … I mean, I don't … sorry, what are you talking about?" I stammered. My mind flashed back to the "dead parents" audition. Great, I thought. Just what I need. The thing I don't want gets me a callback.

She smiled. "I know, you have a lot of questions, and this is all happening really fast." She opened up her desk and pulled out a thick manila envelope. "All of the information is in here."

"Is anyone else from the department going?" I said, mostly because I couldn't think of a better response. My mind was still racing. Did they seriously want to portray real people feeling real emotions about death on a network TV show? Maybe it had been too long since I'd watched TV.

"OK, great … thanks!" I said, gathering up my stuff. "I'll call you if anything exciting happens."

Maybe she could tell what I was thinking. I was almost down the stairs of the drama department building when she called back to me from the door. "Oh … Amy? I'd recommend not mentioning the fact that you don't watch TV while you're in L.A.." She smiled. "These are good people, they have good writers, and from what I've read, it's going to be a show that even *you* might watch. What I'm saying is … this is a really good opportunity, Amy. Don't blow it."

I laughed. "You know me too well," I said, giving her the thumbs up. "I promise to behave myself, and to not mouth off about bullshit TV *or* get a boob job while I'm in Los Angeles. I will make you proud."

I took the long way back to the dorm to try to sort through my thoughts … was it creepy to be going on an audition where I played a character whose life so closely mirrored my own? Was I exploiting the situation? **Should** I have been exploiting the situation? Wouldn't repeatedly revisiting those emotions put me in a permanently depressed state? Was it wrong to sell my emotions to a TV show? Was I getting ahead of myself? I finally decided that an all-expenses paid trip to L.A. couldn't be bad … the odds against getting the part were probably huge anyway, so it couldn't hurt to take the free ticket … maybe I could meet Richard Linklater or Cameron Crowe in a coffee house, and they could give me my big indie film break.

I more than anyone recognized the irony of the situation. I was not "LA" in any sense of the word. I shopped in thrift stores. I loved indie films. I delighted in my pale skin. Because I'd promised to suspend my hatred of the Hollywood bullshit machine for forty-eight hours, I found myself with absolutely nothing to wear.

Two hours later, I was standing in front of my closet in a panic, attempting to pack for L.A. The floor of my tiny dorm room was covered with every piece of clothing I'd ever owned, and I was still not confident about my look. What, exactly, does one wear to a Big Hollywood TV Show Audition?

❀　　　❀　　　❀

"Aim, go with a little skirt and a tank top. You don't want to look overdone."

My best friend Vincent Ferrillo, an aspiring stylist, had been at work on my wardrobe since getting my emergency phone call on my way back to the dorm. He'd shown up with a toolbox full of makeup, a set of hot rollers, and a stack of old *Vogue* magazines under his arm.

"Vince, she said they wanted someone who looks like they live **here** … Don't you think I'm going to look ridiculous if I try to look like I'm from California? Then again, what if they said "Midwest, but they really meant "Hollywood Midwest? Who even knows what they're thinking?" I laid down on a pile of clothes, flummoxed. For the first time in years, I wished that I was more in touch with what people on TV were wearing.

"Definitely the Hollywood Midwest," said Vince emphatically. "Who would do a series about real people who live here? I mean … look around you, Amy. "My God," he whispered in a hushed stage voice. "Did you SEE the photos in the campus paper this week of the spring formal? Tragic! We are leaving here as soon as possible, lady! Get going and blaze the trail to the promise land! Now, decide on an outfit, so I can give you a crash course in *People* and *US Weekly* gossip. Finally—all this information will come in handy."

I laughed. Vince always knew how to make me feel better. I even let him tell me about who Paris Hilton and Nicole Richie were, and why he had a mad crush on a blogger who'd named himself after one of them.

CHAPTER 2

✾

My cell phone rang at five-thirty the next morning. I was barely asleep and answered it right away. "Hello? Are you downstairs?" I whispered frantically. It was so early, my face felt like a potato. "Car service arriving for Amy Spencer in 15 minutes," said the woman on the line.

Even Carrie Ann was still asleep, her red hair fanned out on the pillow like a big red flower. I couldn't believe a driver was waiting to pick me up, and Little Miss Excitement wasn't even awake to see it.

I threw the remaining clothes still strewn on the bed into my suitcase, zipped up my backpack, and headed for the door, trying to make as little noise as possible. Carrie Ann raised her head sleepily at the click of the doorknob. "Break a leg," she said, her head falling back onto the pillow heavily. I really wished she could go with me. I needed the moral support on my trip to Plastic Land.

Out in front of the dorm, it was so dark the streetlights were still on, and the buildings looked like sleeping giants. The car pulled up slowly, looking for me. "This is crazy," I thought. "Is this really my life?" I took a deep breath as I slid into the back of the car, determined to be as Zen as possible.

I wanted to not like First Class so much, but it made me feel like Cinderella. My parents had always been frugal types, and so they would never have dreamed of flying first class, even if they could afforded it. As I walked onto the plane and sat down, I thought of our annual Florida family vacation—my mom, my dad, and my younger brothers, all crammed together in coach, too much carry on luggage, too many wriggly kids. Then I thought about my mom and brothers, sleeping in our house in Bay City—I hadn't even called to tell them what was going on.

       ❧   ❧   ❧

That afternoon, I opened the door of the casting office and walked into a crowd of the most beautiful girls I'd ever seen in person. Each and every one of them was over 5"10, had long hair and perfect skin, and looked about fifteen years old. Tall, giraffe-like girls languished against the walls, in the doorway, and in every corner, like I'd landed on a planet inhabited solely by beautiful mutant aliens, and I was the sole colonizer from the Land of Normal People. I stopped myself from laughing out loud.

If this is my competition, I thought, I am leaving right now. I wanted to tell someone in casting that I had never seen a girl that looked like any of these girls in Bay City, except for one tall, thin girl named Natasha who supposedly moved to Japan to model and was never heard from again. One thing was clear: if any of these girls were what they were really looking for, this was going to be a very short trip.

"Amy Spencer?" said a voice from within the Sea of Gorgeousness. I turned around to see a short white girl with black and purple dreadlocks, chunky bracelets, and an underbite sitting at a desk with a clipboard. Her arms were covered in tattoos, and she had a pierced eyebrow. I moved toward her with relief. Perhaps she would be able to lead me to safety.

She smiled. "I'm Lisha," she said.

"Is this my audition?" I said, still mortified. "Is there some mistake?" She seemed like a normal person, so I considered telling her that the mere presence of so many beautiful girls was not only statistically abnormal, but was kind of freaking me out.

She looked around and laughed. "No, this is a different casting call … they're trying to find the one model in all of Hollywood that actually has rhythm. It's not going well, as you might imagine. Your audition is next door, in the main office. Don't worry … I'll make sure you don't get lost in the beautiful girl forest." She smiled.

I followed Lisha out of Model Land and down the hall. "Bizarre, isn't it?" She said. "But, I guess if you're abnormally tall with wide set eyes and perfect skin, what else are you going to do but become a model? You can't play basketball, and people stare at you all the time, so you might as well try to pimp yourself out while you're still young enough."

"Right," I said, laughing. "Did they tell you any of their model trade secrets?

"Well, I did just learn the disturbing fact that if you eat toilet paper, it makes you full and it just comes right out in your poop," she said.

"What? Are you serious? That is … sick and somehow fascinating," I said, taking mental notes for my upcoming Abnormal Psych paper. An interesting mixture of pica and anorexia, for sure. Picarexia, maybe?

Lisha knocked on one of the doors in a non-model inhabited office. "Kim?" she said. "Amy's here. Are you ready for her?" She motioned me into the room. "OK … goodbye! Nice to meet you," I said, fearful that my new friend was leaving me.

"Oh, don't worry" she said. You'll be seeing me a lot over the next few days."

Kim Wilson was a gorgeous African American woman with skin the color of caramel, shoulder length brown hair, and a gigantic diamond wedding ring. She was immaculately dressed and smelled like expensive perfume, and she had a motherly vibe that put me at ease. She took me into her office and closed the door. "I'm so glad to meet you!" she said enthusiastically. "We really liked your tape."

I sat down in her office. "At this stage, we have what's called a working session, which is with the creator of the show and the director who's going to be working on the pilot," she explained. They'll want to see how well you can think on your feet. So … do you think you're ready to meet the producer and the director?" she said, leading me into a room even smaller than the Studio Theater at my drama department.

In the corner of the room sat two men, who stood up when I came in. One was maybe forty, tall with dark hair graying at the temples and kind blue eyes. The other was shorter, with a shock of white curly hair and a beard. "This is Amy Spencer," she said. "Amy, this is Josh Stein, the creator of **Autumn Leaves**," and the dark-haired man smiled and extended his hand. "Nice to meet you, Amy … we loved your tape," he said. "I'm Paul Jones," said the white-haired man, "I'm going to be directing the pilot. We're just going to do a working session today, to see how you deal with the script, take direction, that kind of stuff. If all goes well, we'll take you to studio, then to network to test."

I couldn't begin to think of the right thing to say, so I shrugged.

"Overwhelmed yet?" said Josh, laughing. His smile reminded me of my dad.

"A little … it's been sort of a whirlwind," I said.

"This is the same scene you did on the tape, only it's more of the script … you've just found out your parents were killed in a plane crash, you go to the funeral, and in the next scene, you have to decide where you're going to live. This next part is when you find out about your gay uncle, and how he and his partner want to adopt you." He smiled. "You really captured the emotion that we're looking for in your audition tape." He looked over at Paul. "Everyone else has been was too … hysterical. You know what I mean?"

"Yes … I do." I said quietly. "I'm glad you liked it."

We read the scenes, then Paul asked if I could improv.

"Like, comedy?" I said. "I can try … but where does improv comedy fit into this show …" trailing off, I could feel them both looking at me, and my face turned red. I am so not getting this part, I thought.

Paul smiled warmly. "We'd just like to see you improvise a dramatic scene, without words, with these chairs as your parents' coffins. Think of whatever you want … just try to convince us of the feeling. A lot of the effect this show is going to be communicated through close-ups on Autumn's face, and we just want to see how you do in the quiet moments, when there's no dialog."

I couldn't tell if he could see the horror on my face as he described this impro-vised scene. Before I could chicken out, I sat down in a chair and basically re-enacted exactly what I was doing at my dad's funeral, for better or worse. And just like that, the working session was over, and Kim was walking me toward the door. "Good job," she said, putting her hand on my arm. "You're really good."

❦ ❦ ❦

Later that same day, I was in a beautiful hotel room (also paid for by the studio) when my phone rang. It was Kim, with good news. "Listen," she said. You're going on to the next level—to the studio to test, then to network if they like you. You're getting really close, Amy ... this is great! Now ... do you have an agent? You need someone to negotiate the terms of your contract on your behalf."

I gripped the phone so as to not drop it from sheer surprise. "I ... don't have an agent," I said slowly, resigning myself to the reality that this meant I would have to go back to Michigan immediately. "Can I not go to the next audition?" I heard myself say. I was disturbed that I suddenly cared so much about this.

She laughed a hearty laugh. "Now that's a problem I can actually solve—any agent would want a piece of this contract if you get the job. Just leave your phone on, and I'll have my friend Todd call you. He's an agent at William Morris."

What seemed like a minute went by, then the phone rang again. "Hello?" I said.

"Amy Spencer?" said a chipper voice. "This is Todd Whitley. Kim told me you need representation, and I'm happy to step in on your behalf."

Then he started talking. There was no time to ask questions, or even to get a word in edgewise. "Listen ... Kim faxed me over the preliminary contract, and I'm glad I came in when I did, because the numbers were really looking a little thin. This network loves to screw new actors that don't have any credits. They've got you on a fifteen thirty deal with a two banger. If you were my client, which for right now you are, I'd say no to this. Can I say no to this?"

"Um ... yes?" I said nervously, not wanting to sound like I just got off the plane from Michigan. Which, of course, I did. When did getting this part suddenly become so important?

"OK great," he said. "I'll call you back if we hit any snags, but there shouldn't be any problems. I've worked with these guys before, and I'm pretty sure I can get them up to twenty forty at least, with a three banger and a suite guaranteed. Talk to you tomorrow! Break a leg, Amy Spencer!"

❦   ❦   ❦

By 9:00 the next morning, I was walking through the lobby of the most beautiful building I had ever seen, following a Gucci-clad assistant in stiletto heels to the board room for the next audition. She led me to the lobby, where I got nervous all over again.

Other people in the waiting area included:

—An impossibly thin, tan girl with tiny hips, long, perfectly straight blonde hair, and sparkling blue eyes (possibly a model, definitely successful at something).

—A similarly beautiful brunette with giant green eyes and curly hair that went halfway down her waist.

—A very tall girl with stripey brownish-blonde hair who looked vaguely familiar

—A dark-haired girl with big pouty lips.

—An older man with bushy eyebrows, who I definitely recognized from movies.

—A girl who looked like Dakota Fanning. Or maybe it was Dakota Fanning.

A mid-thirties brunette with a blunt-cut bob haircut and a square jaw emerged from behind a closed conference room door. She was wearing a beautiful black suit, had perfect red lipstick and tiny round glasses, and was carrying a stack of thick manila envelopes.

"Hello everyone," she said as she found each person and gave them their respective envelope. "Thank you all for coming. First thing, we'll need you to sign the contracts. In case you're not familiar with how it works, this is your offer for employment. If you are offered the role, it becomes a binding contract and you go to work. If you are not, this contract is null and void, and you are released from further obligation. We will ask you to stay through the length of everyone's audition, in case the producers want to see one of you again. Your agents will let you know later in the day if you'll be advancing to the network."

I opened my manila envelope and pulled out the contract, which was legal size and covered in red and blue "sign here" stickers, along with an expensive-looking black pen, which I made a mental note to steal whether or not I advanced to the next audition. What's the difference? I thought. It's probably all just a fluke anyway. Who cares? I unscrewed the black pen and folded the bottom half of the contract over, preparing to sign.

My nonchalance went out the window a moment later when I got to the bottom of the first page, where the salary was detailed next to a yellow and red SIGN HERE arrow. Because I didn't know what to look for, my eyes went straight to the numbers. I read the passage three times, remembered my phone call with Todd from the day before, and finally put it all together.

$40,000 for the pilot ... $20,000 for each episode thereafter, for a total of twenty-two episodes ... increase contingent upon sale of show ... increase contingent upon success and renewal of show ... increase contingent upon syndication....

My heart began to beat so loud, I was sure the perfect blonde next to me could hear it. I looked around at all the other actresses as they looked at their contracts. Why did they all look so calm? Were they seeing what I was seeing? I tried to add all the numbers together ... $40,000 for the pilot, $20,000 per episode ... twenty-two episodes. That sounded like almost $500,000, just for the first year. *This* was the "twenty forty" deal Todd was talking about the night before? Was this some kind of joke?

My eyes filled with tears and my lip started to tremble as I thought of the pressure that much money could take off my mom. My dad had had some life insurance, but on a software engineer's salary there wasn't a lot to put away, so his death had left her with three kids and a mortgage. Plus, my dad's health insurance had only covered half of his medical bills, which had reached just over a million dollars. She tried to act like it wasn't too much pressure for her, but I worried about the bags under her eyes and her increasingly thin face. Late at night, when the boys were asleep, she would talk to me about how worried she was. I knew it was too much for her, and I'd been trying to think of a way to help her. Maybe this was it.

Dammit! I thought, trying to focus. I got this far in the audition process because I didn't even want it ... now that I want it, am I going to push it away?

How can you tell if you're doing that? This job could actually save my family, I thought.

I looked up to see Actor Guy staring at me, and as subtly as I could, I wiped the tears from my eyes and tried to get my cool indie chick vibe back. He smiled.

❧   ❧   ❧

After the audition, I got into a cab. I felt like telling the driver "just drive," like Holden Caulfield did in **Catcher in the Rye**. But … do people really do that? Where would we go? Doesn't everyone need a destination, and not just existentially? I couldn't even take a spontaneous cab ride without questioning the very nature of existence.

Finally, I put the cab driver (and myself) out of our collective *ennui* and had him take me to the closest Starbucks, figuring maybe a double latte would create the Ritalin effect, pushing me past the point of excited agitation and back into the "calm zone." Two hours later though, I was still obsessing when my cellphone started to buzz. One more latte and I could've answered the phone with the power of my mind.

This could be it … don't sound too eager … was it wrong to want this?

"Hello?" I said, trying not to sound too over caffeinated and desperate.

"Amy Spencer! This is Todd. Good job, girl! You made the cut, and the network wants to see you in an hour. Do you need the address?"

The truth is, I wanted to hate L.A. With every audition and every new person I met, I looked for evidence to validate my theory that Los Angeles was the din of iniquity and bad acting that I'd railed against.

Somehow, though, I didn't see it. Everyone was so nice, the weather was beautiful, and the show seemed like it was going to be really good. Plus, there was the money. Maybe I'd been too quick to judge Los Angeles without getting to know it first. Was I rationalizing, was I seeing the real LA, or had it taken me one day to lose my edge?

Everything was moving so fast, I didn't even have time to make up my mind.

❦   ❦   ❦

Every place I went to was nicer than the last. The waiting area in the network was nicer than any nice house I'd ever seen, in Bay City or on TV.

"Um, excuse me.," I said to the woman at the front desk. "Is everyone here who is going to be here?" I mean … is there anyone else coming?"

She looked at her list. "Nope, just the three of you. Good luck!"

So that was it … Pouty Big Lips, Pin Thin Blonde, and I were the only ones left.

A clone of the well-dressed blonde executive from the studio came out to greet us. "Hello, thanks for coming," she said. "As you probably know, this is the last step—you're going to be meeting a number of executives as well as the president of the network. We're just going to ask you to read some more scenes from the pilot. Please stay until everyone is done, and you'll be hearing from your agents later today, whichever way we decide to go. OK, thanks!"

This time, I was the last to go. As we finished the last scene, I looked down at my watch to see the only promising sign of the day—my audition actually took fifteen minutes, which was more than the other two girls' combined.

❦   ❦   ❦

Three hours after the audition, I was back at the hotel, waiting for The Big Phone call. I had, during that time period, made sure my phone was charged exactly forty-two times, packed and unpacked my suitcase twice, and seriously attempted some "mind over matter" meditation in order to will the phone to ring.

Why, oh why do they show you those big numbers? I thought helplessly. Monday I was happy in my life as a broke college student with a crappy part time waitresssing job. Now it was Friday, I'd been seduced by the possibility of fame and money, and I was going berserk in a Hollywood hotel room, waiting for a call from a guy named Todd.

What had I become?

I paced around the room, making a mental list of things I couldn't do as I waited.

—Couldn't go pee, because what if Todd called with news?

—Couldn't take a walk around the hotel, because what if Todd called with news and I was in an unfavorable cell phone area, causing me to miss the call and possibly causing the part to go to someone else?

—Couldn't go for a drive, because I had no car, and besides, I'd probably get into one of those unbelievable traffic jams and never be able to find my way back.

—Couldn't eat, because I was too nervous, and besides, based on the size of my competition, I shouldn't be eating anyway.

—Couldn't call friends, because, being unsure how to work my call waiting, I usually hung up when I tried to switch over and also, didn't want to cause Todd's call to go to voicemail.

—Couldn't take a nap—too much caffeine.

—Couldn't call Todd.

—Couldn't call casting people.

—Couldn't get hopes up.

—Couldn't not get hopes up.

—Couldn't kill myself.

After another hour of mental wrangling, I compromised by lying ramrod straight on the bed, cell phone resting securely on my stomach for maximum reception as well as access, willing myself to breathe in and out and flipping through an assortment of TV shows that could surely only be on during the daytime. Who is Judge Hatchett? I wondered. Did she name herself that?

At 5:55 pm the phone finally rang. I grabbed for it, staring at the screen. It was definitely Todd.

Ring. Don't want to pick it up too fast ... that will make me look desperate.

Ring. Now I didn't want to answer it. Did I really want this news? If I let it go to voicemail at least I delayed the inevitable.

Ring. Don't do it … I told myself … if you answer, then you'll have to go back to Michigan to write your psych paper.

I answered right before the call went to voicemail. "Hello?" I said, trying to keep my voice at a reasonable volume.

"Amy Spencer!" said Todd from what sounded like the inside of a coffee can. "How are you? I have you on speakerphone."

The sound of a cowbell ringing snapped me out of my momentary downward crazy spiral. Then I heard people cheering.

What the …?

Todd came back on. "Congratulations! You got it! You're Autumn! You start shooting on Monday! We knew you could do it!"

Once I had pinched myself enough times to ensure that I was awake and that The Big Phone Call really happened, I composed myself and hit "4" on my cell phone's speed dial.

"Mom?"

"Amy! Oh my gosh! I miss you … how's school going?" She sounded tired.

"Mom, are you sitting down? I have some really good news."

CHAPTER 3

❀

By 9:00 the next morning, there were no less than *four* congratulatory baskets outside my room at the hotel (two fruit, one chocolate, one assorted, containing caviar and fancy water crackers).

An hour after eating Godiva chocolate for breakfast, I was at the studio office building once again, where a lovely red-haired woman named Julie who had been charged with "facilitating my transition" had gotten me into the Screen Actors Guild and arranged of absence from Hudson with "work credit" for being on the show, acting all the while like normal rules of life didn't apply, which I suppose they really didn't anymore. Since the first actress playing this part had already shot the pilot and all the publicity shots had been taken, Julie mentioned that those would need to be redone "as soon as possible."

Just as I realized I was about to be late to the very first "table read" rehearsal, Julie handed me off to Valerie, a studio intern, who filled me in on the latest studio and network scoop as she lead me from one office to the next, opening doors with a keycard attached to her pants with a long chain. Valerie was a serious girl with long black hair, sneakers, frayed jeans, and white Converse. She walked fast. "They're so lucky they found you—this show was about to go right into never never land if they didn't start re-shooting first thing Monday. We were all surprised that the network executives agreed, especially Mindy Steinman. She is truly frightening." She laughed. "Wait till you meet Sondra Smith. I bet she's in her office having an aneurysm right now, since she was done with the marketing and PR plan for the show like, three weeks ago."

Everyone was still milling about and getting settled when we got to the rehearsal, so Valerie and I hung back, standing at the door of the very same conference room where I had auditioned for studio executives the previous afternoon. We stood for a moment, eyeing the group of actors, who already knew each other and were joking around. Valerie filled me in as we drank coffee from the catering table, and I tried to gather up the courage to go over and meet everyone before we started rehearsal and they all decided they liked the other girl better and organized a coup to get me fired.

She leaned against the back wall. "Greg Forster, who plays your Uncle Michael—this is supposed to be his breakout show," she said, motioning with her donut to the man who'd been in my audition the day before. "It's a huge deal for him to do a gay role, you know...." she said, though I couldn't tell whether this meant he was gay or not. "The guy standing next to him is Ross Wong. He's been on TV for a zillion years. He's playing your uncle's partner." Again, no mention of his being gay or not. Was this important? I tried to take notes in my head.

"That's Michele McCann ... she plays your best friend Amanda," she continued, pointing to a dark-haired girl in a short top with amazing ab muscles. "Her father is Robert McCann, one of the producers, but she swears she auditioned under an alias. Then there's Emily Dean, who plays your little sister Jessie, (the Dakota Fanning girl, who I had since confirmed was NOT Dakota Fanning), and Matt Pierce, who plays the "boy next door" Zach, who will possibly become your love interest in upcoming shows. That's it for the regular cast. For one-hour dramas, they usually stick to six characters to form the ensemble ... like, look at *One Tree Hill* or *The O.C.*. Six people gives you the most stuff to play off of and still retain the brand recognition of the main characters. Plus it gives you the most permutations of the traditional dramatic formula."

I nodded, then started to joke that five new people playing five characters would be like ten new people to me since I was just cast the night before. Then I rethought my ironic sense of humor.

After being officially introduced to the cast and told by several executives that they "wanted me the whole time," I was also re-introduced to Josh Stein and Paul Jones. They both smiled and hugged me. "You're what I was waiting for," said Josh. Something about him reminded me of my dad.

By the end of the table read, I thought I might have earned their respect as an actress, though I had entered a level of exhaustion not previously known to man. At 3:00 that afternoon, I moved on to a wardrobe fitting, during which I was informed by the costume designer that I had "four inches and a good thirty five pounds" on the girl playing Autumn previously, for whom all of the costumes had been made. Costume Designer Lady (Lola), who was fifty years old with a bad smoker's hack, informed me that some of the costumes for the still photo shoot of the cast for publicity and marketing purposes would have to be cut up the back and *taped to my body*. She sighed. "I didn't know they were going to go in such a different direction," she said, eyeing my thighs. "I guess we'll just have to make it work," then joked, "Unless you think you can lose twenty five pounds by tomorrow!" At that point, I began to seriously regret the club sandwich and cookies consumed during the table read.

To recap: photos of me as the lead in a television show for a major network were going to appear in magazines, on billboards, and even on buses around the country. Yay! In these photos, my clothing would be cut up the back and taped on to my body to accommodate my being much larger than the previous actress, and all of the pants would be of the "high water" variety. Less than ideal. By 4:00 pm, I had resumed the smoking habit I'd given up the previous summer, after Lola took a smoke break in the middle of the fitting and casually mentioned that "cigarettes might help with your appetite."

That night, we had a catered "meet and greet" gathering at the studio, where I decided to skip dessert and stick to salad in the interest of fitting into my costumes. Ross saw me fretting over the food choices and joked "I see the Hollywood Machine has gotten to you already." I then tried not to act excited that they were actually serving me alcohol, even though I was nineteen, and my character on the show was supposed to be sixteen. Toward the end of the party, I started to feel lonely and wished that Vince and Carrie Ann were with me to enjoy all of this, and I wished my dad could see me.

Things kept getting better. After the party, I arrived back at the hotel to find that my room had been upgraded to a suite, which Todd got the network to pay for as my residence as a condition of my deal. More congratulatory baskets and flower arrangements had arrived, and the staff had kindly arranged them in the foyer. Of my suite. Where I now lived. Having never met Todd in person, I silently thanked him while lying in my posh accommodations, attempting unsuccessfully to decompress from what was at once the most exciting and most terrifying day of my life, and trying to go to sleep because I was called for another costume fitting at 9:00am. By 3:00 am, I decided I would try to survive on coffee, cigarettes, and adrenaline.

❦   ❦   ❦

The next morning, I faced Lola again for costume fitting number two. "We found some more material, and we're going to try reconstructing the clothes we've already made to fit you. It's the only thing that's going to work by the photo shoot this afternoon." After hearing this news, I skipped breakfast in favor of coffee and more cigarettes.

One hour later, I was scheduled for a visit to hair and makeup, where I studied myself in the giant mirror, trying to take a "before" snapshot in my mind before they whipped makeup department mojo on me. My brownish-blonde hair, usually attractively wavy, had settled into a curious "bed head dreadlock" formation overnight, and had blonde streaks from the last time Vince got a little over-ambitious with the highlights. With the proper time and flatiron, I could blow it out to look cool, but that morning it was being unruly and had taken on a "Bride of Frankenstein" theme. Because approaching it with a comb just seemed to make it angry, I had tied it into a knot and hoped for the best. I leaned closer to the mirror, looked at the dark circles under my eyes, and sighed. I hadn't slept much, and I looked a little disheveled and puffy.

First, I experienced the incredible pain of waxing of body parts I did not even know could be waxed ("did you know you have a peach fuzz moustache?"), had an eyebrow plucking that would've put Vince to shame, and got a haircut/dye job that I'm sure would have been $800 in a salon. I almost felt like Cinderella, surrounded by those sparkly mice during her transformation scene, only I was starting to become paranoid that they were going to declare me "Too Ugly for TV" and send me packing. After two hours, though, I looked in the mirror, barely recognized myself, and determine that this, officially, was the Best I'd Ever Looked in My Life.

My elation at looking like a model was short lived, as I was soon reminded that while my face might look amazing, my body still had a ways to go. By noon, I was back in the Wardrobe department a third time, having been fetched by Valerie and informed by Lola once again that "there just wasn't enough time or enough fabric to make all these changes to the wardrobe." I had tried on every piece of clothing made for an apparently elfin-sized actress, finding one skirt and a blouse that didn't make me look like a sausage. To every clothing change, Lola responded with a sigh, and she kept pressing on the meaty space between her thumb and forefinger. "Headache acupressure point," she said, and I wondered if it was my ass that was giving her the headache. When I put on the skirt that the other actress had previously worn in most of the publicity shots, it was so small that it wouldn't zip up all the way. Exasperated, Lola took out a pair of scissors, cut the skirt up the back, and taped the sides to the backs of my legs, exposing my underwear, a tattered pair of Old Navy bikini briefs that said "Angel/Devil" on them. I turned around to survey the underwear/skirt/tape configuration, which from the back was just short of being a horror film. "Just don't make any sudden movements during the photo shoot," said Lola. "We'll make something better for the next round, but for now, we have to get you out there in front of the camera. The whole cast is waiting."

At this declaration, I think I had a stroke. *The cast was waiting?* The second time I was going to see these people, and I was wearing someone else's costumes that had been cut open and taped to my body because I was too fat to fit into them? The whole cast was waiting to see my ass exposed by an ill-fitting costume? They were waiting to see my tragic, faded Angel/Devil underpants—one of the only items of clothing I'd thrown into my duffel bag when I left my dorm and never came back? Despite my incredible looking eyebrows and beautiful hair, tears welled up in my eyes. "Is there nothing else I can wear?" I said desperately. "This is really ... embarrassing." Keep it together, I thought.

"I know, honey, but stuff happens fast here ... just make the best of it, and we'll bring some altered clothes out for the costume change at 2:00. She threw a sweater around my waist. "Just wear this until it's time to take the shot, then take it off. No one will even notice."

Thirty minutes later, the repeat photo call for the *Autumn Leaves* cast was set to begin. I was escorted by Valerie (who did not comment on the sweater around my waist or the fact that I was walking like something was seriously wrong with me) through the labyrinthine halls of the studio from the costume department to a large room that had been converted to a photo studio with a backdrop and many bright lights. Everyone in the cast was gathered, costumed, and ready. My head was spinning, and the tape holding my costume was beginning to pull at my legs. I feared I would not survive the afternoon with my dignity intact.

Miraculously, no one mentioned the sweater, the tape, or the underpants, though I did feel quite certain I was going to die of shame right before the "unveiling" of my outfit and my almost-naked behind. Ross Wong was the only one who even mentioned it. "Don't worry about it," he said. "Things always go wrong. That kind of thing happens all the time. I once played Judas in a production of "The Joy of Christmas" where they had to stop the show because they used live animals, and one of the goats bit the head off of the plastic baby Jesus doll and ran offstage." By the end of the story, the whole cast was laughing so hard, I forgot all about my mortification.

After the photo shoot was over, Valerie gave me a ride back to the hotel. Just before I got out of the car, she handed me a thick script. "The writers just put in some revisions after the table read. You do know that you need to be completely off book for this script by tomorrow morning, right?"

❧   ❧   ❧

Still shell-shocked from the weekend, I arrived at the studio promptly at eight the next morning for Day One of pilot shooting, off book and ready to go. The guard behind the bulletproof glass at the studio barely looked up as he asked for my name and driver's license. "Um … Amy Spencer? Here for the *Autumn Leaves* pilot?" I said. "Amy Spencer," I said again, more authoritatively, trying to remind myself that, underpants incident aside, I was good enough to get the part, I was the new star of the show, and this was my first day of work. I wondered if anyone could tell by looking at me that I was doing little cartwheels inside my head, or that I set the alarm on the clock in the hotel, and the Samsonite travel clock my dad bought me in the ninth grade for summer camp, AND asked for a wakeup call, and I still woke up at 5 am so I wouldn't be late.

As soon as I passed the front desk, a beautiful black girl with close-cropped hair and creamy skin approached me. "Hi … Amy? I'm Joan. I'm one of the production assistants. I'll just be taking you to hair and makeup, getting you the latest script, and taking you to set, since there's so much going on. Welcome! We're so glad you're here!"

"Um … thanks. Hi, nice to meet you," I laughed. What happened to Valerie? Did she say latest script? I think I was supposed to feel important, but really I still felt like someone was going to jump out and yell "fraud" at any time, or possibly mention the underpants. Everything was so new, I didn't know where anything was, and I was pretty sure I was the only one who had never been on the set of a television show before. I'm not Catholic or anything, but for some reason I crossed myself as I walked through the studio doors, thinking that I was about to learn the meaning of the phrase "sink or swim."

❦   ❦   ❦

"Cut! Let's take that again. Amy—wait a second before you start talking. OK, everybody back to one." Paul did not sound happy. I watched as everyone went back to their original places for the scene; I knew they were wondering why the producers went with a total amateur like me, and right then, so was I.

Two days into the shoot, I'd already worked a total of forty-eight hours and was surviving on less sleep than I ever thought possible. Was it the exhaustion that was making me mess up, or the fact that I was learning everything for the first time? Whatever the case, shooting kept getting held up because of my mistakes. Apparently my one student film hadn't quite prepared me for the rigors of shooting a one-hour drama, and so I was learning on the job.

To be fair, I **was** given a crash course in "acting for television" right before we rolled on the first scene. This consisted of Paul Jones, the director, looking over at me and saying "Make sure you keep everything small, no big gestures. It all has to stay within the frame of the camera, but don't look into the camera unless we tell you to."

After another few hours of missed cues and frustrating takes, I was 99% sure I was about to be fired. Since the show was a combination of big name writer/ director/controversial script, the producers had all been on set every day, and I wanted to do the best job possible, but it was a little overwhelming with script changes, blocking changes, remembering when to speak, and getting back into character after they shifted the camera and the lights a million times. So far I'd managed not to lose it in front of anyone, but I was blinking back tears as Jo, the stage manager, came over.

"It's fine," she whispered, patting my arm. "Don't worry. This always happens. Just be patient with yourself, and you'll get the hang of it." I needed a supportive word so badly, I felt like hugging her. She squeezed my shoulder. "You'll see. Tomorrow will be better."

It was Emily Dean, who played my little sister Jessie, who helped me the most. Even though she was only twelve, this was her fifth pilot, and she'd done a bunch of movies. She was a showbiz veteran, and my lifesaver, subtly teaching me how to hit my marks, to tone down my acting for the camera, and how to convey more emotion with just my face. Ross was also great, and I learned just by watching him shoot the scenes that I wasn't in. That's where the lack of sleep came in—when I could have (should have) been napping, I was either learning my lines, watching other scenes, or lying on the couch in my trailer, feeling terrified that this was my last day on the set, and that the next day I'd most likely be going back to Michigan to become an accountant.

We finished the take on the fifth try, and I went back to the trailer, where I had learned to cry silently so as to avoid sparking rumors around the set that I couldn't hack it ("did you hear Amy sobbing in her trailer?"), and to learn the next scene I was in, stopping for fruit and Diet Coke at the craft services table on my way.

I was only through the first Silent Tears Kleenex when Ross poked his head in my trailer. "That was better!" he said, smiling broadly.

Little choking sobs started to clutch my chest. "Ross, they're going to fire me for sure. I've missed my mark at least twelve times today."

He sat down on the couch. The "three banger" that Todd negotiated as part of my deal turned out to be a really large trailer, and I ended up with a sofa-bed as well as a dining area, TV/DVD player, and a chair/mirror. Actually, on Day Two (in another "Pinch Myself" moment) I realized that the trailer was approximately the same size as my dorm room.

"Don't worry … if they see something in you, they'll teach you what you need to know. Nobody gets fired for trying too hard, Amy."

Ross was rapidly becoming my new mentor. "What do people get fired for, then?" I said, hoping he'd dish the Hollywood dirt and take my mind off my imminent unemployment. Perhaps exhaustion was making me shallow.

"Well," he said, "I saw someone get fired after the very first table read for going 'this is where I'm feeling emotion, this is where I'll be crying,' and stuff like that." He laughed. "She was gone the next day. It's better to just go for it, and if it's wrong someone will tell you. Just think—you're already doing better than her, and she's done many more TV shows than you!" He wouldn't give me the woman's name, but he said it was "someone I'd seen on TV before." "She did fine—she got another job," he said. "It all worked out. No one really goes away in Hollywood unless they give up on themselves, or get into drugs, or start taking the situation for granted and burning bridges. Remember that, no matter what happens."

Ross was by far the most stable of all the cast members, myself included. He did yoga in his trailer, followed a macrobiotic diet, and could usually be found reading books in between takes, rather than smoking and gossiping like the rest of the cast. Already I'd decided that if I ever needed to confide in someone, it would be him.

I'd also decided to try to get through the rest of the week with only one box of Kleenex.

❧   ❧   ❧

By the end of the first week, I had managed not to embarrass myself, get fired, or lose the network millions of dollars with my ineptitude. Jo was right; the process was actually getting easier the more I practiced. I had, however, gained three pounds due to stress eating—something I hardly needed, considering I was still feeling the "you're too fat" vibe from the costume department.

I blamed craft services. Having been only recently introduced to this concept, I was surprised at the startling amount of free things that could be found to eat on a set. I started keeping a mental list the second day, just so I would remember to tell Vince and Carrie Ann about it when I saw them again.

1. Omelet bar. That's right. A person, making omelets, for a show in which my character's name was in the title.

2. Fruit. Not just the mealy, questionably ripe kind of fruit that I'd grown accustomed to eating in the dorm. This was good fruit, cut up at regular intervals throughout the day. Plus, on the first day, the chef

asked me what kind of fruit I liked, and now he was cutting it up just for me. Throughout the day. In case I wanted any pineapple, red seedless grapes, strawberries, or even watermelon, balled especially for me.

3. Cheese. Not just the Kraft American Singles kind of cheese like my mom used to make sandwiches out of when I was in the fourth grade. I'm talking about Swiss Cheese cut into fancy squares, a wheel of Brie that seemed to never get hard or run out, and a variety of other amazing assorted cheese.

4. Candy. Free candy. Free M & Ms, free giant Snickers bars, free Skittles, free Sweet Tarts, free Dove Dark Chocolates, FREE CANDY.

5. Popcorn. The one "empty carbs" item that you're never supposed to eat while watching your weight was, much to my chagrin, available in huge buckets all over the set. Carmel corn, cheese corn, regular, lite, kettle corn, and all the rest. It also did not help that every trailer was equipped with a microwave, insuring that the smell of delicious popcorn was almost always wafting through the set from somewhere.

6. Soda. Like, every kind of soda known to man, in seemingly endless supplies. Unfortunately, this cast seemed to go through Diet Coke at an exceedingly fast rate, so unless you hoarded your stash, you were almost guaranteed to end up with a warm can. Full-sugar Coke and Dr. Pepper, on the other hand, were always cold.

7. Sandwiches of every variety: turkey, roast beef, vegetable for the multiple vegetarians on set. Stacked high with your choice of bacon (for the non-vegetarians) and the afore-mentioned assortment of wonderful cheese choices. How do you say no to a free sandwich?

8. Dessert bar. As in, after lunch, a tray of tiny fancy desserts appeared, including many things I had never had before. Pie, chocolate cake, cheesecake, profiteroles, cupcakes, and tiny tart-looking things with gelatinized fruit on top. Why the cruel torture?

9. Muffins. Blueberry muffins, banana nut muffins, cranberry muffins, chocolate chip muffins, brands of muffins I never even knew existed. I swear, there was a "muffin wrangler" just for all the muffins.

10. Bagels, hot bagels, of every variety under the sun. Toasted, un-toasted, sliced, topped with your choice of seventeen varieties of cream cheese.

The first four days of shooting, all bets were off. Then slowly, insidiously, I began to notice that not only was I the only one who could consistently be found at the craft services table as they put out each "course," but that my costumes were beginning to be even tighter than before.

And so, the dilemma: while the "starving college" student side of me wanted to stuff most of these items into my coat and run from the set whooping like a child or someone recently released from a refugee camp, the "newly employed on a Hollywood television show bearing my name actress" side of me concluded that eating all of these things, every day, was producing even more weight, something that had already been mentioned as undesirable. Still, it was a cruel irony to put this amount of fancy free food in front of someone who a) was, up until very recently, poor and hungry, b) ate when confronted with stress, and c) could not, no, **would** not say no to free chocolate cake.

To compound the craft services dilemma, I couldn't shake the feeling that I should've been hoarding this food, in case I woke up from this dream and wasn't making outrageous money as the star of a cool TV show. Still, I didn't want to get the reputation as someone who was stealing food from the craft services table, so I willed myself to walk numerous times per day past three tables filled with food so bountiful and luscious looking, it might have actually been a psychological test.

❦   ❦   ❦

While I was trying to avoid the craft services table, I discovered that the many smokers on set had fashioned a makeshift "Smoker's Lounge" in back of the set for the main house. I started spending some quality time there, smoking cigarettes during the times I was not trying to frantically learn lines before scenes or watching the other actors to try to see what they were doing right. I only had to hang out there for two days before I'd heard the whole story of "The Girl Who Got Fired From the Pilot."

Auditions had been going on for several months for this lead character, with limited success, since everyone was deemed either "too Hollywood" or "too overdramatic" to convincingly play the role. Then a girl had been cast and the pilot was shot, but she was suddenly fired under circumstances that were unclear (rumors ranging from "Josh just didn't like her," to "she wasn't Midwestern enough," to "politics within the network" to "she and the girl playing her little sister Jessie didn't look enough alike"). Since the show had a pre-order for at least nine episodes in addition to the pilot, the network started putting serious pressure on Kim to re-cast the lead in time for the pilot to start re-shooting on Monday so the show could still be released in time for the fall lineup. That's where I came in.

During one of the many other cigarette breaks during the day, I learned that Michele McCann was also a show business veteran at age twenty-one. This was her fourth pilot. Also, she was tiny—5'2" maybe, and easily wore children's size clothes. She had, without a doubt, not an ounce of fat on her entire body. Finally I broke down. "How do you stay so ... skinny?" I said, hoping that I wasn't insulting her.

"Well, you really just cut down on your carbs and reduce your total caloric intake until you've reached your desired weight—of course, it might be a little harder for you, because you've got a bigger frame. You could stand to lose about 10 pounds, to start," she said, taking a drag off of her skinny Virginia Slim. "If the show takes off, they're going to want us to look more ... similar. Do you know what I'm saying? Similar? I mean, this isn't *Ugly Betty*."

Her shiny chestnut hair offset her sparkling brown eyes and clear white skin as she cast a knowing glance across my body.

"Right," I said, "I totally know what you mean."

"I do four or five spinning classes a week" she said seriously. "Then I do the elliptical, then weights. Figure at least two hours a day, or just stop eating and that might get you there, but you're not going to be toned if you just do it that way." She was at least as militant about the daily maintenance of her perfectly taut, muscular abs as she was about finding clothing small enough to show them off. "Your body is your instrument, and you have to have absolute discipline over it, or this business will eat you alive."

This was a lot for me to take in all at once. "When was the last time you had pizza?" I said, praying the answer was "last week."

She crinkled her perfect nose. "Ugh—not for years. I'm completely organic. You really have to be if you want to take your career to the next level. Really, it comes down to this—do you want to eat that crap, or do you want to be successful? If you just want to eat junk food, there are like a million people I know who want your part in this show. In fact, my best friend auditioned for it, and we totally thought she got it until they brought you in at the last minute. Everyone in town was really surprised when the network went with an unknown from Iowa."

I started to say "I'm from Michigan, and in Michigan they consider me skinny" but Josh walked up with one of the suits from the network. "How's it going, girls?" he said. "Just wanted to let you know—we added a new scene this morning. It's at the beach." Michele's eyes went immediately down to the bagel in my hand, and my heart sank. I tried to think of the last time I wore a swimsuit. So unfair! Technically it was still winter when I left Michigan.

Michele chimed in again. "Josh, I was just telling Amy how glad we are to have someone new and so talented in the cast. We're all really excited about the show."

Josh looked over at me. "Great, Michele," he said. Maybe he had some idea how fake she was, I thought hopefully. I tossed my bagel in the trash and went back to my trailer to learn the lines for the new scene while simultaneously vowing to never eat again. Michele was definitely a bitch, but she might have been right: I probably needed to lose weight to stay competitive in this world.

❦   ❦   ❦

"Where's Rodney?"

At 3:30 am on my first-ever Friday (actually Saturday) of shooting, I was half-dead from exhaustion. As I willed myself to stay awake and remember my lines, a production assistant named Rodney was torturing me with his horrific body odor.

Was this the life of a Hollywood star?

We were still shooting at 3:00 am because Friday is the only day of the week that there is no "turnaround time," meaning they didn't have to let us rest before we came in the next day (union rules), so technically, they could make us work for the entire weekend and not let us go until Sunday at 8:00 pm (if we were called back at 8:00 am Monday). Problem was, we'd been shooting since 9:00am on Friday, so we were all getting a little punchy.

Now, back to Rodney. Rodney of the horrific b.o. was the production assistant in charge of "continuity," which was the last part of TV acting that I was having a hard time grasping. Seems that when you shoot a TV show and you do the same take seventeen times, everything has to look the *exact same* in every take, or else it's impossible to edit. That means your hand has to do the same thing, you have to have the same amount of water in your glass, and your shirt has to be bunched up in the same way in every take. During each scene, the script supervisor was furiously taking notes, so that she could instruct Rodney as to how to fix our clothing and hair, where to put all the stuff on the table, and how much to fill up our water glasses.

We were shooting a scene where my Uncle Michael and his partner Peter were taking me out to dinner to get to know me better, and there were food and drinks involved, so after every take, Rodney had to replace everything we'd been eating and drinking with new versions. Also, everyone was required to remember exactly what they were eating and drinking on every single line, a feat made nearly impossible for me by the fact that I was expecting to go home five hours before. Now, as Rodney leaned over me for the eighteenth time with his stinky armpits, replacing dinner rolls with bites out of them and refilling glasses, I wished that 1) I had thought ahead to take a nap, 2) I had taken that Intro to TV Acting class and learned about continuity, and 3) that someone could subtly suggest a nice underarm deodorant to Rodney, or perhaps a doctor.

Ross was attempting to keep me awake by making subtle faces in response to the smell of Rodney. Trying to keep from laughing at this was really my only link to consciousness at this point. He hadn't told me yet whether he was actually gay, but I'd decided that if he wasn't, I was definitely going to offer to make out with him when we wrapped shooting for the day, I was so grateful.

❦   ❦   ❦

Mercifully, after the initial panic and crash course in TV acting, I found that I enjoyed the whole routine, and the by the beginning of Week Two, things started to go smoothly. Because of some odd gift for hand-eye coordination, I was almost freakishly good at hitting my mark every time, my sense for continuity was rapidly improving, and my skill for fast memorization was often complimented.

My appearance, on the other hand, still left much to be desired. Even though I had by some miracle managed to stop thinking about the craft services table every five minutes, I was still faced with the fact that, at 5'7" and 135 pounds, I was probably "too fat for Hollywood."

It started in the wardrobe department. Every day when I arrived on set, my costumes were already in my trailer. Having been told on the first day that it was customary to try on all the costumes when you arrive (thus giving the wardrobe ample time to make needed adjustments), I optimistically tried on the first one, which was invariably too small, then moved on to others (also too small). After a few discouraging days of this, I surmised that the wardrobe department was still holding on to the hope that I might go from a size six to a size zero overnight, and they'd been neglecting to make the necessary alterations. This resulted in a never-ending trek between my trailer and the wardrobe department, holding my tiny costumes in my hand and praying that we wouldn't have a repeat of the "underpants incident."

A few days into the second week of shooting, I faced Lola with a forced smile. "This one doesn't fit either," I joked. I was getting sort of fed up with the whole "we didn't have time to let out your costumes" thing, but I figured she had enough to deal with. I certainly didn't want to ruffle any feathers by pulling a diva move like complaining about my costumes during the shooting of my big break. Also, I really didn't know the hierarchy of anyone on the set, and I didn't want Lola narking me out to the network, claiming I wasn't a team player. My only consolation was that no one at the studio or the network had ever mentioned my weight, even though I was clearly larger than the rest of the actresses. Michele speculated that the probable reason for this was that they were going to "try out my angle" for the test audience, and then they'd let me know. "It happens all the time," she said. "My friend got called in for a pilot, and at the end they asked her to come back to test, but they said they wanted her to be 'more attractive' by the next day. I mean, isn't that weird? Like, aren't you your most attractive every time you go into an audition?"

One thing was for sure—if they expected me to be "similar" to Michele McCann by the time we started shooting Season One, I was going to have to throw away all the craft services food I'd been amassing in my trailer and swear to never eat pizza again.

CHAPTER 4

❀

A week after shooting wrapped on the pilot, I was still trying to sleep off the exhaustion when suddenly there was a furious knocking at the door of my suite. Since I was positive I put the "do not disturb" sign on the door after dragging myself back to the hotel at four am on the last Friday night of shooting, I could not imagine who could be knocking on the door, especially at 11:00 at night. In my experience (at least in the past three days, when I'd actually been at the hotel and not the studio), housekeeping came in the morning.

"Go away!" I groaned. "I'm sleeping!"

More knocking. Good Lord. I felt like a grumpy three year old on the verge of a tantrum. I pushed my sleep mask up onto my forehead, pulled on some pants, and flung open the door in a rage. "What do you…."

I stopped abruptly as I beheld Vince, complete with many bags, on my doorstep.

"Vince? What are you …?"

I trailed off as he grabbed me up in a huge hug. "Hello darling!" he said excitedly. "How's my movie star?"

"Oh my God!" I screamed. "What are you doing here? How long are you staying? Isn't this place amazing?" I wanted to cry from relief to see a familiar face, and to immediately tell him everything that had happened since I'd been gone.

I was screaming, and he was screaming, and after a minute, I thought maybe we'd woken up every guest at the hotel. I pulled Vince and his suitcases into the room and shut the door, in case the security guards came looking for the source of the noise. He was as excited as I was. "Aim—I turned in my final project, filed my paperwork, and I'm done with school. I … live here now!"

At all once I forgot all about the fatigue, we ordered room service, and he gave me the scoop. He'd been amassing credits for a double major, but then the guidance counselor for his department had told him he had taken enough to finish his degree. The dean of the business school had called Vince's father, a prestigious Hudson University alumnus himself, to congratulate him on Vince's success, after which Vince's father had promptly called to inform him that he was to start the following Monday as a marketing manager in the family business. After which Vince had filed his paperwork, taken the rest of the money from his college fund, and ridden a Greyhound bus to Los Angeles.

Carrie Ann and I had been friends with Vince since we all moved into the dorms freshman year, when he was dating our next door neighbor, a beautiful dancer named Scott. After he and Scott broke up, Carrie Ann and I had gotten Vince in the friend divorce and had been living happily ever after. An aspiring fashion designer a year ahead of us in school, Vince was always on the verge of giving it all up and moving to San Francisco, Los Angeles, or New York to "be with sane people." Growing up gay in Michigan, the son of a wealthy businessman—not a cake walk, to say the least. Only the allure of the free tuition and cigarette money promised to him by his wealthy father in exchange for a college degree in a "normal" subject like business had kept him in Michigan. And now he was free.

"What you going to do for work? I said. I knew his father had probably cut him off, and Vince would never accept my offer to just move in with me.

"You know what?" he said. "Something will work out. This has already been an amazing month—for both of us!" he said, still high on having broken free from the Midwest. "It's about time I started living my life for me. I'm totally going to find Perez, and we are going to live happily ever after."

And with that, Vincent Firello became a permanent resident of Los Angeles and I got 100% less lonely.

❦   ❦   ❦

A few days after Vince's arrival, I came home to find my first paycheck from the network waiting for me. Since I knew it was going to be more money than I had ever seen in one place my life, I took the still-sealed envelope up to the suite so I could have my conniption fit in private.

Even after taxes and many other things taken out, I was pretty sure this one paycheck accounted for more money than my mother made in a year. Mostly, I was excited to have the big paycheck so I could start helping her with the bills, get a car, and to buy some new clothes. OK, so I wasn't totally altruistic in my intentions, but my heart was in the right place.

With Vince by my side, here's how I spent my First Big Paycheck:

1. Bought three pairs of fancy jeans (one Blue Cult, one Citizens of Humanity, and one Rock & Republic). Was surprised to discover that, despite my procrastinatory attitude toward dieting, I was already wearing a smaller size than when I left Hudson. Maybe all of Lola's wishful thinking was actually working by osmosis.

2. Leased one brand new BMW X5 SUV, white. Physically could not stop myself after Vince told me that this was the exact car driven by Maggie Gyllenhaal (though he may have been making this up just to make me get the car—not sure). Perhaps also attempting to make up for the fact that in high school, I had an old Chevy Cavalier that looked like a shoe—a car that didn't even make it to my freshman year of college. Yay for my fancy new car!

3. Took Vince shopping for celebratory outfits. Despite my newfound wealth, I declined to purchase a $2,500 jean jacket with mink at the collar and sleeves that he suggested. "Who am I, J. Lo?" I said. Vince just laughed. During this shopping excursion, I actually consented to visit several thrift stores on Melrose. Usually I was bored after five minutes of pawing through used, stinky clothes, but somehow Vince always unearthed some rare and valuable treasure to add to his amazing collection of vintage clothing. On this trip, it was a lovely Hermes scarf, discovered just as I was hitting my thrift store limit.

3. Paid off one of my dad's hospital bills

4. Made one advance payment toward my mom's mortgage

At first, my mother sounded mortified that her teenage daughter was offering to pay for these things that a parent should pay for, but as soon as I'd made it clear I wasn't taking no for an answer, I could hear the relief in her voice. After the checks actually arrived, she called at a time she would usually have been asleep. "Amy," she said," I just wanted to say thank you. Your dad would be so proud."

❦   ❦   ❦

Owing perhaps to his powers of sheer determination, in two weeks' time, Vince had an ancient silver Honda with a vanilla air freshener scent so strong we nicknamed it "The Douche," a working knowledge of the freeways of Los Angeles, **and** a part-time job as the assistant to a tiny Japanese fashion stylist named Nina Yakimoto. Since he was working only part-time, he still had time to hang out with me before Season One started shooting. With Vince's encouragement, I began to explore parts of Los Angeles outside my five-block radius, which until then had consisted mostly of The Coffee Bean, the hotel, and the Virgin Megastore. He totally motivated me to get out and see more of the city. With that in mind, we started a "New Things" list, and added to it every time a new insight came up.

The Los Angeles List:

1. Even the people who work in Starbucks are beautiful in L.A. Even the people who sell you shoes in the Adidas store are beautiful in L.A. Even the busboys are beautiful in LA. Perhaps this is because in Los Angeles, everyone is just on the verge of getting their Big Break.

2. There is never, ever a good time to make a left turn in L.A.

3. Also, there is never NOT traffic on the 405 Freeway.

4. "I was stuck in traffic" does not work as an excuse in L.A, since everyone is always stuck in traffic.

5. If you meet a person who is the same "type" as you, don't think you're going to be friends, because you're not. Similar "types" cannot be friends because of the potential for vicious backstabbing and the competitive nature of the industry. Groups of actor/actress friends

can include: One Blonde, One Fat Brunette (Funny Optional), One Redhead (Funny Required), and One Ethnic Girl, and one gay guy, ethnicity open. One of each only, not more. This theory was cultivated at the Coffee Bean, where we observed a shocking amount of backstabbing among actress-wannabe type girls.

6. In Los Angeles, it is not uncommon to hear the phrase "do you have this any smaller than a zero?"

7. Despite indications to the contrary in movies, Hollywood Boulevard is just sad and depressing. Especially the Popeye's on Hollywood and Cahuenga, which could be renamed "Epicenter of Broken Dreams." Side of desperation, anyone?

8. Unless you have a freakishly good sense of direction, you are not getting anywhere with a fold-out gas station map of Los Angeles. Even Google Maps is sometimes wrong. The Thomas' Guide is the only solution to this problem.

9. A Mocha Light Frappucino without whipped cream has 140 calories, a fact shared with me by a (beautiful) female Starbucks barista after I ordered a "regular Frappucino" and she looked me up and down, then said "Are you sure?" Ouch.

10. When everyone is always talking into a BlueTooth or other hands-free device, it is really hard to tell who is insane and who's just an agent.

11. Only two types of people still smoke in L.A.: actors and homeless people.

CHAPTER 5

✿

After another few weeks enjoying my friend and my newfound wealth, I got a call from Sondra Smith.

"We need you to make an appearance at the Network UpFronts in New York next week … that's when the pilot is debuting, and we want to make 100% sure we have the green light for Season One," she said. "We're putting the cast on a private jet … we'll have a car pick you up on Tuesday morning. Oh, and Amy—when you come back, we'll need to have the first of several meetings about your media strategy."

Even after the extremely personal Sondra interview on the first day, the grueling hours shooting the pilot, and the snarky comments from Michele and Lola about my appearance, I was definitely still not at the "jaded" point yet with the job. In fact, if Sondra had told me I had to go to Alaska and carve the name of the show into a block of ice while dressed as an Eskimo, I would've gone willingly. The fact that I had to go do something for work AND I got a free trip to New York out of it was just more icing on the already-delicious cake. Private jet? Chocolate sprinkles on the icing on the cake.

If I was excited about my first "First Class" flight on the way out to California for the audition, I was positively geeked out about the prospect of flying on a private jet for the first time. In fact, every time something like this happened, I tried to remind myself not to get used to it, that indie film people didn't need money for their art. Still, I had to admit—it did feel good to have money. I was in the middle of a chorus of "I hit the big time … I'm on a private jet! Whoop whoop!" when my phone rand and I saw Carrie Ann's number.

"Hello? Carrie Ann?" I said. "Are you in New York right now?"

She was. Carrie Ann had sailed through auditions for "Broadway Bound," a program put on by the Hudson University drama department every year to get theater kids "in touch" with the Broadway experience by sending them to New York during summer break. Since school was over, she was due to start Broadway Bound any minute.

"Yes I am!" she said … "I was just calling to give you my New York address! I've been here for three days, and I love it already!"

"Well, guess what?" I said excitedly. "I'm coming there in two days, on a private jet, and my show is putting me up at the Pierre Hotel, baby! Can you stay with me for three days? We can eat room service, catch up, and watch movies! It will be so fun! I can't wait to see you! Say yes!"

She shrieked. "Oh my God … yes yes yes! I'm so excited to see you and hear everything about the pilot, and Vince, and everything! I'll meet you at the Pierre when I'm done with class. Amy, wow … this is going to be great! I can't wait to see you! We can explore the city together!"

Two days later, I felt cooler than ever when the network sent a limo to take me from the hotel to LAX. I was taken to a secret part of the airport I didn't even know existed, which I immediately dubbed "Airport Room of the Rich and Famous." This is the room where celebrities have their passports/IDs checked, go through security, and wait for their flights so the paparazzi won't get to them. After all, Catherine Zeta-Jones can't be seen doing things that common people do, like waiting in line for baggage claim.

The private jet was beyond everything I ever thought it would be—a whole plane of First Class! Fancy leather seats, food that you requested before the flight, and a flight attendant to bring you things like freshly-made skim cappuccinos and just released issues of **People** magazine and **US Weekly** for the flight. The air even seemed smoother when flying in a private jet. Is it possible that for more money, you can fly even higher, up to the really good air? I'd heard that Air Force One flies at 45,000 feet. Maybe that's where we were.

My lack of knowledge of the trappings of the rich and spoiled never ceased to amaze and amuse Michele McCann, who I wanted to kill 99% of the time. "Have you never done anything?," she laughed when I picked up the phone and stared at it. I gave her a "ha ha, you're so funny" look as I dialed my mom's number (from the plane!). I wondered what Michele was like in high school. Was she fat? Was she a cheerleader? Was there anything about her that would allow me to ever get the upper hand? I knew it was taking all of her available acting skill just to pretend like she liked me, and that she was longing to see me get fired so her friend could take my job. Still, I was determined to enjoy every moment of my newfound success, her snarky Hollywood attitude aside.

My mom was excited to hear from me, though she seemed appalled by the concept of the phone in the plane. "Isn't that expensive?" she kept saying. "Don't waste your money!"

I cupped my hand over and phone and my mouth at the same time in a lame attempt at privacy, whispering "It's free, mom—it's all free," to which she replied "I still don't believe this job, Amy." Finally, she relented. "Send me a postcard from New York, and tell Carrie Ann I said hi!" she said. "I can't wait for your show to come out! I've told everyone in my office to watch for it in the fall!"

During the mandatory marketing meeting in the conference room at the hotel, Sondra whipped out another bullet-pointed list, explaining that the "upfront" is the chance for the advertisers to preview the shows, that it was really important, and that we all had to make an effort to talk to as many media people as possible. There was also something about us posing in an **Autumn Leaves** photo booth at the after party at a restaurant called Cipriani. I tried to take it all in, even attempting a few notes, but I was still so excited about the private jet, seeing New York for the first time, and seeing Carrie Ann that already I was tired from smiling.

🍁   🍁   🍁

Two hours later, Carrie Ann and I had made a picnic of expensive room service food on one of the super-fancy Pierre Hotel bedspreads.

"I can't believe they're paying for all of this, Aim," she said, her mouth full of $20 chopped chicken salad. "You are, like, the ultimate rags to riches girl."

I laughed, nodding my head. Apparently, my being cast in the show was still the talk of the school, even though the news had had a few months to cool off.

Carrie Ann caught me up on drama department gossip as we dug into sweet potato fries lovingly laid out for us on a silver platter. I was thrilled to be eating again, since the wardrobe department had taken my real measurements and had time to make costumes in the right sizes before we started shooting Season One. Contrary to Michele's doomsday theories regarding my weight, I hadn't heard one thing about it from anyone since shooting wrapped on the pilot, so I figured I was home free.

"Throw me the key to the mini bar," she said, climbing over the pile of rubble. "I want to see what kind of wine $35 buys you in this place." She laughed, pulling out a mid-sized bottle of Merlot and holding it up for examination. "Did you see this list of prices? Good Lord! You know, we could go down to the corner deli and buy, like, seventeen bottles of Strawberry Hill for the price of this little guy."

"Yes," I said. "But then we'd be wasted, and we'd have to pay for it ourselves. Besides, who would leave the comfort of The Pierre Hotel? We should move in and live here forever like queens."

Carrie Ann laughed, attempting a pirouette on the bed. Even though she was only nineteen, everyone was convinced she was going to end up on Broadway in the next couple of years—her nickname in the department was "Baby Bernadette." Hanging out with her was the one thing I missed about school.

"Oh, I don't know—my two bedroom, five roommate apartment in Inwood has its charm, especially if you like Dominican food," she said, laughing. She was determined to replicate life of a Broadway hopeful, right down to the noisy third floor walkup apartment above a restaurant that smelled like *empanadas*. "It's the 'humble beginnings' part of my Biography story on A & E," she said, jumping up and down on the bed. "Wait till you see the place I'm taking voice class—it's right down the street from where they do **Phantom of the Opera**!"

That night, we stayed up way too late, talking about our dreams and watching movies on pay-per-view. "Naomi Watts," Carrie mumbled as she nodded off. "There's a girl who never gave up on her dreams."

❦   ❦   ❦

"Just follow Greg and I," said Ross, putting his arm around me. I must have looked nervous as we waited backstage to go out and introduce the show at the UpFront. Perhaps this was due to the fact that somehow, in the bullet pointed list she'd distributed the very night before, Sondra had neglected to mention that our first-ever public appearance as a cast was to be held at 2:00 pm, on a Wednesday, in **Madison Square Garden**.

We were to follow the cast of the network's most popular one-hour drama—an order strategically planned by the network to leave the audience as excited as possible by the time they saw us and our brand-new pilot. "What if they hate it?" I whispered, and Michele shushed me. She looked nervous too, but apparently it was easier to focus her energy on making me feel stupid. I craned my neck from the backstage area to see the audience members, trying to calm myself down. Suits, as far as the eye could see. Oddly, the suits were being worn by people who looked to be my age or a little older. Why were all the advertisers twenty two years old?

"Agency people," said Greg Forster, sneering. It was 2:00 pm, but he already smelled like the Johnnie Walker Green Label he always seemed to have handy. "Like some fucking kid in a suit knows what constitutes good TV." I looked over at Michele incredulously, as if to say "I get shushed and he doesn't?" but I already knew she'd be avoiding my gaze. She wouldn't dare say anything to him, no matter how belligerent he got. In the Hollywood Hierarchy, at least for that moment, Greg outranked her, and she was nothing if not aware of her place in the system (even though she was constantly trying to ascend to the top). "Shits in suits," he kept muttering, leaning against the wall, and I silently prayed he'd pull himself together for the speech. "Shits in suits!"

The order was set: Greg and Ross first, then me (the newcomer), then the rest of the cast walk onto the stage, they say a few words about how we're really excited about the new show, how it's great to be here, and how we're looking forward to meeting them in person at Cipriani. Standing next to Ross, I said a mental prayer that he'd be doing most of the talking. All we needed was for Greg to start shooting his mouth off about how much he hated network executives. I was no expert, but "Shits in Suits" sounded like something people would remember when it came time to make important decisions about advertising dollars.

The emcee for the afternoon was a comedian named Dave McGinnis, and I could hear his witty onstage banter wrapping up. "Get ready," said Ross. And just like that, we were walking onstage and introducing ourselves. Greg was even cordial and funny, which somehow made me respect his acting skill a little more.

♣   ♣   ♣

I'd been back from New York for two days when I came home from a solo shopping excursion to find Vince packing excitedly. "Aim—I found an apartment," he said. "It's a one bedroom, it's in West Hollywood, and it's *mine mine mine*! There's totally room for both of us, in case you can't sleep and want to stay over. We could get a Chinese curtain thing, and a fold out couch. It will be just like Three's Company."

"Wasn't Jack NOT gay in that show?" I said, laughing. I was excited that he was having good luck in L.A. too, if a little shocked at the speed with which he'd found an apartment. "Where's the place?" I said, pulling a Perrier out of the mini-fridge and plunking down in one of the overstuffed chairs. I couldn't believe he was actually **choosing** to leave the hotel.

"It's right down the street, at Fountain and Laurel," he said. "I already have a cute neighbor who was laying out by the pool when I went to sign the lease. I actually think he's on that show *Passions* … I love it already!"

I understood the need for independence, but I was a little sad to hear that he was leaving. As roommates, Vince and I had been a surprisingly good match, and I was sort of not encouraging him to get a new place, for selfish reasons. Having a roommate again, even for a short time, had somehow made the experience feel more real and more permanent.

"You're going *now*?" I said. "Don't we even get one last night together, my darling? How will I survive the shock of living alone again?"

"No time to lose," he said in a phony French accent. "I have furniture to buy, wall dressings to hang, fabric to drape! Plus, I have my first-ever private client meeting tonight." He stopped, lowering his voice and looking around. "It's one of the ***Desperate Housewives***."

I laughed. "Congratulations!" I said. "I don't think you have to sign a 'stylist-client' confidentiality agreement, though." He made a face and went back to his business.

I was in the middle of watching Vince pack up the (surprisingly large) amount of clothes that he'd amassed since arriving in L.A. when my cell phone started to buzz. "This is Elizabeth from Mindy Steinman's office at the network," said the serious voice. "Can you come down for a meeting at 4:00 today? Mindy just has a few things she wanted to discuss with you."

With that, I made Vince promise not to leave without writing down his new address and headed down to the posh network offices, where I got a secret thrill from being waved in at the golden gate.

I checked my watch as soon as I arrived at the network, noting with surprise that it was 3:30 pm. This meant that a) I had actually made it all the way to the west side, parked, and found the right office in under forty five minutes, even in mid-day traffic and on the 405, and b) I was actually early for a meeting, an occasion rare enough to warrant a self congratulatory pat on the back. I was sitting on the leather couch in an otherwise-deserted looking office, in the middle of a copy of the ***New Yorker*** I had in my purse for just such waiting occasions when I heard her voice through the crack in the door.

"This just won't do," it started. Then, more: "Did you go to college?"

A terrified voice replied meekly "Yes, Ms. Steinman. Harvard."

"And … Harvard is still teaching English, I'm assuming?"

"Yes, Ms. Steinman." I cringed on Elizabeth's behalf.

"I'm just wondering then, Elizabeth, how it is that you have not yet mastered the basics of English that it might take in order for you to write a simple memo. Please be aware of the fact that if you feel you're not up to handling this job, there are probably at least 10,000 film students out there who would do it for free."

"Of course, Ms. Steinman."

A disgusted sigh, then: "Elizabeth, Amy Spencer from **Autumn Leaves** is on her way in now. Please make sure she's brought directly to my office when she arrives, and let me know if she's late."

My watch said 3:45pm, and I was starting to get nervous. If I kept sitting outside the office and the door opened, Mindy Steinman would know that I was already there, and this poor Elizabeth girl would get in even more trouble. However, if I left and tried to come back, *I* might get in trouble. What was the right answer?

The berating continued, and I couldn't bear to listen anymore. Finally, I made an escape to the hallway, where I stood outside the main office reading and re-reading an article on the evolution of Wikipedia until exactly 3:55 pm. As I opened the door to go back in, I felt a sense of relief to see that Elizabeth had made it out alive and was sitting at her desk. "Hi there," she said flatly. "You must be Amy. Just have a seat, and Mindy will see you soon."

4:00 pm came and went, and I studied Elizabeth. She had longish blonde hair, and was wearing a white cotton tailored shirt and black pants. Since she was typing what I was pretty sure was an "I hate my boss" email, I surmised that she was not illiterate. She looked upset, but I wasn't even supposed to have heard the conversation, so I kept my nose in my magazine for what seemed like forever, checking my watch in five minute intervals. What was she doing in there? Why did she want me there right at 4:00 pm? Was this some sort of psychological game? Was I waiting for a fate even worse than Elizabeth's?

At 4:42 pm, Elizabeth's phone rang. She answered it and looked up at me. "Mindy will see you now," she said. As she hung up the phone, I thought I saw a look of dread on my behalf in her eyes, or maybe it was "better you than me" look. Elizabeth had all the classic signs of an abused wife from my Psych 101 textbook, right down to being unsympathetic if she saw that someone else was going to get it.

"Amy, nice to see you. Shut the door and have a seat," said Mindy Steinman, executive producer. Maybe because I was so nervous at the final audition, I didn't really notice anything about her, but as I walked into her office, I came to realize all at once that Mindy Steinman was an impractically large and somewhat unkempt woman. With long, dishwater brown hair curling around her round, pasty face and down her back, she was easily three hundred pounds. Because my parents trained me to think nice things about people of all sizes, I decided that she would have been great in a Boticelli painting, all fleshy curves and pale skin. Actually, she looked a little like Fran, the woman who owned the junk shop back in Bay City. Like Fran, she wheezed and lumbered like a freight train as she got up, poured herself a glass of water from a bar on the wall of her office, and settled herself back behind her large oak desk. As I watched her holding the water up to her fat lips, the thought of her eating made me a little nauseous. Suddenly, I felt trapped, and all at once I realized that Sondra Smith was, in fact, just the gargoyle at the gate of Mindy Steinman Hell.

"As you know, the network just confirmed they're picking up **Autumn Leaves** for a pre-order of thirteen episodes, which means we start shooting on July 4th for Season One."

"I know … that's great!…." I said trepidatiously, then immediately doubted myself. I thought it was great. **Was** it great? Did she want twenty episodes? Did things usually get picked up faster? Why did I let her make me so nervous?

She made a face like she'd smelled something bad. "Great? No, Amy, that's unheard of. She spat the words out like the unexpected and unwanted pits of grapes she'd thought were seedless. "Great," she repeated again, chuckling.

"Oh, I didn't know … I thought … I mean … that's fantastic! I'm really excited to be working on such a great show!" I stammered as I try to dig myself out of the hole I'd gotten myself in. When did this meeting take a turn for the worse? I remembered the overhead Elizabeth conversation, and vowed not to speak again until spoken to.

She'd already moved on to the next thought. "There are just a few … changes that the network has asked us to make, in order for the show to be as successful as possible. You want the show to be successful, right?" She leaned forward in her chair, scowling over thick black glasses, which had formed a dent in the fat on the side of her head.

I nodded. I wasn't sure I got whatever hidden meaning she was trying to convey. I started to squirm in my chair. What was she saying? Had **I** not mastered the English language?

"First off, we've decided to go a different direction with the writer of the show," she said. "So, we won't be working with Josh anymore. The network thinks that the show has more potential as the next **Beverly Hills, 90210**, or **The O.C.**, and Josh wasn't on board with that. So, we've brought in a different team to re-tool." She paused momentarily, to see if I was getting all this. "This is going to mean we have to make you as commercially appealing as possible. Do you get what I'm saying?"

A sinking feeling began to grow in the pit of my stomach. Josh was gone? Could they just arbitrarily change everything like that? What did she mean by "commercially appealing?" I nodded.

She leaned back in her chair, which groaned. "Listen, I'm not going to lie to you. I think your look is too "regular folks," to work for the long term and the new direction. But Josh got his way with his "authentic Midwestern girl," and now it's too late to re-shoot again.

"So," she continued, "If this is going to work, we're going to have to make some changes, and make the best of it. We'll need to do some serious thinking about your weight."

As she lifted her arms in the air to gesture for emphasis, I watched in horror as the fat on her arms shook like pink wings, and resisted the urge to stare. She paused for a moment.

"We focus grouped the pilot, and I'm telling you, you barely squeaked by … I mean, this isn't an "issues" show with one overweight character. Do you follow what I'm saying?" She stopped and leaned forward again, and I thought I saw a grin hidden somewhere in the fat rolls in her neck.

I felt my heart drop into my stomach. She didn't want to cast me? Did she just call me fat? Was it even legal for her to be saying these things to me? I felt like vomiting on her expensive desk. Somehow, I fought through the panicky feeling growing inside me long enough to smile weakly.

"OK," I said … "Sounds great."

She leaned forward again, propping herself up on chubby, trembling arms. "The first thing we'll need you to do is lose at least fifteen pounds. I don't believe you're really a size four … I had Lola in the wardrobe department send over your clothes, and they're all at least sixes."

My head started to spin. Yes, I had gained the freshman fifteen and not lost it, but isn't that what everyone does in college? Didn't they originally want a real Midwestern looking girl? Was the new direction about a girl with an eating disorder?

She was dead serious. "We need you to be committed to the show, and that starts with your look. We start shooting Season One in four weeks, and we need you to be *max* 115 pounds by then, or we really are going to have to replace you." With that, she opened up her desk drawer, pulled out prescription bottle and tossed it across the desk at me. "Here, try these. Once we get that weight down, we'll also need to develop a new persona for you, including your hair, your style, and your name.

I could feel Elizabeth's eyes on me as I walked out of the office. I knew she'd heard everything, and I expected at least a sympathetic glance from her, since now I new what she faced on a daily basis. Instead, she simply cast a disapproving glance at my thighs, then pursed her lips and sighed, as if she couldn't imagine how I could be thin enough in four weeks.

From that day on, Mindy Steinman was known to me only as Attila.

CHAPTER 6

✦

"Turn this music off ... my God!" said Vince, hitting the pause button on my iPod with the toe of his boot. "1,500 songs, and all you can play is "*Agnus Dei*" over and over again? This shit would make Richard Simmons want to commit suicide."

The day after my "we're going in a new direction and you're too fat" meeting with Attila, I was lying on my bed surrounded by diet books, listening to Rufus Wainwright and trying to figure out the best way to lose fifteen pounds in thirty days WITHOUT taking the Mysterious Black Pills or ending up in the hospital. The meeting and her proclamation about how little she liked me had thrown me into a semi-funky funk, which I was drowning in Diet Coke and frozen York Peppermint Patties I kept in my freezer, just for occasions such as this. I was mentally gearing up preparing to never eat anything delicious, ever again.

"I'm having a food funeral," I said grumpily. Clearly, the only way for me to keep my job was to lose the weight, and the only way to lose that much weight that fast was to stop eating entirely, or to eat only things that tasted like cardboard. "Go away, Mr. Six Pack Abs Despite Eating Taco Bell," I said, hitting "play," then making a face at him and turning the music up even louder. I couldn't wait until he heard the "I'm Depressed" play list I'd put together for that evening. "It's impossible!" I wailed. "I am trapped in a Hell of my own making." I couldn't even imagine the thought of telling my family that the only good thing to happen to us in three years was gone because I couldn't suck it up.

"Ugh—bite your tongue!," he said. "A million girls would kill for this job, and you have it. You'll figure it out. We're going out. And brush your hair, Sasquatch. If any celebrities happen to be there, I don't want you embarrassing me." I had to admit, having an overdramatic gay best friend was handy sometimes. He would never me go outside until I was at least presentable, and somehow, he could tell me really offensive stuff without it sounding so bad. I'm pretty sure I would have killed Carrie Ann for that Sasquatch comment, but Vince could pull it off. I was in the middle of thinking how I wished *he'd* been the one to break the "you're too fat" news to me the day before, when remembered that I'd promised to go to some after-hours party with him at Maxfield, and instantly I began trying to strategize ways to get out of going.

He anticipated my every excuse. Before I knew it, he'd picked an outfit for me, I'd pulled a fashionable scarf over my still-unruly hair, and we were out the door, leaving the diet books strewn on the bed.

❦   ❦   ❦

"Order something good, like the fried Portobello mushrooms," I said to Vince, gazing wistfully at the appetizers menu. So much delicious food, all of which was forbidden to me.

After three weeks on my Attila-mandated diet, I had lost exactly eight pounds (mostly from depression and stress) and gained a near-obsessive desire to eat vicariously through other people. I had accompanied Vince to Dolce, so we could both check out the restaurant for the first time, and so I could watch him eat. Since I'd been on food restriction, I'd tried four different diets, one involving grapefruit and hotdogs, and had endured two ill-fated days on the Atkins diet, after which I decided that I'd rather get fired from the show than ever see another piece of steak again. The Perricone Diet was out too, as I cannot even stand the smell of salmon. Finally, I arrived at a modified "South Beach" style diet that allowed me to eat enough to keep from going insane.

Vince ordered a cheeseburger, and I made do with a Chinese Chicken salad, but without bread, dressing, or those good crunchy things. I was also looking forward to some black coffee for dessert, which had become one of the main parts of my new food pyramid, along with Diet Coke, water, and cigarettes.

Jon Voight walked by. "Do you think he'd introduce us to Angelina if we asked nicely?" I whispered to Vince, who laughed. "Yeah, I bet he's never heard that before. Besides, aren't they estranged?" he said.

The people at the next table ordered fried calamari, and I watched with the intensity of a peeping tom as they dug in, dipping crusty fried bits into the cream sauce. This weight loss thing was hard—just when the pressure was on the most, it seemed like I was surrounded by delicious free food everywhere I turned—like when you learn a new word, then you hear it all the time. I knew that this was probably the previously unidentified price I'd have to pay for this ridiculous good fortune falling my way, but somehow that concept wasn't making me any less hungry.

"Did you try the pills?" said Vince, sipping a beautifully frothy full fat latte. "I'll try them for you if you're scared." Vince had always been known for his fearless attitude toward the consumption of anything questionable, from food to drink to pharmaceutical. He never got sick, went crazy, or lost his good attitude. In fact, Vince was the only person I'd ever known who had tried every kind of drug there was and was still not afraid to try the newest and latest.

I hadn't tried the pills Attila had given me, partially because I found the idea of taking drugs out of some unmarked bottle from an executive's desk creepy, and also because I was considering this weight loss a "will power" thing I should be able to just do on my own. Still, if I didn't start losing more weight fast (like nine more pounds in the next seven days, to be exact), I was totally screwed. I finished the last of my salad and took a sip of Vince's latte, vowing that if I didn't lose two more pounds by the very next day, I was biting the bullet and trying the pills.

❧   ❧   ❧

By the next morning, I'd GAINED a pound and was starting to panic. I knew Attila (or at least one of her evil emissaries) would be there on the first day of shooting, if for nothing else then just to check on my weight loss progress. Now I **had** to take the pills.

I got out the bottle, which I'd been carrying around in my purse since The World's Most Awful Meeting, trying to work up the nerve to take one, or to call the police and report Attila as a drug dealer. As I rolled the unmarked bottle back and forth in my hands, I wondered what sort of clandestine transaction had to go on behind the scenes that ended in her having pills in her desk drawer, all handy like that. She was obviously not taking them herself, so maybe she just had them on hand for all the people she considered "over-weight." But—where did they even come from? Did the network have its own doctor on staff, just for this sort of problem? Did she have a meeting with him or her first, to discuss how fat she thought I was? Moreover, if I needed medical marijuana to combat the stress of having her as an executive producer, would they be able to prescribe that? The curiosity was killing me. Still, despite the "new direction," I didn't even want to entertain the fact that they might give the job to someone else. I had bills to pay. This thing was bigger than me.

After twenty minutes of trying to work up the nerve, I finally opened up the bottle, shook out one of the black pills, and swallowed it with water, hoping it didn't make me go nuts or have any other bad side effects. I then went up to the roof of the hotel to smoke cigarettes and watch the cars go by. Where were all those people going? Were they all taking pills too?

After an hour or so, the gnawing hunger in the pit of my stomach had started to subside. "This could work," I thought, noting that I'd gone at least fifteen minutes without thinking about how much I wanted a Cinnabon. I did feel a little like I'd had too much caffeine, but that wasn't an unfamiliar feeling for me—in fact, I kind of liked it.

After a few days, I struck a balance with the pills—one in the morning, one in the afternoon, and one if I was going out at night (to keep me from drinking too many Cosmos). The steady stream of pharmaceutical goodness success-fully calmed my food obsessions. I kept the black pills with me for if I got hun-gry, the white pills given to me by one of the lighting guys with me in case I got too jumpy from the black pills, and the blue pills prescribed by the doctor on set for insomnia beside my bed for when I really needed to sleep. I wasn't proud, but by July 4th I was a triumphant 114 pounds, a weight I couldn't remember being since the seventh grade.

❦   ❦   ❦

When we showed up on set to start shooting Season One, the first thing I noticed was that the living room looked different. "What happened to the nice furniture?" I said to Ross, as we gathered around the main house set for a kick-off meeting with one of the producers.

"New direction," he said, sighing. "Focus groups thought that Peter and Michael were too rich ... apparently having too much money is even worse than being gay. They toned it down during the break," he said. I laughed, relieved that he wasn't thrilled about the changes either, and that my weight wasn't the only thing the focus group people didn't like. "Won't people be confused when they see the pilot, then your house looks different in the very next episode?" I said, trying not to sound naïve, bitter, and hungry, all at the same time.

He laughed again. "Pilots are the most rarely shown of any of the episodes ... they're where the studio and the network decide what works and what needs to be changed. Did you ever see the pilot of *Sex and the City*? Sarah Jessica Parker had a bob haircut, she talked straight into the camera, and one of the scenes had the four women eating Chinese food while sitting on the floor of Carrie's apartment. Most of that was changed by the first episode, but by the second season, it was all gone."

"What else did they change? Do I still have a sister? Do we still live in Malibu?" I said, half kidding.

"Oh yeah ... changes like that would require that they re-shoot the pilot again, which they couldn't do. But ... things like people's professions, or sets, or people's appearances ..." He trailed off, sounding embarrassed. He'd obviously noticed my weight loss and was trying to avoid drawing attention to it. I loved him for that.

Michele McCann walked up beside us, and I could feel her eyes surveying my body. "Hi guys," she said enthusiastically. "The new set looks great, right?" Ross excused himself immediately; privately he'd told me that he found Michele "chaotic," and that he tried to stay away from her. I had vowed to do the same if possible, though I was in most of her scenes. I noted with disappointment that she looked exactly the same—apparently the elusive focus group had approved of her, which was sure to only make her attitude worse. "Wow, you've really made a lot of progress toward your weight loss goals, Amy," she said coyly.

I waited for the other shoe to drop. "Only ten more pounds to go!" she said. Wham!

I couldn't tell if she was being cruel and sarcastic, or if this was just her version of cheerful encouragement. Maybe I was too weak from lack of food to come up with an appropriately biting retort.

❧   ❧   ❧

We'd been shooting Season One for about three weeks and the show's fall premiere was rapidly approaching when I got the call from Sondra Smith. "We'll need you in the office at 8:00 am sharp on Saturday, Amy. We've got a team assembled to focus on marketing and branding of your persona," she said. "We've got a lot of work to do on you before the show premieres!" I noted with irritation that a) she knew Saturday mornings were the worst time to schedule meetings because of the long Friday night shoots, and b) I had never received so much as a "good job" for the not easy task of losing weight before shooting resumed, and now I was being reconstructed like the Bionic Woman.

While I'd been learning to subsist on amounts of food heretofore only tolerated by prisoners in P.O.W. camps, Attila had assembled a team of people to make me "marketable" enough to carry a major network show when it launched. Apparently making a brand out of me was going to require the services of more than a few professionals.

❧   ❧   ❧

I arrived at the network early on Saturday morning delirious from shooting all night and was immediately handed a thick, spiral bound report. I was shocked to find my own name of the cover. As I read over the agenda for the day (page one in the "Amy Spencer report"), I was surprised to find that not only was the entire day dedicated to me, but that I had meetings scheduled approximately every ninety minutes until 7:00 that night. What was going on here? I thought. Was I joining some kind of cult?

"Um, what is all this?" I said to Kristen, the one girl in the marketing department I found remotely friendly. "Can this really all be for me?"

"Oh, yeah," she said, looking serious. "There have been so many meetings about you, making your strategy, crafting a new look, the whole thing. This is "Super Saturday!"—the day when it all comes together!" she smiled excitedly, and I tried to smile back. I so wished someone had warned me about "Super Saturday!"

The kickoff meeting for Super Saturday started promptly at 9:00 am. Sondra Smith was the captain of this ship, and Attila was nowhere to be found. I imagined that, in typical Jabba the Hut style, she existed only in her office at the network, her tentacles of influence and evil reaching far and wide.

Sondra opened up the "Amy Spencer" book, which made a cracking sound as she turned the pages "As you are all aware from yesterday's informational briefing, the success of this show rides on our branding of Amy." She looked pleased with herself for the strategies she'd come up with, as well as completely uninterested to hear what I thought. In fact, as she looked around the table to the no less than fifteen men and women assembled in the conference room, she made very little if any eye contact with me, as if she'd really prefer I not be there at all. I turned the pages of the Super Saturday book, stopping on a page called "Life History." It contained, in bullet pointed form, everything I'd told Sondra at our first meeting, from my dad's death to who I'd had sex with to what high school I attended. Super Saturday indeed!

"I'm just going to jump right in with one of the big line items to accomplish for today—the name change. Now, as we've discussed, we as a team feel that 'Amy Spencer' is not a powerful enough name for the girl who has the lead in this groundbreaking network show. While we thought 'Spencer' could work with anything, we agreed that 'Amy' is just too bland, so we've decided to change just the first name. I've asked you each to come up with a list of alternatives, and I wanted to jump right in with some brainstorming."

I looked around. Was she talking about changing my name? I watched in horror as each executive produced a list. They'd thought about alternate names for me? Was this for real?

A pale, blonde haired man of about forty threw out the first shot. "I was thinking Carmen" he said seriously. "Carmen has power, and a little bit of Latina mystery."

"Hmmm...." said Sondra. "Might be tough to sell to the Latina market. She doesn't have any Latin relatives, nor does she speak Spanish."

"Well, neither does Christina Aguilera, and she enjoys that market share," said Blonde Guy. Still, no one looked at me.

"I was thinking more "Old Hollywood Glamour," said Sondra. "Who has something along those lines?" I sat back in disbelief, waiting to hear the next suggestion.

"What about Lana?" said Kristen. "Like Lana Turner. Lana Spencer could be our new Hollywood starlet." I tried to shoot Kristen an "et tu Brute?" look, but she carefully avoided my eyes. She'd obviously known about this for awhile and hadn't said anything.

"Interesting, but sounds a little too much like a porn star ... any others?" said Sondra. I sat back, relieved at least for the moment, since I hated the name Lana.

"What about something unconventional, like Guinevere?" said another of the young executives, this one a young-looking brunette in a suit. "Strange names are really big these days. At least that would get her name in the papers. I've got Guinevere, Pixie, and Faberge."

I laughed out loud at the prospect of introducing myself as "Pixie Spencer," and was met with several uncomfortable glances. Was I not on board? Was I not being a team player?

"Simpler," said Sondra. "Too complex, and then she seems inaccessible, like Samaire Armstrong. She's cute, but her team should have changed that name. "Also, Faberge might be too "urban," she said, being careful to make the politically correct finger gestures.

"What about Star?" said another non descript executive. "Star Spencer is the perfect combination of Hollywood and real folks." A hush fell over the room as everyone nodded their heads. "Star Spencer is perfect," said Sondra, continuing to not look at me. "We'll go with that."

My mind was racing. Could they just change my name like that? Weren't there court papers involved? What about my driver's license? Did I have to start calling myself Star from now on? What was I going to tell my mom? Amy was her mother's name … she was not going to like this. Shouldn't I even get a vote? Is this how it went for Portia de Rossi (Amanda Lee Rogers), Carmen Electra (Tara Patrick), or even Bob Dylan (Robert Zimmerman)? Did I even have a choice in this matter? Had I even lost control of my name?

I was just about to raise my hand to ask a few of these questions when Sondra started again, already using the new name like they hadn't just decided on it the moment before. "Another objective of this meeting is to introduce Star to the individual members of her team, her points of contact for things like appearances, endorsements, and things like that. Kristen, you've been assigned to media—magazine requests, promotional appearances for the show, and requests for interviews. Offers for other types of work can be referred directly to Todd Whitley at William Morris. You know Todd, right?" Kristen nodded, looking over at me guiltily.

"Now," Sondra continued. "Many of you will recognize Brynn Harper, a great stylist who has worked with everyone from Brittany Murphy to Mandy Moore and everyone in between. Brynn is just great at finding the swan in the ugly duckling!" she said cheerfully, casting a glance in my direction. "Brynn will be working with Star this afternoon, just getting the hair, skin, and makeup choices up to speed for casual appearances and off hours, and also working on poses for candid photography."

I looked around at everyone taking notes. What, exactly, was the definition of "casual appearances and off hours?" Did they mean the grocery store? Did I have to adhere to some sort of standard outside of the eighteen hours a day I was on the set? Was I contractually obligated to wear makeup at all times? I started to sweat.

She continued. "Gina from wardrobe will be coordinating with Brynn on an ongoing basis, regarding designers' requests for placement on the show, fashions they'd like to see worn in the off hours, exclusively and non exclusively, and appropriate fashions for casual use. Gina works with Lola, so she'll be making a weekly report of Star's weight and measurements."

I wanted to crawl under the table. If I had a personal version of Hell, I'm pretty sure it would include a brand new name and a weekly report of "weight and measurements."

"Tim here is going to be working with Star on media training. As we all know, this is a controversial show for the network with some challenging content, and we want to make sure all of the cast members, especially Star, are on the same page so the press doesn't misinterpret any of our messages based on off-handed comments. Tim's team also coordinates the placement of promotional items like **Autumn Leaves** merchandise, so if you need an "I Love My Two Gay Dads" sweatshirt, go to him."

Everyone at the table chuckled, and I realized that I had just seen Sondra Smith make a joke.

"I'll be handling Star's etiquette, both on the set, during appearances, and after hours. That will be the last meeting of the day. On Monday morning, we'll reconvene here with individual reports on progress and next steps, and coordinate this into a full-scale presentation to Mindy by the close of business on the status of this situation. Are there any questions?"

I left the first meeting with a creepy feeling. Maybe I was finally seeing the reality of the Hollywood life, but it was definitely too late to do anything about it. There really was no turning back.

❦   ❦   ❦

Four hours later, Brynn Harper and I sat at a table strewn with Polaroid shots of my face. "Listen, I'm not going to lie," she said, pointing at one of the photos. "When you smile with your mouth open like that, you look like someone's retarded cousin. Your tooth to gum ratio is all wrong, and your smile creates three folds in your neck. We really have a lot of work to do to get you ready."

My first session with 'Stylist to the Stars' Brynn Harper had not begun well. After what must have been 100 Polaroids taken in an attempt to capture and refine my best "angles" for future photographic and publicity purposes, I was told that the smile I had used in every school photo since I was five made me look like I was both mentally challenged and fat. She also hated my hair and informed me that my "personal style was absolutely tragic, and not in a Kelly Clarkson before picture kind of way."

"You need to go home and practice your "good faces" every day in the mirror, so when you do personal appearances, the magazines have a number of good shots to choose from," she said earnestly. "If you keep making that face, you are going straight into the "star bloopers" edition of the *Enquirer*. Have you noticed how much more press Keira Knightley is getting now than when she first started? Somebody obviously told her that she looks much better when she keeps her mouth closed. Have you seen her giant teeth?"

I was trying not to be offended—Brynn knew everything about the construction of a celebrity image, and the network was paying her big bucks to "streamline" me before the show premiered. However, she was acting like I was her biggest-ever challenge. In fact, I thought the Hair and Makeup department was doing a pretty good job on my hair, and I knew I didn't have anything glaringly wrong with me, like a big bump in my nose. I was thinking about telling her to get over herself when she started in again, taking out a magnifying glass and holding it up to my face.

"Your skin is bad … not Cameron Diaz bad, but broken out and blotchy nonetheless. What do you use to wash it … a washcloth and Dial soap?" she laughed. At me.

"Um … yeah, that's exactly what I use," I said, laughing. "Actually, I'm not kidding. It's always worked for me."

"Oh, you're killing me," she said. "I can't believe the makeup department on your show hasn't told the producers about your skin problems. We need to get you to a dermatologist to get some of those pimples injected right away. Here's the number of the guy Leo DiCaprio uses," she said, scribbling the name in the top of a pad of pink Post-Its that had previously been used only to stick the words "Don't Make This Face!" on the Polaroids.

"Also, you need to get on a regiment of products, so when the magazines ask you, you can tell them what you're using. I'll have La Mer send some over, and you'll probably like Dr. Hauschka as well. If nothing else, you could just start using Proactiv like Jessica Simpson—maybe they'll use you in their infomercials!"

I started to internally panic at the list of products and services that seemed to grow longer by the minute. The big paychecks *had* started to come in regularly, but I had vowed to help my mom and my brothers and bank a lot of the rest for the future, and I wasn't sure if I would have to pay for this stuff myself. How to ask without incurring her wrath?

"Do I have to pay … I mean, how much is all of this stuff?" I said, attempting to choose words with the least potential for mockery.

She laughed again. "Oh, that is so cute. Honey, don't worry—it's all covered. If your show gets big, you're not going to be paying for much of anything. You'll see."

Brynn had also brought a huge collection of designer clothes in an attempt to construct some kind of personal style for me before the show launched and I embarrassed the entire network with my collection of colorful vintage t-shirts which now included "I'm a Pepper," "Silly Rabbit … Trix are for kids!" and "My Little Pony." "Ugh—so last year," she said, picking up the shirt I'd worn to the office that day. "You should really never go out in public wearing the same thing twice anyway."

For the record, it's not that I didn't care about fashion. I cared enough. It's just that, when you're a college student in Michigan, a $700 pair of shoes doesn't even *exist in your universe*, and so fashion was like a spectator sport for me—a sport that I wasn't even remotely rich enough to participate in. Anyhow, I got the feeling from Brynn that even if I *had* made an effort up to this point, I still would have fallen short of this new world.

"Next, your hair. I'm getting Ken Paves to come over to do blonde highlights on you. He's Jessica Simpson's best friend, you know … we want to make you blonde, but not too blonde … you still have to be the believable as the All American Girl. Look at Sarah Michelle Gellar. When *Buffy* first started, she had dark hair, and by the end, that show was a huge hit and she was practically a platinum blonde. It just goes to show—blondes make for good television." She stood behind me, picking up individual sections of my hair and then tossing them down again, making clucking noises with her tongue. "Your hair is dry and frizzy, and you obviously just haven't had a haircut in a long time. It's got no shape at all!"

As she circled me, I silently thanked God that I'd started with the getting of the part, then the shooting of the pilot, THEN the weight loss and the makeover, because I'm pretty sure I would have killed myself if Attila and Brynn were the first people I saw when I got to L.A.

Just when I thought she'd lost hope and was going to recommend to the network that they have me killed so they could focus the show on someone less monstrous, she said: "You have really expressive eyes. Let's focus on those, and really play those up for now."

I walked out of the conference room that now looked like a Level Five disaster area, carrying a giant pile of clothes and noting bitterly that the one thing she liked about me was something over which I had absolutely no control.

❧   ❧   ❧

The "style" meeting was followed by media training ("try not to say 'gay' if you can help it—the proper term is 'homosexual'), product placement ('if there's a Coke in the scene, be sure to hold it so the logo is facing the camera'), and magazine photo shoot/interview requests ('stick to bullet points, don't let them put you in anything too revealing that would compromise your brand equity'), and several others. By the end of the day, my main focus was willing myself to stay awake, since I already knew I was going to forget most of what they were telling me. My last meeting of the day was "etiquette and standards," with Sondra herself. Though I arrived in her office fifteen minutes early for the meeting, she was already a few hours into her "I Hate Everyone" face.

"OK, now I'm going to go over some basic "rules"—just try to keep these in mind when you go out, talk to people or give any interviews. At first, we're going to try to just limit your exposure, to make sure we start positioning you in a way that's appropriate to your target market."

Since I felt a little like I was still in school, and since I understood one third of what she was saying, I got out my black and white composition notebook, wrote the headline *RULES FOR CELEBRITY,* and started taking notes.

1. No smoking. "You can smoke in private, but it's better overall if you don't let anyone take photos of you smoking," she said. "You'll end up on websites and in materials of those "anti smoking" organizations, you just don't need that, especially since Autumn is supposed to be this wholesome Midwestern girl, and that's what we're billing you as. It's not that big a deal—just something you want to watch out for because it does you more harm than good." I wondered if she knew that without a constant stream of nicotine, I'd be getting a lecture from another department on my "weight issue."

2. No Trash Talking. "You're going to be media trained by the marketing department if you're doing interviews about the show … this is more for in your regular life. The media loves to create feuds between hot young stars (Nicole Richie vs. Paris Hilton, Lindsay Lohan vs. Jessica Simpson, etc.). So, if a reporter asks you, even casually, if you like someone, always just said "yes," don't comment, or change the subject to something fun, like clothes, music, or a movie you just saw or a book you just read. Actually … we'll make a monthly list of music, movies, and books you can mention in the media. That's a good idea," she said, making a little note for herself in her portfolio.

"If you give them one tiny comment, there's going to be a whole spread in the center of *Life & Style* magazine the very next week. Trust me. Even though there's no such thing as bad publicity, it's better if they focus on something good. This also applies to working on film sets … even if you hate everyone you're working with, don't *ever ever ever* go on record saying that you don't like a director, or your fellow actor has bad breath, or anything like that. You'll see."

3. Don't Be a Drunk. "There will be a lot of opportunities for you to drink, even though you're not twenty one yet, and that's fine—just don't to be photographed drinking, or you'll end up in some big exposé. I mean, look at what doing that did to Tara Reid's career, and she was that cute little virgin girl from *American Pie*. So sad." She paused for a moment, as if in reverie. As she talked I considered my brief and unsuccessful attempt at becoming a Hudson drama department party girl, which ended with Vince and Carrie Ann carrying me home, and two days in bed. "OK," I nodded.

4. Don't talk about your plastic surgery. "Have it—everybody does—in fact, you might need some," she said, making another note, "But definitely don't admit to it. And don't 'out' anybody else, or speculate publicly on who has had it. Stuff like that will come back to haunt you. In this area, it's best to just *deny deny deny*!" At this, I wondered what surgery she thought I needed, but I just kept nodding and taking notes.

5. Don't get caught doing drugs. "If Kate Moss taught us anything, she taught us that it's a bad idea to snort cocaine if there's anybody watching. Matthew McConaughey is another good example of this—yes, he's hot, but somewhere in the back of people's minds, he's always going to be 'Stoned Naked Guy with Bongos.' I don't even need to mention Farrah Fawcett or Courtney Love. Some directors will not work with you if they think you're just going to be high all the time or bring drugs onto their sets, because it will make their insurance go up, and if they think you're just going to freak out and hold up their shooting schedule, producers are not going to back a film that you're in. Just be aware of what you're doing at all times when you're out in public and someone might have a camera. It's much easier to deny if there's no proof, or if it's just some nobody's word against yours. That we can spin." I kept nodding. Some of these theories Vince had speculated about during late nights in the dorm with his *US Weekly* and *People*, but it was like an all-access backstage pass to actually be hearing them from an industry person's mouth. I wanted to call Vince and scream "YOU WERE RIGHT!" Instead, I just kept nodding and writing, trying to keep accurate notes.

6. Always Be Thinking. "In other words, every time you're not alone, you're working. Things can change in a heartbeat, your show could go off the air, you could get cast in an action movie and become as big as J-Lo overnight. Make sure you make as many friends as possible when you're starting out, because you never know when you're going to need help.

7. Don't Be a Weirdo. "It's really simple—being weird to a certain extent can be your strategy (think Drew Barrymore), but if you do it too many times, you get a reputation as a loose cannon. Remember Sean Young? No? That's because she supposedly went crazy and stalked one of her co-stars. Now she can't get hired as a P.A. Look—Joaquin Phoenix gave this weird red-carpet interview about a frog eating through his skull, and then he didn't win the Academy Award for *Walk the Line*. Philip Seymour Hoffman might be totally weird in private, but you'd never know it—thus, he won for *playing* a weirdo, Truman Capote."

I stopped nodding for a moment. This particular item was so multi-faceted, I felt like I needed the Cliff Notes. I made a mental note to Google "Sean Young" when I got home.

After quizzing me on different made up situations ("What do you do if Lindsay Lohan comes up to you in a club and slaps you in the face?"), Sondra was satisfied that when the show premiered, I could be counted on to not go crazy and embarrass the network. "OK, we'll call you in again if we feel like we need to do any follow up with you," she said. I noticed it was already dark outside, and I longed for my sweet bed. I was totally exhausted, and all I wanted to do was go back to the hotel where it was safe, smoke cigarettes, drink some vodka, and process all of this new information. Hopefully, I wouldn't be in any of these situations anytime soon. Maybe the first few times, I could just bring my notebook with me, for reference.

❦   ❦   ❦

An hour after the conclusion of Super Saturday, Vince was listening wide eyed in rapt attention as I told him about the day of meetings and the truth about everything. "They changed your NAME?" he said in disbelief, grabbing a Camel Light out of his messenger bag and lighting it. "Can they just do that?"

"Well," I said, "It went by so fast … I don't know. I didn't feel comfortable objecting. Besides, "Star" is kind of a cool name. Maybe they're right … Amy Spencer *does* sound like the name of a girl who milks cows."

He laughed. "Cows? Whatever. You will always be my little Amy." He paused. "They're right about your hair, though … it still needs work. And for the record, that thing about Lindsay Lohan is a trick question. She would throw a drink in your face, not slap you!" he said, blowing smoke rings and laughing.

❦   ❦   ❦

In further anticipation of the premiere, Super Saturday was followed by an afternoon of media training for the entire cast. Since the premise of *Autumn Leaves* was a revolutionary one for a network show; we were warned that we would soon be besieged by media scrutiny. Sondra was tasked to media train each of us to make sure we were all "on message." During an uncharacteristic break from shooting, the cast was gathered at a mahogany table in a huge conference room at the network offices.

"I've prepared a list of topical bullet points," she said. I noted that I had never actually had a conversation with Sondra that did not contain the word "bullet points." Ross made a hash mark on his notepad, and I stifled a laugh.

He'd noticed too.

CHAPTER 7

❀

The premiere of the show was officially the first time I'd ever been on TV, and I was beside myself with excitement. Carrie Ann had taken a few days off of school and flown out for the party, which she, Vince and I (and the rest of the cast) attended at Greg Forster's fabulous house in the Valley.

The day after the series premiere, we were sitting at King's Road Café near Vince's new apartment having brunch when two teenage girls ran up. "Oh my God ... Star Spencer ... it's you! We totally loved your show! Zach is so hot! You look so much smaller in person! Can we have your autograph?"

I glanced over at Vince who was putting serious effort into not laughing as I signed my name on the girl's math homework. Since I had never really gotten around to practicing the signature of my new name, it ended up looking like a combination of my old signature and like that of a fourth grader. "Omigod ... thanks!" squealed the girls, skittering off down Beverly.

The girls' presence drew scattered glances from the other people in the restaurant, some of whom began a game of "Where have I seen that girl before?" Quickly, they all decided that I must be some B-Level star at best and went back to their frittatas. I reminded myself that two weeks ago, Vince and I had seen Famke Janssen there and debated doing that very same thing.

"That was weird," said Carrie Ann, digging back into her salad.

I started to obsess about what those young girls were saying about me as they walked away. Why had they said I was smaller in person? Did they think I was fat? The makeup person had to work on me for two hours just to cover my acne for the pilot. I made a mental note to eat better and work out more, and to try to integrate more of Brynn Harper's style tips into my daily going-out preparations. This bothered me, though—how come I couldn't just focus on the good? Was the Hollywood game getting to me already?

After lunch, we walked down to the nail salon for manicures. Carrie Ann seemed a little quiet. "What's wrong?," I said.

"I don't know," she started. It's just … those girls … I just think the show is going to be really huge. On the one hand, I'm really happy for you, but … I just have a feeling that you're never coming back now, and I'm just kind of freaking out for you. It all just seems so random, you know?"

"I know, it's totally weird," I said, just to fill the silence. Vince made a face. "No it's not," he said. "It's fucking great! Hello … Amy is living the American Dream right now, Carrie … of *course* she's never coming back," he said. "She's famous, she's rich, and she belongs here. Come on! You know it's what you want too!" he said, poking her in the ribs. I laughed, happy that he was trying to break the obvious tension, but Carrie Ann seemed determined to be serious. Was she jealous?

In truth, the whole roller-coaster aspect of it was freaking me out a little bit too, but there was no going back. I mean, wasn't this the reason we majored in drama in the first place? How could she be mad at me for being successful and happy? The problem was, I actually didn't know what I did to get the lucky break, and I wasn't exactly sure what I could do to keep the luck going. From the first audition, it had all seemed somehow beyond my control, and I really felt like it could all end at any minute. Every time I tried to tell someone this, they'd just tell me to "enjoy the ride," and that I should feel lucky, because 90% of Screen Actors Guild members were unemployed. It's not that I wasn't happy and excited. In fact, I was **beyond** happy and excited. But … how do you enjoy a ride when you have no concept of its turns, when it will come to an end, or where you're going? Was Carrie Ann just pessimistic, was she jealous, or was she right?

❉   ❉   ❉

Two weeks after the show's premiere, Michele decided she wanted to be my friend, taking me to Robertson Boulevard on a Saturday afternoon for some celebratory shopping. "I can't believe you've never been here," she said, leading me into Lisa Kline. "You have so much to learn." I noted with little surprise that her "I'm being nice" voice was hardly different from her "I don't like you" voice. Maybe I needed to lighten up about her. With Vince always out and busy developing his client base and Carrie Ann not returning any of my calls or emails since she went back to school, I was feeling lonely, and I wasn't even at the top.

One of the reasons I'd never been to Robertson was the money. Even though I'd started receiving regular paychecks that exceed most peoples' annual salaries, I still cringed when I saw flimsy t-shirts adorned with glitter, $200 price tags dangling off of them. Something about it just seemed wrong to me. Besides, I was still getting the "you're too fat" vibe from everyone on set, so I felt bad buying anything in my real size. Still, I was curious about the "West Hollywood shopping" that everyone on set talked about, so I finally gave in and went with her.

We stepped out of Lisa Kline on the way to Ghost when I noticed them—two guys with cameras, trying to be subtle while they followed us down the street. "Do you see them?" I whispered to Michele. "Are they following us?" We tried slowing down, and the guys slowed down too. Once they realized we knew they were following us, they got out a set of even larger cameras and started blatantly snapping our every move. All at once, I was totally self conscious, trying to remember all of my good camera angles. I knew they were trying to capture us in our "normal life" moments, but the very act of having cameras trained on me rendered me totally self-conscious, as if having the camera there had changed the act of shopping into a mini-performance. Right then, I developed a whole new understanding of those weird people on COPS as I realized it actually *is* impossible to "act natural" when you know you're being observed.

"Omigod! It's our first stalkerazzi experience!" Michele said, taking out her cell phone and dialing furiously. "Rachel! You're never going to believe who's following me right now," she said into the phone. "Don Jackson! Yeah … that sleazy guy who used to sit outside the Miramar Hotel last summer, waiting for

Britney to come out? … yeah! I know! Really good, I know! Yes, I will totally get you on the show! OK, bye!"

"Don't smile at them," said Michele. "Don't even look at them … pretend like you don't see them. That's what big stars do." We kept walking, proceeding quickly into Ghost. The camera guys stayed outside, but they were photographing us through the window, trying to capture what we were looking at, what we were buying. It was weird and exhilarating and fun, all at the same time. "This is so great!" said Michele. "This means the show is a big hit … why else would they care what kind of shoes we're looking at?" We went in four more stores, and the crowd just got bigger.

She was right—four days later, photos of our shopping excursion appeared in a few of the magazines, alongside a giant headline that screamed "*Autumn Leaves* Stars Are Just Like Us!" The day after that, Michele and I each received a box full of shoes and bags. I tried to match each item with how much it was at the store, and I came up with $5,000 for one box.

"We should go shopping together more often," Michele laughed. "We made out like bandits! I wonder if this is what happens when those girls from *Grey's Anatomy* go out together on the weekends?"

I laughed. If this was what being famous was going to be like, I loved it already. Let the photographers follow you a little, get free stuff? What was the big deal?

❦   ❦   ❦

The day after the shopping photos came out, my phone rang with a number I didn't recognize. It was Attila, calling from a cell phone. I tried to imagine a Blue Tooth hiding within the folds of her fat face as I tried to think of the right things to say. Why did I let her get to me? I was the start of a hit show!

"Hello, Star? I'm looking at a photo of you and Michele in Lisa Kline, and I don't like what I see. Why are you wearing an "I'm a Pepper" t-shirt? Obviously, your work with Brynn wasn't enough, so we're going to try a different direction. We're going to need you to be a little more upscale, to reflect well on the show. We're building a brand, after all. I've booked you an appointment with Jennifer Rosen for Saturday at 2:00pm. She'll be pulling together some looks for you. She's in Silverlake." I was determined never to make the mistake of making small talk with her ever again, so I didn't mention that I had only been to Silverlake once and it had taken me four hours to get home. My car had a killer GPS system that had recently gotten me all the way to Santa Monica and back. I took the address and hoped for the best.

Vince was beyond excited to hear this news. Apparently, Jennifer Rosen was the best stylist in town with a list of celebrity clients a mile long. "You are so taking me with you!" He screamed. "Jennifer Rosen is the SHIT! She makes like, $7,000 a day being a celebrity stylist. If I work with her, that would totally be *my* big break!"

Armed with GPS and strong coffee, we arrived only slightly late at Jennifer Rosen's groovy Silverlake townhouse, the entryway of which was packed to the rafters with designer clothes. She opened the door on the first ring. "Star!" she said excitedly. "I'm so glad you're here!" She was early forties with blonde hair, stick thin arms, a golden bronze fake tan, and smoky eyeliner.

She and Vince shook hands, and I said a little prayer that they hit it off. I silently vowed to do whatever she said, just so I could get in good with her on his behalf.

"So, Mindy sent me over the photos, which I had already seen of course. Do you want a Diet Coke?"

"Sure," I said, trying not to read into the fact that she offered me a Diet Coke instead of regular. Despite the black pills, I had actually GAINED back four pounds since we started shooting again, and I was hungry all the time anyway—this woman looked like she hadn't eaten since the 1980's. She was maybe 100 pounds, with protruding hipbones, a bony clavicle, and absolutely no boobs. I seriously doubted she would able to relate to the fact that if I even *looked* at a cupcake, the next day I gained a pound. I started to get nervous. Were all the clothes in her jam-packed foyer the same size as her? Good Lord. Why is everyone in Hollywood so freakishly tiny? Did I have any hope of ever being this size?

We stood in front of a giant mirror framed in gilt gold that was set up in her living room. I wondered how many of her celebrity clients had stood in that same spot while she constructed a carefully crafted image for them.

"OK, we need to start with your hair. I know they worked on it a little bit for the show, and the cut looks all right, but I think you could safely go much blonder, and much longer. I like my girls to have long, blonde hair and tan skin. Also, when you go out, PLEASE don't pull your hair back in a messy ponytail or one of those buns, unless you've just been to the gym. We want your hair long, and blonde, and flowing down your back. That way it'll make your face look thinner. I've made you an appointment with Byron Williams for tomorrow for extensions and color, and I've cleared it with Mindy."

I nodded, hoping that my hair didn't fall out from all the bleaching. I was sure she'd say that baldness was definitely not star-like.

"The problem is, you don't have a cohesive sense of style," she said. "What are you going for, in terms of a look? Old Hollywood glamour like Catherine Zeta-Jones, boho chic like Kate Moss or Sienna Miller, or modern elegance, like Carolyn Bessette Kennedy? Do you even know? You need to have a goal for the style we're creating, you know? Right now, when you're not shooting, you just look like a regular civilian on the way to the mall or something." She laughed. "We just need to step you up a notch."

"I totally agree," Vince said, nodding. "No one's *E! True Hollywood Story* ever starts with the girl in a corduroy blazer and an 'I'm a Pepper' t-shirt, Aim." I was so glad the two of them were on the same page regarding my utter lack of style. I knew he meant well. Her, I wasn't so sure about. I was rapidly growing not to trust stylists at all.

"I have no idea," I said meekly. In fact, I really didn't know. Was it really not okay to go out in sweatpants if I was just getting gas or buying milk at the store? Did I need Rock & Republic jeans and Alexander McQueen heels just to go to brunch?

Apparently I did. Next, she directed me to the first of about 100 outfits I would try on that day. "Put this on, and we'll see what looks good on you." I changed into what looked to be a very expensive Balenciaga top, and she took a Polaroid. "That looks great—you need some earrings though," she said, pulling out a drawer that was full to overflowing with jewelry of all shapes and sizes. "The network wants you to look more put together. There is big money behind that show, and you're the face of it, whether you like it or not. You should be committed to building your brand," she said as she draped gold necklaces over my head. "There you go … very Mary-Kate," she said, turning me around and plunking gray aviator glasses on my face.

"OK, what about your skin?" she said.

"Yes," I sighed. "I'm seeing a dermatologist about the acne, and I'm still looking for the perfect concealer for the eye bags" What more could she say? I felt like already, I'd heard it all before.

"What? No! That's not what I mean … that stuff you can cover" she said, laughing. "You're too pale, girl! You need to look like you go out in California sun! You're not in Michigan anymore!" She pulled out a small pot of powder that said "Gold Coast" on the side, produced a puff out of thin air, and started brushing it onto my face. I thought we must have been almost done when to further compound my horror, she pulled out a tape measure, which she wrapped around my hips, clicking her tongue. "What's your diet plan?" she said. "You really should be thinner. Like, I have all of my clients in size 25 jeans—are those 27s? Those have to go."

Once again, I felt like crying. 27 was the smallest size I'd worn in three years. There was no possible way, short of an actual miracle, that I would be able to fit my ass into a size 25. I knew she would tell Attila I was being difficult, so I looked at Vince and laughed. "OK," I said, sighing. Would I ever win this game?

In fact, most of the clothes sent by the designers were too small. "Sample sizes are a zero," she sighed. "That's what you should be in order to wear the most names and get the most press," she said. "You should work on that. They didn't tell me you still had weight issues." She stood back, taking a Polaroid of me wearing a too-small size zero skirt. "We can make this work for now, but you'd look really good if you lost another ten pounds. I'm sure you get that all the time."

I wanted to tell her that I'd **been** working on that—that, in fact, the "weight issue" was **all** I'd been working on, that I actually had to will myself not to eat Cookie Dough ice cream the night before, and that I was, in fact, so constantly hungry that I might be justified in killing her. Instead, I just said "yes, I understand … I'll work on that," and continued to sift through endless piles of clothes I knew wouldn't fit, hoping to find a nice jacket or scarf.

She looked at me quizzically. "Yes, thinness is an essential part of the Young Hollywood look. Let me know if you need more help."

I looked at Vince again. I was already taking the secret black pills from Attila. Did she know that? What did she mean? I wondered what magic trick *she* had—she certainly looked like she had mastered the art of thinness.

Curiosity got the best of me. "Hey, if you have a secret for getting into size 25 jeans, you just let me know," I laughed. She pulled out a small packet of white powder, pressing it into my hand. Her eyes lit up. "Just for emergencies," she said, "like size 25 jeans." We spent another four hours trying on outfits and taking Polaroids, working on a style for me. Finally, we settled somewhere between "Kate Moss boho chic" and "classic" style. Who knew that clothes could be so complicated?

The next day I spent four more hours in the salon of Byron Williams, who straightened, extensioned, and colored my hair into Hollywood Fabulous Oblivion. I had to admit, I looked cooler than I ever had in my life. I barely recognized myself. I was famous and rich, and now I was *hot.*

Now there was just the matter of getting into those size 25s. At least I knew how she got there. Next stop: Jay Leno.

❧   ❧   ❧

There was no time to be nervous as I prepared for my first-ever guest appearance on Leno. I stood in my dressing room, surrounded by people I barely knew who I guess could have been described as an "entourage"—*my* entourage. Jill (the makeup girl) was applying last minute touch ups to my face, the foundation of which was already thick enough a) to make me look like a drag queen and b) to be sliding off my face from the stress and the heat of the lights. "Seriously, stop sweating!" she said, her voice rising a little too high. "What girl sweats this much?" Already, I could tell it was not going well.

I tried to stand as still as possible while the hair guy put the finishing touches on a blowout of my newly-blonde hair as Jennifer draped me in dangly necklaces. Sondra handed me a typewritten sheet of questions and bullet points, which I tried to read without smudging my freshly painted nails. "Read it!" She barked. "You're on in five!"

Autumn Leaves was one of the most popular shows of the fall season—thus, me on Leno. Sondra pushed the paper precariously close to my face, leaning in after it. "Listen, Star, I jotted down some likes and dislikes for you, along with an outline of your eating and workout plan in case he asks why you've lost weight since the show first started airing."

I didn't dare laugh out loud. I looked over the list. "Golf?" I said, looking up. "Sondra, I don't even play golf. I have never even been on a golf course."

"Hey, watch your eyelashes!" said Jill. "The mink ones take longer to dry. We want your eyes to pop on camera!" Her voice had risen even higher; perhaps Sondra made her as nervous as she was making me. She came at me with the bitey end of an eyelash curler. "Stay still! Stay still!"

"Right," Sondra interrupted. "We don't care if you don't actually *play* golf. We're building a public persona," she said, making the little quote marks in the air with her fingers. She was on a mission that would not be thwarted by mink eyelashes. "Your persona is named Star, and she plays golf. Golf expands your market and makes you attractive to all the dads of Middle America. We'll get you a golf coach, set up a photo op out in Palm Springs. You'll love it. Cami Diaz plays golf. Cathy Zeta-Jones plays golf … golf is the new cardio!"

For the record, "golf is the new cardio" is definitely a statement I would have furiously mocked, were the context at all different. But, since I was trying not to get any further on Sondra's bad side, I simply said: "OK, I'll try to fit golf in there somewhere. Anything else? I want to be sure to be prepared!" I tried to act interested and engaged. I needed at least one advocate on the network's marketing team.

She perked up. "Well, I've also prepared a fun story about moving into your first house, since we all know you lived in Michigan until six months ago."

"Sondra, what's the story about? I still live in a hotel," I said. Were they just making up everything now?

"Yes, I know, but people don't relate to that. This is just a little story about how you moved into this new place, and you didn't know how to work the alarm system, so you ended up calling the police on yourself. It makes you look lovably scatterbrained and accessible."

"OK." I said, giving up and taking the questions and answers into the bathroom, where I began trying to figure out how not to pee on the ruffles of my Chloe dress while I learned as much about my life as possible.

Somehow, I'd always thought being famous came with a certain amount of "devil may care" freedom, but I was slowly discovering the truth.

A bout of furious knocking interrupted my momentary bathroom respite. "Star—what are you doing in there?! You're on next!" Sondra was even more worried about her job security than I was … after all, *my* firing would require changing the entire storyline of a major television show, but if she was found responsible for this, she might actually have to join the Witness Protection Program.

So, maybe she had it worse than me. Still, I was the one about to make a fool of herself on Leno. I paced backstage, going over and over the bullet points. This was just like a pop quiz in college, only the subject was my life.

I heard Jay introduce me, and I felt a little like I was melting. Was this my life? Somehow I managed to talk about the show, tell my cute alarm anecdote, and keep my legs crossed so no one could see my underwear, all while adhering to the bullet points. My only iffy moment came when Jay ad-libbed, which Sondra had guaranteed he wouldn't.

"So … Star … this is the most exciting time of your life right now, huh? What do you like to do when you're not shooting the show?" he said.

And just like that, my mind was blank.

I knew I was supposed to have a witty response—this *was* the most exciting time of my life, for sure. Was I allowed to say that though? I searched my brain for a good answer, vaguely remembering something about golf. Then I froze.

"I … um … I.…" I said, laughing a little. The little voice in my head was going: *Say something! You're on Jay Leno!*

"I like cheese." I said, and Jay laughed. Cheese? Where did that come from? I thought frantically. I then tried to back pedal my way out of the weirdness by explaining that since we started shooting, I'd had no free time, blah blah blah, but Jay took it and ran.

"And there's a lot of cheese backstage at **Autumn Leaves**?" He said jokingly. "You and your two dads are having cheese tastings?" I knew he wasn't trying to make me nervous, but I really wanted to crawl under the couch, and I could definitely feel Sondra's eyes boring a hole in the side of my head from the "backstage" area. I could already feel the memo coming—*Dear Star, regarding your recent Leno appearance, the network would appreciate your limiting your comments to bullet points only. Please see Sondra Smith for more details.*

"And golf." I said weakly. "Definitely golf."

❦   ❦   ❦

Following the "I Like Cheese" Leno appearance, I was surprised to find that no memo appeared to castigate me on my obvious lack of adherence to the bullet points. My fellow cast members actually complimented me on the good job I did.

In fact, it appeared that my Jennifer Rosen/Vince style plan had finally sunk in. I was thinner than ever, and two weeks later, I arrived on the set to find a memo from Sondra underneath my trailer door.

To: Star Spencer
From: Sondra Smith
cc: Mindy Steinman
Re: Teen Vogue

Teen Vogue has requested cover shoot for holiday issue. Photo shoot is Saturday the 14th, 8:00 am at Smashbox Studios, Culver City.

Please arrive early if possible, and stick to prepared, show-related bullet points (attached), and previous media training for interview. The reporter is a freelance writer, and the interview will be conducted during the shoot.

Have fun!
Sondra Smith

I held the paper in my hand. Me, on the cover of a magazine!? Who made these decisions? Who should I call first? I wondered if the *Teen Vogue* people were going to change their minds when I get to the studio and they saw my eye bags.

I pushed # 2 on my cell phone's speed dial. "Vince—you're never going to believe this. They want me to be on the cover of *Teen Vogue!*"

Vince screamed so loud, I had to hold the phone away from my ear. When he was done, he accepted my invitation to accompany to the shoot—his first job as a solo stylist. He gasped, and I thought I heard him choke back a little sob. "Thank you thank you thank you, Amy! Your star is rising, baby! You won't be sorry!" he said, then hung up.

Sometimes, you really need a friend to put things in perspective for you.

❧   ❧   ❧

The show had only been on for a few months when we were shooting a party scene on a set built to look like a country club, and the extras were restless. There were about fifty of them, waiting to spring into action, pretending to eat the fake food and looking like they were having a good time.

Michele and I were sitting in the Smoker's Lounge, which was next to the set for the country club where all the extras were waiting, so to kill time we were eavesdropping on a conversation between a short, balding guy with glasses, and bleach blonde woman with enormous fake breasts. They were standing in front of a middle-aged black woman, and all of them were there for a party. Never let it be said that the country club in **Autumn Leaves** didn't let in people of all races, creeds, and sexual preferences.

"Yeah, I've done extra work on all the shows, and now this. I'm going to casting workshops all the time, and I'm doing the mailings to try to get an agent, you know?" said Big Breasted Blonde. I'd heard other actors talk about the so-called "casting workshop," which sounded to me like one marginally-influential intern charging twenty actors to watch them read.

"It's tough, but you've just got to keep going and eventually you'll get your big break. My acting teacher said I'm good enough to be auditioning regularly, and to just keep at it." We also learned that the balding guy had been "working toward the Hollywood dream" for eleven years, and despite having never gotten even close to a speaking part, he was optimistic that his "big break was right around the corner."

Bleach Blonde replied with an even more disturbing tale. "I just got a chin implant and a brow lift, and now I feel like I'm really ready to take on the modeling industry," she said. I heard Michele stifle a snicker. "She's got to be forty years old," she whispered. "Shouldn't she have tried to take on the industry before now? I'm pretty sure it's too late for her." I smiled, praying that the extras couldn't hear her over the sound of the crew members talking and the giant fan that was turned on between takes to cool the set down. All of the extras had been instructed not to make casual conversation with the regular cast members, and in fact, once the scene was over, they'd be going to a holding area where they would not even be able to use the same bathroom as the regular cast.

I wanted to stop listening, but I couldn't; their conversation was like a train wreck. In the absence of some positive affirmation like a speaking role, I was sure that I would have gotten discouraged. Every time I heard a story like this, in fact, it made me even more superstitious. Did these people "just know" they wanted to be actors, and if so, why weren't they more successful? I had wanted to be an actress since I was a kid too, and now I was one. Simple, right? Did some people "miss" their fate? Were some people just destined to be mediocre, and no matter what they try, they will never succeed? Why do some people (like me) get a "big break" with almost no effort at all, while Joe the Extra toils in obscurity for eleven years with hardly a speaking part? If I said or did the wrong thing and got fired and lost the keys to Oz, would I ever be able to get back? These thoughts terrified me.

Finally, the stage manager indicated that the crew was finished with the lights and called the actors back, and the director came back to set. Thankfully, this meant that we'd be able to start shooting the scene soon, and I wouldn't have to listen to the extras talk about their careers anymore. Somehow, being in the presence of desperation of that magnitude never failed to make me depressed and uncomfortable.

CHAPTER 8

❁

Having slept exactly two hours since shooting wrapped for the night (an epic no-turnaround Saturday), I picked up Vince at 7:00 am for the highly-anticipated *Teen Vogue* Shoot.

He climbed into the BMW and handed me a very large cup of Starbucks coffee. "Is it wrong for me to say I love you right now?" I said. He laughed. "I don't even want to see what's under those glasses, missy." In my first-ever "diva" move, I'd insisted that they hire Vince as my stylist for the shoot. He needed to build up his clientele and reputation, and I needed someone to keep me awake and sane all day. Plus, Vince had been styling me since Hudson, when I wore flannel shirts, took myself way too seriously, and (perish the thought) didn't pluck my eyebrows.

"I made you a Google Map, and called ahead to ask for grilled chicken salads for lunch," he said, shaking sugar packets into the coffee balanced between his knees. "I am telling your WeHo friends that you drink black coffee with sugar. That is SO not a gay boy's drink," I said, laughing. He smiled. "Only in front of you, baby. Everywhere else I'm a mocha light Frappucino like the rest of my people."

We sped down the 405, quickly leaving Mulholland Drive behind, passing the Getty, and speeding toward the west side. Funky music was already pumping through the studio when we got there. In fact, this photo shoot felt so much like a party, I was rapidly overcoming my "photo shoot phobia," (underpants incident, anyone?). There was the perfect amount of food, but not so much that I'd be grouchy from trying not to eat the Famous Amos cookies all day. Vince had outdone himself.

My fear was almost conquered—that is, until it was time to try on potential outfits. After pulling on a cute skirt/sweater outfit, I noticed that each of the items was too small.

"Does this brand run small?" I said, a feeling of dread beginning to creep into the pit of my stomach. I had already wrestled my body down to a size two/four. How much smaller did clothes get, anyway? "This doesn't fit." I peeled off the tiny, ill-fitting skirt, throwing it onto the chair in the makeshift wardrobe department. "What's next?"

Vince picked up the skirt. "This is a size zero," he said, sounding annoyed. "I said twos and fours, and I called yesterday to confirm the wardrobe. I even called with her measurements." He riffled through the different clothes hanging from silver clothing racks. "These are all size zeros."

Vince looked pissed—his first official solo stylist job was rapidly circling the drain, and I was precariously close to tears. "What's going on here?" he said, trying to get the situation under control. "I'm so sorry," said the wardrobe assistant, a well-meaning but frazzled girl named Lisa. "After we pulled the wardrobe, a woman from an executive's office at your studio called. She said you'd been dieting a lot lately and you were actually a size zero now, so we got all new stuff." She looked like she was about to cry right along with me.

I felt the anger rising to the top of my head. Even in her absence, Attila was making her presence felt. I'd been hearing rumors that she'd started to audition other actresses to replace me. I knew Michele wanted me out too and that she was reporting to her father on every line I flubbed and everything I put in my mouth. Even though things were good on the surface, I still felt like the bottom could drop out at any minute.

I was three seconds from total hysteria when Vince took charge. "OK, there's obviously been a misunderstanding," he said calmly. "We can use some of this stuff, but most of it has to go." He looked at me. "Go to hair and makeup and do the interview with the reporter while Lisa and I figure this out. Don't worry about it." He winked at me. "Be sure to stick to the bullet points."

Now I felt like crying from relief. "Really? No cutting the clothes?" I whispered as he walked me to the makeup area, his arm firmly around my waist. "Honey, when have you ever known me to cut the clothes?" He smiled.

Sure enough, my fairy godfather came through. By the time it was time to change into my first outfit, Vince and Lisa had managed to pull together a complete new set of size four outfits, including a beautiful geometric print Diane Von Furstenberg wrap dress. "How did you …?" I looked at Vince. "I worked stylist magic, baby. That's why they pay me the big bucks," he said. "I am a fashion super hero … able to make Diane von Furstenberg dresses appear out of thin air!"

I never did find out where he got the new clothes. Perhaps in some sort of karmic reward, he'd soon acquired two more clients just through word of mouth. By then, I was on another diet, still trying achieve the Mindy-mandated size zero.

❧   ❧   ❧

One week later, Vince and I were watching *Say Anything* for the millionth time when I got a call from the front desk at the hotel. "Ms. Spencer, you have packages waiting. Should we bring them up?"

The boxes turned out to be huge "care packages" from different companies wanting me to endorse their stuff. Jennifer told me she'd be contacting them on my behalf, but she didn't really say what would be in them or what I should do with them when they got there.

Once the boxes arrived in the room and the door was closed, we ripped into them one by one like hungry wolves with raw meat. Vince was in his element. He was taking notes, writing down what was in each box, what designer it came from, and who the contact was for the company in case we ever needed more. "This is unbelievable," he said, breathless. "There's $50,000 worth of stuff here, at least."

The next thing I knew, he was assembling outfits for me out of what was in the boxes, making outfits that showcased two or three designers at a time. There were eight boxes in all, sent from different designers and stores.

"This is like, the greatest thing I have ever seen in my life. I am never, never leaving L.A." sighed Vince. I agreed, secretly wishing I didn't love the trappings of celebrity quite this much. Did I lose some of my edge every time I accepted free clothes? I really hoped not.

❦   ❦   ❦

"How hard can it be? Just pick a charity from the list, and let's go. Mr. Chow is waiting!" Vince waited impatiently in front of the door as I paced back and forth. "Sondra wanted this done weeks ago … she's going to kill me," I said. The Charity List had been plaguing me since Sondra dropped it off in my trailer. I knew it had been weeks because the day she dropped it off, we were shooting the "Autumn's uncle catches her kissing a boy and has to give her the sex talk" scene, which might have been one of the most embarrassing days of my life. Not only was it my first on-screen kiss with a guy I had just met (terrifically awkward), but I was also baffled by the multiple layers of subject matter—getting a heterosexual sex talk (embarrassing) from Greg, a straight actor pretending to be embarrassed because he's gay and knows nothing about heterosexual sex (mortifying) … then I ask what the difference is between hetero and homo sex, and the whole thing devolves one big uncomfortable weird scene. I didn't want to cry every five minutes like I did while we were shooting the pilot, but the day had required a number of takes, so by the end we were all exhausted from laughing and trying to get the scene right. Since nothing like this show had ever been done before, the executives were always on set trying to make sure that the scripts don't go too far, that we were on the right side of the political correctness line.

Apparently, "balancing" an episode like this one required an amplified PR strategy. That night when I got back to my trailer, Sondra was waiting with The List, which had everything from a Mexican orphanage devastated by an earthquake to Tsunami relief to a long list of medical conditions. "What is this?" I asked.

"Here's the deal," she said. "We need a good story on you in the press in about a six weeks to distract from the Middle America backlash we're going to get from this episode. We've got to put a photo shoot together ASAP, so be sure you pick something sooner rather than later."

"What's my cause?" I said. "Like, did I volunteer at my church or something?" I couldn't believe anyone was really going to care about my extracurricular activities. Was I applying to college again?

"God, no ... religion is totally out. Disease is in these days," she said, her face getting serious as she laid it out for me. "It's better if it's personal to you, like if your mom had breast cancer like Brittany Murphy's mom, or if you were in the Tsunami like that model Petra Nemcova, or you're from New Orleans and can talk about Hurricane Katrina. It's also better if you pick something that has sick or starving kids, but not too sick, because no one wants to see photos of you with kids that are too sick. It would be great if you had time to go to Africa, because your skin would look amazing contrasted with the little starving African kids, if you know what I mean. She winked, and I tried not to roll my eyes. Oh, and don't pick the ones that are crossed off. Some of the other cast members are doing those, and we can't have more than one of you on the same cause at a time—*that* looks contrived."

I stared blankly at the list. "Sondra, are you serious?" I said. "Can't I just pick something good, like raising money to fight poverty in inner cities? What about health insurance for the working poor?" I tried to remember some of the issues I'd heard my parents discussing at the dinner table when I was in high school.

Sondra wrinkled her nose and let out a huge sigh. "Listen, I am NOT going to some filthy Boy's and Girl's Club with you in Home Town America just so you can be a do-gooder. It is my job to get photos of you out there that will give people warm feelings about you. We have to give people a reason to like you and to keep watching the show. I don't want to spend a lot of time on this though—find a ribbon to cut in Santa Monica, or go hug some babies in a Pediatric Oncology Unit. Do not make me get dirty, or put me in danger. Just stick to the list, and don't get carried away."

And so The List had been sitting in my trailer, gathering dust and making me tense as I wracked my brain for things that had an actual connection to my life. No one in my family had ever had cancer, my grandparents were still alive, and I'd never been in a natural disaster. The more I went through my family tree and decided I was totally boring and normal, the more I dreaded the inevitable Sondra phone call asking what charity I'd picked.

I scanned the list for the hundredth time. The Myasthenia Gravis Foundation? What even *is* that? Africa was out, as I was unlikely to get a long enough break in shooting to allow me to go back to Bay City for the weekend, much less another continent. I'd never known anyone whose house was destroyed by a hurricane, and no one I knew had lupus, so I was out of luck. Some people get all the good diseases. Damn that Lance Armstrong! The heart defect my dad died of was so rare it barely had a name, much less a foundation. Also, I knew this wasn't really how it worked. Ross was on the board of several charities in LA, did it because he loved it, and helped a lot of people in the process.

And so I was lying on the bed, totally incapacitated, as I knew Sondra was coming by the set the next day and was going to want my choice. For a moment I considered writing "Eating Disorders of the Rich and Famous" on the list, but I knew this would get back to Attila, and I didn't need the headache. What I needed was a nice cousin with scoliosis or a paralyzed veteran uncle. What I had was nothing. Zilch. Zero.

"What about gay rights?" called Vince from the living room of my suite. "Gay rights are huge these days, your show is about gay issues, and you happen to have a gay best friend. We could get you some rainbow bracelets to pass out. Problem solved. Let's go." He put my purse next to my limp hand on the bed and tried to put my fingers around the handle.

I handed him the list. "Sorry … no gay rights causes on here." I didn't want to tell him that I'd already asked about this, and (even though the show's theme focused on two homosexual men adopting a teenage girl), Sondra had strictly forbidden me to speak out about gay and lesbian issues. "Are you kidding me?" she'd sneered. "The minute you attend the opening of some Podunk Gay, Lesbian and Transgender Rainbow Queer Center, I'm going to have to do WEEKS worth of work to combat all the gay rumors that are going to start about you. You don't want to be on the cover of *The Advocate* your first year in Hollywood. I don't care if your dad is gay, which by the way, Anne Heche's was, and that didn't even come out until she'd been with Ellen for two years. Don't even think about doing the gay thing, Star. Seriously. I'm going to have enough trouble keeping the gay media off Greg, who has played an action hero in every show he's been in up to now. Look at that poor Jennifer Beals in *The L Word*. She's married with a baby, and still there's all this speculation about her because that show is so popular. We can't have that with you right now … Please just pick something simple—I'm totally swamped trying to do individual PR for all of you guys as well as the show itself. Seriously, if the show gets much bigger, we're going to need you to hire your own publicist. Ask Greg—he's already got his own."

I surveyed the list again, determined to pick something immediately and get it over with. This shouldn't be so difficult. Dogs … I liked dogs. What about the Humane Society? Finally, I settled on a charity that rescued dogs, which seemed like the cause least likely to incur the wrath of my team. "Great, that's totally great. I'll arrange a photo shoot," said Sondra when I called to tell her. "Just don't go all 'Bob Barker' on us."

❧   ❧   ❧

The fact was, despite how much I wanted to think of myself as an edgy indie girl, being a TV star was fun, and got more so every day. Case in point: Vince and I were at a magazine stand on Hollywood Blvd shopping for our weekly gossip fix when we spotted my *Teen Vogue* cover, already on the newsstands. "Oh my God … it's you!" he screamed, grabbing the magazine. We stood there, absorbing the shock and poring over every picture. "Wow," he whispered. "That doesn't even look like you." He paused. "But in a good way … you know what I mean. Is *that* what they do to Mariah Carey?"

"I know," I said. It wasn't just that I'd changed so much since Michigan—the weight loss, the new hair color, and the makeup alone made me look like a super-enhanced version of my former self. It was the retouching that we really marveled over—they'd completely gotten rid of my eye bags, shaved at least three inches off my waist, and had even managed to make me look taller. I turned the pages slowly, staring at the photos inside … I *did* look totally hot, but I almost didn't recognize myself in the mass of hair, makeup and airbrushing passing for me in the photos. The only place I could really see myself was the eyes, and even then I looked like myself wearing a "beautiful girl" Halloween costume. I shouldn't have liked the fake me so much, but I did.

"You were there, right? I slept for two hours the night before … I have never looked this good!" I said. I was completely amazed and impressed at the result. "I am so in love with this picture, I am carrying this around with me all the time," I exclaimed, putting one of the pages over my face. "This is my new look!" We started to read the short article that accompanied the photos. The reporter had also interviewed one of the makeup artists about working with me, and she'd said: "Star needs almost no makeup … her skin just glows." We laughed. Ah, if only that were true. I could hardly wait for *People* magazine to dig up old photos of me from high school to do the inevitable "then and now" comparison issue. Between the frizzy perm, the braces, and the bad skin, I could just see an "Ugly Duckling turns Into a Swan" story on the horizon, like the ones they're always doing about Kelly Clarkson.

We marveled over the amazing photos until the newsstand guy gave us a dirty look. "It's her—in the magazine!" Vince said excitedly, pointing to me, then to the picture. We bought every copy at that newsstand, and we each walked toward my car holding a big stack. My mom was going to freak!

The crazier it got, the more I tried to remind myself that this whole life was fake, and to not get too attached. Slowly, though, I could feel myself getting sucked in. I tried to stay cynical about the Hollywood scene, but I had to admit—I really, really loved it.

Added to the growing list of "amazing Hollywood moments," I noted that it was totally surreal to be driving down Hollywood Blvd, in a BMW paid for by my huge paycheck from my starring role on a TV show, passing under a big billboard of that show, on the way to FedEx a bunch of magazines with my own face on the cover to my family in Michigan.

For the record, I still think it's a good idea to make a "celebrity mask" out of retouched photos, and just wear that out in public.

❦   ❦   ❦

We'd barely recovered from the excitement of my First Big Magazine Cover when the phone rang even earlier than usual one cold morning in December. "Have you seen the news?" I heard a perky voice say. It was Kristen from the marketing department.

I looked over at the clock, which said 8:30 am. "Ummmppnnnhhhh," I grunted from beneath my fortress of pillows. I wasn't called until 11:00am, and had taken a time-release Ambien someone gave me in order to guarantee that I made the most of every resting moment available. "Star, wake up!" she shouted, "I have news!" I sat bolt upright in bed. She hadn't called me this early since before Super Saturday! and every time the marketing department said "news," it always meant I had to do something I wasn't going to enjoy. My stomach clenched. "Wha ... what's going on?" I said, trying not to sound drugged. Could I get fired for sounding drugged?

"Omigod ... they announced the Golden Globe nominations, and *Autumn Leaves* is up for four!" she shouted. "This is HUGE, Star! You should go in to the set early ... the producers are going to be there, there's a party tonight, the whole thing." She was breathless with excitement, and I could hear shouts in the background as she hung up. My head was spinning. I wanted to call her back ask if I was nominated ... or did I? I picked up the remote from the nightstand, quickly turning on the TV and flipping to E! to see if their ticker had picked it up.

I held my breath as I watched the list of nominees go by, counting the nominations in my head as they came up ... Best Drama ... that was one ... Best Actor Greg Forster ... two ... Best Supporting Actor Ross Wong, three ... Best Supporting Actress ... Star Spencer.

Oh my God! I thought, I'm nominated for a Golden Globe Award! I jumped up on my bed, then started to run around the room. The phone started to ring again. Vince. I answered the phone while at the same time yelling "Did you see it?"

"Oh my God!" he screamed. "How excited are you right now? You're nominated for a Golden Globe Award! Call your mom! Call your mom! Arrrgghhh-hhhhhhhh so excited!"

I laughed. Finally, an event worthy of Vince's power of hyperbole. By the time I got to the set, there was already a party going on. Since *Autumn Leaves* was now bigger than *Desperate Housewives*, the cast had already been asked to make an appearance at the Golden Globes, and to present an award. Was this my life?

The day after the announcement, I arrived on set to find my trailer filled with flowers, gift baskets, and dresses. By noon Vince was packed in between the frothy designer dresses, looking like a kid in a candy store. "Aim, *everyone* is sending over samples," he said excitedly. "So far, Roberto Cavalli sent over this amazing gold beaded gown, Elie Saab sent a sea foam green dress, and Roland Mouret sent a whole rack of stuff. We've just got to get you into a couple of these, so I can start working on a "hair and accessories" strategy. We've only got a couple of weeks to plan, and there's no way I'm letting you end up on the "What Was She Thinking?" list for your first big awards show."

Vince had become the stylist for many other celebrities, and this was his first event season too. He was sharing my feelings of extreme excitement. We pinched each other at two hour intervals as the designer clothes and gifts continued to pour in throughout the day.

"This … is … unbelievable," he said, paging through a million-dollar jewelry catalog. "This necklace is worth $5 million," AND they send this hot security guard to follow you around all night. We both win! Omigod … and have you even considered the Presenter Gift Bag? Epic! Mink sleeping bag epic! One of my other clients already got a presenter pre-gift bag, and she's not even nominated!"

During one of my breaks from shooting, I started trying them on, discovering that I was either a) now small enough to fit into the sample sizes, or b) now important enough for people to know my real size. I couldn't tell, since most of them didn't have sizes in them anyway.

"Who cares?" said Vince, holding up a short black dress that had just arrived by messenger. "Do you think they'll let you keep the dresses you don't wear?"

❦   ❦   ❦

More exciting, perhaps, than the Golden Globe nomination, the fancy dresses, and the never ending stream of gift baskets was the anticipation of reclaiming Christmas. Winter break from the show was about to start, and I was *counting down the minutes* until I could go home to Bay City, sleep in, and have Christmas Dinner with my family. I had spent a ton of money on Christmas presents for everyone, and I was really excited to finally be able to give my mom and my brothers the great Christmas they deserved, to erase the bad memories from the holiday.

Christmas in my family needed a lot of help. It was December 17th three years earlier when my dad got sick. They'd taken him to the hospital, where he'd lain in a coma for seventeen days, then died in the middle of the night on Christmas Eve. The rest of my senior year was a blur of sympathetic faces, awkward conversations ("I'm so sorry," or "He's in a better place now"), and practicalities. My mother had insisted I start college anyway, saying that it's "what my dad would have wanted." Adam was two years behind me in school and Ian, the youngest, was just twelve. We were all shell shocked. We'd skipped Christmas every year since then.

Really, this was a subject that my family never stopped thinking about, and I felt like I had to be the "strong one" to keep everything from falling apart. It was almost a relief to go away to college, away from the never ending memories of my dad, people who knew him, and well-meaning neighbors who were forever asking us if we needed anything. But now, things were different. I was different. I was on a hit TV show, and I was determined to make this Christmas the best one ever.

The last day of shooting, my bags were packed, the presents were shipped, and I was ready to go when I was summoned to the network offices. I sped down there after shooting wrapped, praying that whatever they wanted me to do could wait until after the holiday.

"Shut the door, and sit down." said Attila. I wondered how long it would take her interns to notice if I bludgeoned her with the chunky wood paperweight on her desk, then left her body there. Actually, from the disgruntled look of her office staff, I was pretty sure they'd help me. Besides, I was leaving the next day for Christmas break, and nothing could spoil my mood.

By my third sit-down, I already knew that whenever she told me to shut the door, it was going to be nothing good. She did these meetings one on one so she could deny they ever happened. Despite the Golden Globe nomination, she was going to find a way to blame something on me. I braced myself and looked at my watch. Sixteen hours until my plane … what could be so bad? She'd yell, I'd cry a little on the way home, and then Christmas Break would be underway. No problem!

She sighed methodically, her chubby hands riffling the weekly ratings reports. "I just don't understand it," she said. "People in your age group should really be relating to you more. I mean, those girls from *One Tree Hill* have popularity ratings that are twice yours. I guess you're just not as "universal appeal" as we thought. Really, Star, it's just going to come down to numbers, and eventually we're just going to have to get rid of your character in favor of someone more appealing."

I wanted to ask her if she'd heard of a little thing called the "Golden Globe Award," or if she'd picked up a magazine lately, or maybe mention that the paparazzi were following me like mad when I so much as went out for brunch, but I already knew this would have no impact, and would most likely backfire. Talking common sense to Attila was the rough equivalent of trying to teach Swedish to a Grizzly bear. In my mind, I knew that most of what she was saying was not true, but I also assumed, possibly erroneously, that she wasn't allowed to make up stuff like this just to torture me.

"What can I do to help?" I said, choosing my words carefully.

"Frankly, Star, I don't see anything that will raise your appeal, except maybe…." she trailed off. Sometimes, she really reminded me of the grand-mother I didn't like.

"What? Mindy, I'll do anything!" With fifteen hours, forty two minutes until my plane took off, I might actually have been serious.

She leaned forward as if to let me in on a trade secret, and slowly opened her thin lips, which I noticed were a delicate shade of coral. She looked at me seri-ously. "Star, I'm glad you said that. It's about your teeth."

That was not at all what I thought she was going to say. My teeth? What could I possibly do about my teeth?

🍁   🍁   🍁

I was sorry I asked.

The next morning, instead of being on a plane back home, I was in the office of cosmetic dentist Dr. Ryan Davis. "OK, open your mouth and let me take a look," he said. "Your producer said your teeth were too 'real people' to work for television."

I lay back in the chair with my mouth open, wondering what he could do about my teeth that would still allow to me to get on the plane that afternoon.

I'd had a few cavities like every other kid in the U.S., and had some fillings. I brushed twice a day, and sometimes even remembered to floss. What else was there? Whitening? Filling replacement? Braces? I kept my mouth open while the dentist poked at my teeth with a little pick, hoping it wouldn't hurt too much and wondering when I could catch the next flight back home.

"Your teeth are a little bit yellow for camera … you've never had braces, right?

"No," I said hesitantly. I didn't know what he wanted to do, and I wasn't sure I had the power to said no. Would they have to write the braces into the show?

"You'd definitely look a lot better with veneers. Your producer wants you to get a whole new set over the break."

My eyes started to glaze over as he described the process of getting a complete set of veneers—a series of procedures that did not sound easy. He took a mold of my teeth as "before and after" slides of formerly snaggle-toothed people flashed on the computer screen in front of the dental chair. In my mind, I could hear my mom telling me that my teeth were "one of my nicest features." I wondered if she always said this because we didn't have the money for expensive dental work. Did my teeth look that bad?

I tuned back in to what he was saying just as he got to "… then we file down your teeth, you come back in a week or so, and we fit the new porcelain veneers on."

At this, I snapped back into full listening mode. Did he say "file down your teeth?" That didn't sound good. Did he say "come back in a week?" Oh no no … I was going to be long gone, sleeping in my old room by then. I didn't quite know which one was more disturbing.

"Wait … what? Am I going to look like Dracula? Why would you file my teeth?" I said frantically. "And … what about Christmas? I can't wait around here for a week … that's, like December 22nd! That's my whole break!" I couldn't stop my voice from cracking, and I felt the tears coming on. Why did Attila have to ruin everything? I was saving Christmas! I wished I wasn't one of those people who cried in response to stress.

Dr. Davis put his arm around me reassuringly. "Well, we want the veneers to fit as closely as possible to your regular teeth, so we file the old ones down completely—we just shave the teeth right off. You don't need them anyway … porcelain is much better, and then you can never get cavities. We can have them done in maybe four or five days … that's faster than we ever do it, but for you.…"

He seemed disturbed when I started to hyperventilate at the mention of "four or five days." Anxiety quickly gave way to anger as I thought of Attila, enjoying her … whatever she did at home. This was insane. New teeth? Over Christmas? Is this what they did to Hilary Duff? Now I had more sympathy for her. I read this interview where she said one of her front teeth fell out during a concert (because she's a singer now) and she had to get her teeth capped in Arkansas. So … they filed down her teeth first? The thought of little Hil Duff (who I had met once at a club) with tiny Dracula-like teeth sent me into a fit of giggles. Then I started to laugh for real. I was missing Christmas for vampire tooth filing, then Chiclet teeth? "Are you okay?" said Dr. Davis apprehensively. "I'm fine," I said, composing myself. I could tell I was starting to make him nervous, and I didn't want anyone in his office calling the tabloids to tell the world how weird I was.

"Go ahead … I'm ready." I sighed.

Dr. Davis gave me a few shots of Novocain to numb my mouth, and then he hit me with the laughing gas just to be on the safe side. Dust flew for what seemed like three hours as he "shaved" my teeth, getting them ready for the new veneers. After awhile they started to make that "burny" smell … even with the shots and the gas it was starting to hurt. I tried to say so, but with the suction thing in my mouth, it just came out "eeee huurrrrrs." Finally he seemed to understand, took a little break, and gave me a tranquilizer. At that point, I would have taken anything to get rid of the raw discomfort of the tooth shaving. Through the haze I looked at my watch, which said 9:00pm.

At midnight they woke me up and handed me a mirror so I could see the temporary teeth. They looked good, but I felt like I was holding up a mirror in order to look at someone else's face. The teeth I'd had since my grown up teeth came in were *gone*, and in their place a perfect set of straight, white replacement teeth. Would anyone in Bay City notice how different I looked? I felt like I needed an owner's manual for them … could I floss them? Could I still said the letter "S" without sounding like I had dentures? Would the show start getting letters about my teeth now? Did they get letters before? Why was it so important to do this now?

As I was leaving the office, the nurse handed me a small slip of paper. "What's this?" I said, stuffing it in my purse.

"Oh, you should read that … it's a list of foods you can't eat from now on," she said earnestly. "You don't want to break the new teeth!"

"You mean the temporary teeth, right?" I said. There was no way I was limiting my diet for the rest of my foreseeable future. The new teeth had to be stronger than that.

"Um, no …" she said. "Once he puts the porcelain veneers on, you'll need to be careful with them from then on, or else they'll break and you'll have to come back."

My mind started to race. Foods I couldn't eat? Why was this not mentioned before? It was Christmas, for God's sake! I figured it was going to be some random list, like when my friend Karen got braces in the seventh grade, and her orthodontist gave her a list that said "don't eat popcorn balls, candy apples, or corn nuts," like Karen lived at the state fair.

But it wasn't. The list consisted of hard foods like nuts, chips, popcorn, hard candy, chicken, ribs, and celery. At the top of the list, I saw the word "carrots."

My eyes welled up with tears. When I was a little kid, I loved carrots so much, my dad started calling me "Bunny Luv," after the girl rabbit on the outside of the carrot bag. In fact, "Bunny" was his nickname for me, and he kept calling me that, even when I was 17 years old. Carrots were my favorite food … I think I consumed at least a bag of baby carrots every day on the set. If I gave up eating this, my staple food, I would have little else to eat.

"Is this a joke?" I said to the nurse. "I'm not giving up carrots."

"Oh, but you have to … carrots are the worst. You're for sure going to break your teeth if you keep eating them. You can eat strained carrots, like baby food, if you're really desperate, or a carrot muffin, but you are probably never going to be able to, like bite into a carrot ever again." She said this all so calmly, she could hardly have been prepared for my reaction.

Despite my best efforts to the contrary, I burst into tears. Suddenly, I feel like one of my fondest memories of my dad had been stolen. Also, was she crazy? I hadn't eaten a muffin in five months.

After two more visits to Dr. Evil, Bunny Luv was gone, and in her place was a perfect-teeth having replacement. Here's the thing—you really CAN tell the difference between your teeth and artificial teeth. I mean, once they're gone, you can totally remember what your old teeth used to look like, and it's a little bit sad. Yes, they looked great—perfect, straight, white Movie Star teeth. But, this was how they'd look forever now … teeth never grow back, so they'll never look the way they did the last time my dad saw me. I wondered if you could hold a funeral for teeth. I wondered if it was the Percoset that was making me all philosophical. I wondered how quickly I could get to the airport.

I arrived at the Detroit airport at 10:30 pm, exactly two days before Christmas, face swollen, jaws and teeth aching. Who knew your gums actually swell on the airplane? Still, I was glad to see my family, and glad to be able to let my guard down and not feel like I was always being watched.

❈   ❈   ❈

It was after midnight when we finally got home from the airport. My mom looked so tired, I almost offered to drive when we pulled over for gas. My youngest brother Ian and I settled back in to our old friendly kidding and banter, but my brother Adam, who had just turned 18, was sulky and silent.

I felt a nostalgic pang when I walked into my old room, which Adam had turned into a music studio. The next fall he'd be going away too, leaving my mom and Ian in the house. I wondered if, when Ian was gone, she'd decide to move to L.A. with me, or live somewhere else. It was weird to have everyone in the same house again, and even weirder to think about not having that house at all anymore. I had started paying the mortgage regularly, but I wondered if she'd be one of those moms who decides that "the house is just too big," and moves into some condo. Part of me wanted her to keep the house, just so I'd have a place to come back to. I looked around the room … Adam had taken down most of my movie posters, replacing them with posters from The Killers, Panic! at the Disco, and The Strokes. My stuff was still on the ceiling, though … I laid down on my old bed, staring up at posters of ***Waiting for Guffman***, *sex, lies, and videotape*, and of course *Say Anything* and thinking about high school, which seemed like a million years ago. Things seemed so much easier when I was an idealistic indie film chick.

Adam was not thrilled about me reclaiming my room. "Don't touch the iMac," he said, grunting as he lifted my suitcase onto the bed. "It's got ProTools on it, and I'm mixing our album. If you touch it, you might mess it up." His face looked more and more like my dad's, especially his eyes, and I wished he were nicer.

"What if I have to check my email?" I said, tempted to mention that my job had PAID for his fancy computer. "I don't think I can live without the internet."

"Use the one in Ian's room … seriously Amy, I'm going to know if you touch it. Why can't you sleep in the guest room?"

"Um, because I live here too, this is my old room, and I'm older than you?" I said, pushing the suitcase with my toe and looking up at him. "Now, go away so I can get some sleep." Adam's competitiveness with me had intensified since I'd been away and gotten my job on *Autumn Leaves*. Ian and I had actually become closer and emailed several times a day, but I only knew what was going on with Adam through second-hand reports. I knew he had applied to colleges and was waiting to hear. I knew he was hoping that his band would become the next Strokes before that so he wouldn't have to go to college. I knew that my mom was going to force him to go.

He rolled his eyes. He was taller than me and had the choppy faux-hawk hair I always saw on rocker kids at the hotel. I almost told him that if he were nicer to me, I would convince our mother to let him come live with me in L.A. when he graduated, but the look on his face was so snide and resentful, I decided to keep my mouth shut and let him be forced to go to college.

"Get out!" I shouted. "Why do you do this?" He muttered something under his breath.

"What?" I said, standing up. "What did you say?"

"I said you're fake now, Amy. You went to L.A., you got the Hollywood car wash, and now you think you're better than everyone else. You look like you have fucking anorexia, you're blonde, and you totally sold out. You look like Barbie. You're on TV, which up until two years ago you didn't even watch … what happened to you?"

"Hollywood car wash?" I yelled. "What even is that? Is that a term you and your poser friends made up? Give me a break. You're not going to last five minutes in the real world, Adam. You have no idea what people are going to want from you if you ever get YOUR big break." My jaw throbbed, and I felt like crying, but wasn't going to give him the satisfaction. He loved to make fun of me for being the "crier" in the family.

Adam's faced turned red and he opened his mouth to yell something else, but Ian's face appeared in the doorway. "Adam, oh my God … she just got here. Can you leave her alone?" he said, looking over at me plaintively. We'd had many email discussions about Adam's attitude.

"Whatever," Adam said, turning and walking out. "I'll be shocked if she eats anything at Christmas dinner."

Ian sat down on my bed. "He's just jealous," he said. "You figured out the mysterious code for success, and he's wondering how you did it."

I laughed. Ian was the smartest of all of us—fifteen years old, and studying physics and calculus. He was going to be the one who ended up making our mom the proudest.

"We should totally watch something," he said, walking over to the wall that was lined with bookshelves full of DVDs. "Did you see **The Secret?** It's pretty deep—not as good as **Mindwalk,** but really engaging."

I was struck with the sudden urge to hug Ian and never let him go. "I need to sleep," I said. "But definitely tomorrow."

"OK," he said, walking toward the door. "Don't worry about Adam. Tomorrow I'm going to bulk erase his hard drive."

I laughed, laying my head down on my pillow. "Ian, I love you." My head ached and I tried to go to sleep, but I couldn't get Adam's words out of my mind. Had I really sold out?

The next morning, the pain in my gums had subsided long enough for me to try eating by chewing with the back of my mouth. My mother had managed to hold off on the "you're too thin" comments so far, but I could tell she was concerned.

She turned around when I came into the kitchen. "Did you sleep well?" she said, hugging me. "Did Adam yell at you? I don't know what's going on with that boy. He's going through a phase. Now Ian is mad at him … I just want all of you to get along."

I laughed. For once, I didn't mind the family drama. It was good to think about something other than scripts, or calories, or who was doing what with whom in L.A. I noted with some surprise that I actually missed Michigan.

"Any good gossip?" she said, stirring the mashed potatoes. Though she'd casually enjoyed her weekly People magazine before *Autumn Leaves* started, now she was celebrity obsessed in a way that I found extremely amusing. "Are you seeing anyone yet?"

I rolled my eyes. "Mom!" I said, pouring coffee into a mug shaped like a tulip. I neglected to mention the semi-affair I'd been having with Matt, the actor who sometimes played my love interest on the show. He was cute, but I barely knew (or saw) him, and he definitely wasn't "bring home to meet the family" material. I also neglected to mention that Vince had finally started hanging out with Perez Hilton, the most famous pink-haired gossip blogger in the world, and probably knew enough underground Hollywood info to blow her mind.

Ian ran in behind me. "Amy, I'm glad you're up … I have discovered a way to make a smoothie out of carrots that retains the original flavor without tasting like baby food. This you are going to like … I have several versions in the fridge for you."

I sat down at the kitchen table. "Ian, you are the best brother ever," I said. "I need more coffee before I try a carrot smoothie, though."

After the initial blowup with Adam, things quickly settled back in to about what they'd been before my dad died. We spent the afternoon wrapping presents, watching *A Charlie Brown Christmas*, and making a very long popcorn string for the tree. By that night (Christmas Eve), the pain in my teeth was gone, and I got my first drug-free night's sleep in months. Adam even stopped calling me Barbie after a few days, and we discovered the one thing we had in common—the fact that our mom didn't know that either of us smoked. Before long we were dragging Ian on impromptu "trips" to the mall, the grocery store, and Adam's friend's house, where his band rehearsed. "I'm glad you guys are getting along so well," said my mom as we walked out the door one afternoon. I punched Ian in the arm before he could tell her the real reason.

During the course of the week, I was thrilled to find that no one from my hometown seemed to give a crap that I was famous.

It was good to be home.

CHAPTER 9

✿

By the time I got back from visiting my family, I was totally conflicted about my Hollywood "transformation," as if I'd been living among a tribe of African pygmy warriors and had adopted all of their customs, then gone back to civilization and had to deal with the local townspeople pointing out the war paint and nose rings that had seemed so normal in my quest to fit in. Was I better the old way?

On the one hand, it was true. I had been starved, my hair bleached and straightened, and my face had been injected, de-acned, and bronzed. My teeth had been shaved and capped, and I was eating less and smoking more than I ever had in my life. I was a rich and successful Hollywood star, I was a Golden Globe nominee, and I had a killer wardrobe, two stylists, and a personal trainer. But ... wasn't I still the same person inside? Wasn't I still a good daughter, paying off medical bills and tuition, taking care of my family like my dad would have wanted?

To compound the paranoia, with each successive step in the "Star" transformation, I wondered a little more—wouldn't people who Tivo'd the show start to notice that things were gradually different about me? Would I ever be able to go back to just being a normal person, or was I destined to end up one of those pinched, overly plastic surgered ladies that everyone talks about at parties?

I mentioned this to Michele on the first day back from break. She snorted derisively. "First of all, America expects us to look good. Secondly ... everybody does it. Look at the people on *Friends*. Jennifer Aniston, Season One is, like, a totally different animal from Jennifer Aniston, the 'Brad and Jen' edition." That transformation took serious teamwork, and now she looks hot. I hope she cleaned up in that divorce. Can you imagine, a guy as hot as Brad Pitt living in freaking Namibia? Good Lord. They don't even have indoor plumbing there, Star! I bet you can get AIDS just by skinning your knee there!"

She was an idiot, but she had a good point about Jennifer Aniston. You wouldn't catch a regular person with flaws on a show like **Friends**. One thing is for sure—there was no one who looks like they're from Bay City on TV, then or now. Even me.

❈   ❈   ❈

A few weeks before the Golden Globes, word came from the network that since it was our first awards show, we could bring our families, after which I immediately got my mom and my brothers tickets, outfits, and seats in the "family" area of the auditorium. My mom and Ian were beyond excited, and even Adam seemed grateful to finally coming to L.A., even if I was because I bought him a ticket.

"Who are you bringing?" I said excitedly to Michele during a cigarette break.

"Oh, I'm not." She sniffed. "My dad is busy, and my mom is …" She lowered her voice and looked around … fat. I don't want her on the red carpet with me. I mean—can you imagine the photo captions? I don't want the tabloids doing a story about how I had to 'overcome my fat genes,' like they always do with Jessica Alba. I'm not even going to tell them they could have come," she said, casually going back to her **Variety** magazine.

I laughed, then was immediately horrified at myself. I wanted to tell her to go to hell, that if I could have my dad back for one minute, even one second, I wouldn't care if he weighed 500 pounds. It didn't register with her, though—she was so lost in her own narcissistic world, even having fat parents was out of the question. Besides, I didn't want to share too much personal information with her, since I never got the impression I was seeing the "real" Michele McCann behind the carefully constructed persona. She was like a master craftsman who had skillfully molded herself into a "success in show business" robot, from the perfectly sculpted body to the mind trained to be as aggressive and opportunistic as the plague. Not that she even had to try—she'd been in her father's shows since she was eight. Maybe being born into the business meant that you just lack any sort of sympathetic or "real person" genes.

❦   ❦   ❦

With six days to go until the Golden Globes, the awards show prep had taken on a life of its own. We'd just finalized the outfit (Zac Posen dress, Louboutin heels, Fred Leighton necklace and earrings), the hairstyle (messy half up do), and the makeup (smoky eyes, pale lips, and medium bronze fake tan) when Sondra's office called. "We're sending you to We Care Spa for the weekend," said Emily, her eager assistant. "Just a little insurance to make sure you look amazing in all your Golden Globes red carpet photos! You'll just go down there, detox, get massages, and relax. You'll come back glowing!"

"Sounds great," I said. "What should I bring?" I wasn't sure what she meant by "detox," but I didn't care. We'd been shooting marathon days, and I was in desperate need of a massage and some sleep.

"Oh, they'll take care of you," she said. "Let me know if you see Giselle or anyone else there. That place is crawling with models and celebrities right before awards shows."

I was released from shooting uncharacteristically early that Friday night, and by midnight, I was in the back of a car going out toward Palm Springs. On the way there, I read the informational package that Emily had put together for me.

The We Care Philosophy

At We Care we base our programs on the theory that most people are taking on an excess amount of toxins through today's diet which is composed of processed foods with many additives and preservatives. These toxins tend to be difficult to breakdown and build up in the colon where they have long lasting negative effects on one's health and contribute to disease. These effects include low energy, digestive problems, decreased mental alertness, fatigue and weight gain. Our approach at We Care is to cleanse the system (specifically the large intestines and colon) of these toxins which have accumulated over the years through use of a natural all liquid diet.

Liquid diet? Colon? Large intestine? All at once, I realized that this was a network-sponsored trip to celebrity fat camp, aimed at getting me to look better in my Golden Globe photos.

Liquid Diet

The We Care liquid diet is rich in nutrients and offers many specific ingredients to address flushing various organs including the liver and kidneys which act as filtering systems for the body. As the body easily accepts the natural liquid diet, it allows the digestive system to utilize more energy in cleaning out the life long accumulated waste products and toxins. This process is accelerated through the use of colonics: a safe, effective measure for accelerating the emptying and cleaning of the colon and large intestine.

Some of the specific products used as part of the We Care natural liquid diet include Kyogreen, Spirulina, Wheat Grass, Barley, Acidophilus, freshly squeezed vegetable juice, lemon water, enzymes, liver and kidney teas and blood purifying tea.

I momentarily considered having the driver turn around, or at least having him stop at In N Out Burger before dropping me off. But because a) I had no way to escape from the car and we were already halfway there, and b) I feared incurring the wrath of both Sondra and Attila if I attempted a prison break, I sat back, lit a cigarette, and attempted to get my head around "detoxing" my body on a liquid diet for the entire weekend. My mind raced. Could you die from fasting? How hungry would I be by Monday? What was a "colonic," anyway? I bet Attila was sitting in the office laughing.

I arrived to find the We Care Spa very quiet and placid, not at all like the diet jail I'd been expecting. On the way to my suite, the only famous person I saw in the community area was not Giselle, but Colin McManus, a hot Scottish actor who had been appearing with some regularity in industry magazines and who I'd seen around town. He came up to me immediately, and my heart skipped a beat. Did he recognize me?

"You're Star, right?" he said, his Scottish accent sounding evening sexier in person than it did in the movies. "Can't fit in your party clothes either, eh?" he said. "Fooking bollocks if you ask me—$2,000 to drink swamp juice and have people shite for you!"

I could barely make out what he was saying, but the whole "detox" thing sounded even more absurd when he said it. I couldn't tell if he was flirting—he was supposed to be engaged to a British actress, though they were seldom photographed together. Michele had once told me that they were staying together for the publicity because they both had movies opening—a strategy she seemed to really admire.

I laughed, trying to act cool and not star struck. "Yeah," I said. "Tight dress. I'm focusing on the spa part, and trying not to think about the liquid fiber diet and how hungry I'm going to be by the end of the weekend. Besides, what's a colonic?"

He told me, and I couldn't believe I was actually discussing poop in any way with a famous hot guy, though I decided if anyone needed "internal cleansing," it was probably him. I'd never seen him in a picture without a beer and a cigarette, no matter what time of day it was.

"I'm in the villa in the back," he said, winking. "Call me if you get lonely or hungry. I smuggled in a secret emergency stash of cigarettes, beer, and Hostess cupcakes. Fook healthy living!" He took my cell phone number, immediately texting me what would be the first of many flirty text messages over the next forty eight hours.

By the next afternoon, I was grumpy, had a raging headache, and was in desperate need of a cigarette. Having just had my first colonic of the day, I felt a little violated and like I needed a shower. A colonic is probably not something I would have ever done willingly. In fact, it IS a little you're paying someone to take a crap for you. While she was pumping my insides, my "colonic technician" Ermina (who smelled strangely of coffee beans) made chatty conversation.

"Wow, you have a ton of buildup. Do you eat a lot of protein?" she said, calmly not acknowledging the fact that she had just inserted a tube into my (ahem) private pooping area.

"No, I eat a lot of nothing. Thanks for asking." I said, unable to disguise my discomfort and annoyance.

"What's going to happen on your show? Does Seth come back?" she said nonchalantly, and I laughed a little bit. It's true, there really is no escape from your fans.

Needless to said, I was in no mood to scoop the crap lady on upcoming plot points. I tried to stay as quiet as possible by pretending to doze off for the rest of the "procedure," but mostly I was just faking through an uncomfortable silence. Although I promised myself I would be one of those "totally down to earth" celebrities, I found that Sondra was right—I should really stop chatting with service people—I was only opening myself to stupid questions that I couldn't answer anyway, and for everyone wanting to get their niece into the business.

Afterwards, I had to admit that my system did feel "clean," though I was light headed and dying for coffee. How did people fast for two or three weeks? I was going on twelve hours, and I felt like a truck ran over me. How was I going to be Golden Globe fabulous in four days?

With hunger gnawing at my stomach and my head throbbing, I skipped the liquid kelp lunch and went back to my room to lie down. Since there was a "no TV or radio" and a "minimal cell phone use" policy in effect, I was forced to send many emails to Vince, then attempt to get the tiny browser in my Blackberry to work so I could at least keep up on the news. I was waiting for the New York Times website to load when I head a tapping at the door.

It was Colin McManus, holding a six pack of Diet Coke. How did he know?

I'd thought he was kidding when he invited me to his villa, but as it turned out, he wasn't. "Where ya been, girlie?" he said, looking into my room. "What ya been eatin'?" He pulled a Hostess cupcake from behind his back. "Yee must be hungry by now, eh?"

I laughed. He smelled like cigarettes and beer and was covered in tattoos—not really my type, but still hot. It wasn't like I thought he was going to tell anyone—no one was supposed to know either of us were there anyway—the very definition of a "Lost Weekend." I laughed to myself as I thought of how horrified Attila would be if I showed up to the Golden Globes on his arm. Colin McManus had a reputation as an international party guy, to say the least—definitely not "supportive of my brand equity." Still, they'd sent me here against my will, so why not have a little fun until Sunday?

After weighing the pros and cons, my stomach was growling so loud I agreed to accompany him back to his villa, where he claimed to have a huge stash of contraband food. When he kissed me, I actually thought 'Oh my God … it's my first Hollywood hookup!" I skipped the second day of fasting in favor of coffee, cigarettes, and Colin McManus.

Something must have worked. By the time I got back to the set on Monday, I was repeatedly complimented on my post detox glow, and I'd actually lost two pounds.

❦   ❦   ❦

Two days before the Golden Globes, the cast attended a mandatory "Awards Show Etiquette" seminar put on by the marketing department. Rather than do the presentation herself as we'd been expecting, we were pleasantly surprised to find that Sondra had hired Cindy Harrison, a comedian/former red carpet commentator from E!—turned consultant whose specialty was keeping famous people out of the "Celebrity Oops!" section of magazines. It took me ten minutes to stop staring at her face, trying to discern what plastic surgery she'd had. Her face was truly a wonder of nature.

"I know some of you have done this a million times," she said, uncapping the lid on a dry erase marker. "We're just going to do the basic overview, and then some of you are scheduled for one on one time. I've created "Awards Show Boot Camp" to basically be a fun way to keep you guys out of the tabloids." She laughed. "Even if you don't win, the night of the awards show can still be fun, if you follow certain guidelines."

I was so excited about the Golden Globes, I didn't know if I could actually retain anything, but she seemed funny, so I made an effort.

"OK," she said, writing "FOOD" in red marker on the dry erase board. "As many of you are aware, the Golden Globe Awards are presented by the Hollywood Foreign Press Association, and the actual awards show is a formal dinner. I would not recommend eating during the ceremony, for several reasons. For one, the food is your standard "rubber chicken" type dinner, and we don't want the cameras to catch you making a "I don't like this food" face if they pan over to you while you're eating. Secondly, you run the risk of being photographed chewing on a big piece of steak or chicken, and that is never attractive, even for you, Mr. Handsome Golden Globe Nominee" she said, pointing at Greg, who laughed.

"Also, even though the dinner is usually served before the televised portion starts, you still don't want the camera to pan over to you and you've got a napkin bib on, cleaning off the last of the gravy on your plate with a roll. Not good! Also, ladies—please do not think you're going to be able to be nervous, eat, and stare at George Clooney at the table next to yours, and manage to avoid getting A-1 steak sauce on your $50,000 dress. Not gonna happen. Do yourself a favor, and eat something before you put on your dress, so you can politely sip your sparkling water when the awards are going on.

"Any questions?" she said, pausing momentarily. She wrote MENTION DESIGNERS under FOOD, and quickly moved on.

"Next, your stylists will tell you this, but while you're on the press line, try to remember to always mention the name of the wonderful individuals who designed your dress, shoes, jewelry, etc. Remember, you're wearing their styles for free, and this is the best advertisement they get all year. So, even if someone like Joan or Melissa Rivers or Isaac Mizrahi doesn't ask during your mini-interview, try to fit it in there anyway. Sentences can be started with "Well, I'm wearing Ungaro, or "I'm wearing Prada," etcetera. You can even throw in kicky expressions like "I'm wearing _____, so I'm just really comfortable tonight!"

"Anyone want to give this one a try?" she said, and Michele raised her hand. "OK … I'm wearing Dolce & Gabbana, so I'm really comfortable tonight?" she said timidly. Michele was all about the calculated perfection, and I could tell she didn't want to screw up the press line at her first Golden Globes.

"Good try," said Cindy. "But everybody knows Dolce stuff is notorious for NOT being comfortable. I haven't seen your dress, but I'm going to guess it has a few straps and laces, am I right?" she said, and Michele laughed. "Right," she said.

"So just say 'I'm wearing Dolce & Gabbana, so I'm having a great time tonight!'". This is ambiguous yet positive, makes you sound knowledgeable about the designer, and easily leaves you open to talk about your shoes, jewelry, and what your life is like now that you're on a hit show!

The next thing she wrote was LIE, and we all laughed.

"For the record, I have personally coached hundreds of celebrities before, during, and after the red carpet, and one thing is always true: People spend a lot of time getting ready, and everyone, and I do mean everyone says it took less time than it did. Now hear this: on the red carpet, you are perpetuating the image that Hollywood people just look that good when they roll out of bed in the morning, which of course I know you do! So, even if they needed a crane, a can of spackle, and a team of wild horses to get you into your girdle, you will NEVER say you spent seven hours getting ready. That, my dears, would make you sound like you NEED a team of people in order to look this good, and that is bad for your image. Just duck and cover when a reporter asks you what time you started getting ready, and say something clever like 'I just spent the morning with my family, relaxing.'"

Next item on the list, WEIRD FACES. "The red carpet is an opportunity for you to get great exposure, but beware … they take so many photos in such a short period of time, if you're not careful you're going to end up with a lot of goofy angles that can be used against you in the future in a "Weird Faces" photo montage. Therefore, you must practice your good camera angle 100 times every night in the mirror over the next few days. You know that little turnaround, peek over the shoulder thing that Paris Hilton does? Definitely rehearsed. Practice your poses at home, people."

She opened up the pen again, this time writing AVOID LECTURES "Listen, I'm not going to lie—if we catch you making one of those "smile with your full mouth" double chin faces, you will get a "post awards show" lecture, probably from me. If you end up in the "what was she thinking" section of *US Weekly*, you will see me again. If you forget to say the name of the person who designed your dress, your stylist will give you a lecture. Generally speaking, you want to avoid these lectures. That's why you have me here now!"

She wrote a few more large words on the dry erase board, stopping for further explanation and jokes after every one.

JEWELRY "Regarding expensive jewelry. If jewelry exceeds the price your parents paid for their house, this guarantees the fact that you will think of nothing other than the jewelry for the entire night, whether or not you're sitting next to Gwyneth Paltrow. However, it is likely if your jewelry costs that much, it will come with its own security guard, so try to let them worry about it for you. Believe me, they'll notice if it falls off."

THE BATHROOM. "Listen carefully—if in fact it did take a team of wild horses and a crane to get you into your dress, don't kid yourself and think you're going to sit around drinking wine all night. Because you know what? Those people aren't going to be able to help you when you're in the bathroom crying because you can't get your dress off (or back on). Also, even if you have a dress with a zipper down the side, when they call your name, you NEVER want to not be there to accept it, then say "I was in the bathroom," even if you're Renee Zellweger. The American public does not want to think about its celebrities relieving themselves in a public restroom. You are America's Royal Family—remember that!

GREAT! "When a reporter asks you if you're having a good time, you have only a few possible answers. A) Great! I'm so glad to be in the company of so many great actors! B) Great! I just saw Reese Witherspoon! I'm so excited to be here!, or C) Great! I feel so lucky to be included in this amazing evening, and I'm wearing Ungaro! Anything that sounds like jealousy, intrigue, or rivalry will end up a sound byte on E! the next day, and a sound byte will get you a lecture."

"If you're singled out and ambushed by a reporter, just say something like "This year has been a crazy roller-coaster! then move on," said Sondra, who up until now had been quiet.

Cindy continued, writing CIVILIANS on the board. If you have a boyfriend/girlfriend who is a "civilian," don't bother bringing them on the red carpet with you. The more times a photographer said "can we just get your picture … alone?", the madder your significant other will be at you once you get inside." I made special note of this, since I was planning to bring Vince and my family.

Next up, SMOKING. "You must never, never NEVER smoke on the red carpet. If you're going to smoke, do it out on the balcony with Scarlett Johansson and that whole crowd, but definitely don't do it in front of a photographer, and DEFINITELY don't burn a hole in the dress. Valentino will not understand."

❋   ❋   ❋

By the day of the Golden Globes, I felt like my mind would explode from all the new information and the excitement. Shooting was even cancelled for the day. I woke up at 10:00 am, trying on my dress first thing in the morning to make sure it still fit (it did). After that brief moment of calm, Award Show Day Chaos kicked in.

My mom, who was staying in the suite next door, was the first to arrive, then Vince, then the hair and makeup people. Sondra had arranged for the cast to arrive in the same limo so we could all enter, walk the red carpet, and sit down as a group. "Create a unified front," she'd said as she gave us each our pickup times and bullet points. Mine was 3:30 pm, which meant I had exactly four hours to get ready, eat, and hopefully not spill anything on the dress.

"Wow honey, this is like getting ready for a wedding," said my mom, who was watching the flurry of activity from the couch as she ate a muffin from the brunch we'd ordered. "When your dad and I got married, I swear I remember putting on the dress, then eight hours of whirlwind, then we looked at each other and said "Oh my God—we're married!" she laughed.

After being girdled, plucked, sprayed, pinned, and taped by a team of "Don't Try This at Home" professionals, I barely had time to eat before it was time to put on my dress and go downstairs for my pickup. "OK, how do I look?" I said, coming out into the living room to show off the results.

"You look like a princess," said my mom. "But … do you have a shawl? I think you're showing too much skin. And you're so thin … don't you want to cover up your arms?

Vince and I laughed. "It's fine, mom," I said. "This is how everyone in Hollywood looks now. OK, see you at the show!" I said, hugging her. "Wave to me on the red carpet!" With that I ran downstairs, the limo pulled up, and we were on the way.

When we actually got to the auditorium, all I could think was that I hope I don't make a mistake, I hope my dress doesn't come off, I hope I don't end up on "E!'s 50 Biggest Celebrity Oops!". "Have fun, but remember—nothing off message!" said Sondra, smiling, then steering us toward the first reporter. The press line at the Golden Globes was much longer than I'd imagined, and bleachers filled with cheering people lined the sidewalks. Though I'd been photographed before, the hundreds of cameras taking our pictures at once were blinding.

Greg Forster, who had in fact done this a million times before, did most of the talking. The show was a hit, and people were loving him. We followed the usher to our table, and Ross seemed to know or to have worked with everyone we passed. He worked the room, but not in a phony way. He just seemed to know everyone. I was impressed.

Even though they made my mom and Vince sit at a table in the back with some of the other relatives (there are no cameras back there, because the networks don't air footage of the 'civilians'), it was still a thrill to see her in a beautiful dress, makeup done, her face shining with pride. I hadn't seen her that happy since my dad died, and it gave me a secret joy to be able to make her smile. Granted, I was a little disappointed when I didn't win (the only award of the night went to Ross for Best Supporting Actor), but I was beyond thrilled to be there in the first place, having conversations with real celebrities who actually watched our show.

Backstage, I noted with surprised amazement that the gift bag presenters/nominees was so big, it actually came in a rolling suitcase—a medium size monogrammed Louis Vuitton suitcase, to be exact, which I'd recently seen at Bloomingdale's for $2,000. I couldn't tell what was most exciting—sitting at a table next to George Clooney, being nominated for a Golden Globe, or the wealth of goodies that I knew was waiting for me in The Gift Bag when I got home.

CHAPTER 10

❀

Two days later, The Gift Bag was still on my mind as Vince and I drove my family to the airport, then sped back to the hotel to crack open, catalog, and admire the sweet swag. Even though we'd been in L.A. for nine months, when it came to really expensive free stuff, we were both still in the honeymoon phase.

We ran immediately up to my room, where The Gift Bag was laying on the bed like that suitcase from *Pulp Fiction*. Vince unzipped it slowly. "I feel like I need special music for this." he said reverently. "Do you have to send thank you notes?"

"I think the places get good press if I show up there," I said. "Sondra would probably be horrified if she knew how impressed we were right now."

He flipped open the cover of the suitcase. "Interesting," he said. "A lot of paper in here." He pulled out a monogrammed leather portfolio and opened it up, pulling out a fancy piece of paper from the top of the stack and holding it up. "Gift certificate for an 'amazing Antarctic adventure package worth $25,000. Includes kayaking, wilderness treks, and extreme camping," he read. "Oh my God—I can totally see you as Nanuck of the North, cute little fur lined parka!" He laughed. Neither of us were camping types, so the thought of us in snow boots, sleeping in a tent, or kayaking sent us into fits of convulsive laughter.

"Yeah, probably not going to use that anytime soon," I said. "No time, and besides, can you see me camping? I think not." I made a mental note to see if I could transfer the gift certificates, because the trip sounded like a great Christmas present for my aunt and uncle.

He pulled out another sheet of paper. "Mr. Handyman gift certificate for one day of free service?" he said, and we laughed again.

"Keep it for when I buy a house," I said, realizing that soon I might actually be able to buy a house. Good Lord.

"Gift certificate for spa treatments at Bliss?" he said. "$1,000 value."

"Throw that over here," I said. "I am calling about that one right now."

"OK, this is good. Swaravski crystal-encrusted bra and thong set. Sexy!" He said, holding them up. "You wear them or I will."

"Yes, I will wear that," I said. "Though, I wonder how uncomfortable a crystal-encrusted thong is—ouch!"

He pulled out a gold box. "What about specially made gold M & M's with *Autumn Leaves* stamped on each individual M?"

"Are you kidding me?" I shouted. "Get out! How do they even do that?"

"I don't know, but there's also a box of truffles in here with your face painted on each one." He produced a gold box with a cellophane lid from the magic Louis Vuitton suitcase. Each one did, in fact, have a tiny picture of my face painted on it. They even got the teeth right.

"Oh, we're keeping those," I laughed. "We are totally getting drunk and eating my face." Oddly, the pamphlet that came in the box with the individually painted truffles also advertised the fact that the company can paint ANYTHING on your truffle, including an ultrasound photo. "That is positively gory!" said Vince, laughing. "I'm going to eat your baby!"

After two hours, I was wearing the crystal-encrusted bra and a pair of brand new cashmere pajamas, and Vince had wrapped himself in a vintage raw silk kimono and had a Frette cashmere leather-trimmed blanket thrown jauntily around his shoulders. We'd been through everything in The Gift Bag and had separated each item into piles labeled "Regift" (for friends or family), "Use" (too fabulous to pass up), or "Keep for Later" (like the gift certificate for dog training and daycare, if I ever came up for air and had time to get a dog). One of the beds was covered in wrapping paper and ribbon rubble, the piles, and empty boxes. We lay on the other bed, exhausted from laughter, excitement, and too many custom-made M & Ms.

❦   ❦   ❦

Sadly, being rich and famous does not exempt you from catching viruses. Two weeks after the Golden Globes, I woke up from a nap in my trailer freezing, teeth chattering and feeling dizzy.

I so should have gotten that flu shot.

Unfortunately, unless you're getting some kind of transplant, there's no calling in sick and halting the shooting schedule of an hour-long drama, even if you're the star and you feel like hell.

By 11:00 am, word had spread around the set that I was sick, a doctor had been called, and Juliet the Second Assistant Director had been to my trailer twice to assure me that she was trying to rearrange the day's shooting schedule, but that they were "definitely going to need me by 4:00—"Is that doable? Can I tell Mindy 4:00?"

I tried to nod my head and say "I'll try," but even the thought of getting up made me tired again, so I just stared at her and groaned. I wanted my mom. I wanted Vince. I wished I had time for a boyfriend, just so he could come take care of me. I whimpered quietly, closed my burning eyes, and tried to sleep, so feverish, I had lost all concept of time.

Sometime later (or maybe it was five minutes), a doctor came into my trailer. "Star—I hear you're sick," he said, and I could only slightly move my head in acknowledgement. "Headache?" he said, and I nodded. "Let's take your temperature." He put the thermometer in my ear, and even that was uncomfortable. "103," he said, whistling as he breathed out. "I'm going to start you on an IV, and give you a megadose of acetaminophen to see if we can't bring that fever down."

I recalled an article I read once about a girl who took too much Tylenol and then needed a liver transplant, but I felt too sick to mention it. I just wanted to fall into the folding parts of my sofa bed and die; I think I would've allowed him to give me an IV filled with anti-freeze if it would make me feel better. Through my fevered delirium I began to wonder—was this the doctor who prescribed the seemingly endless supply of black pills that were keeping me thin? Was any of this really happening? On the bright side, for once I had absolutely no appetite.

Two hours later, I felt well enough to sit up and watch TV, and Vince had arrived with some chicken and broth and crackers that I refused to eat. I still saw little chance of climbing down the stairs to my trailer, walking across the lot to the "main house" set, or shooting my scenes. I felt like I'd reached another dimension of illness, and was so uncomfortable all I could do was writhe and whimper on my couch, the sheets of which were now soaked in sweat.

More time passed. Juliet poked her head in again. "Any better?" she said hopefully. I tried to think of ways to get her as close to me as possible, so I could breathe on her. "MMMmmmhhhnnnnn," I said from beneath my pillows.

"We've been holding the scene for you … they even did a rewrite so you can shoot all of your scenes in bed, if that helps at all, but we need you to come over in the next fifteen minutes, or it's going to push the crew into overtime." When I didn't respond, she said, sheepishly, "OK—they told me to do this if you didn't come to set."

Momentary silence, then I heard her say "Ms. Steinman? It's Juliet. I have Star here. Hold on."

I looked up deliriously at Juliet, who mouthed the words "I'm sorry." I felt the cell phone slide onto the pillow next to my face, and then I heard Atilla's voice.

"Star … what's going on over there? I hear you're holding up shooting for the day. Money down the drain because of delays caused by the talent is unacceptable, Star. Do you hear me? Unacceptable."

I mumbled something incomprehensible about the fever and how I was delirious, and this made her yell even louder. "Star—are you listening to me? When Martin Sheen was making *Apocalypse Now*, he had a heart attack … a heart attack! And Coppola had him back on the set the next day. Did you have a heart attack, Star?"

"No," I said weakly. "Flu." She wasn't on speakerphone, but was screaming so loud I could hear her just as clearly. "If you're not on the set in ten minutes, you are in breach of contract, and we are filing suit. Call a lawyer." she said. The phone flashed "Call Ended." I shut my eyes and saw spots.

Since I thought I might need a liver transplant after the mega dose of acetaminophen and couldn't afford to be unemployed and without health insurance, I performed a small miracle, willing myself to get up, put on my costume, and walk to the set. Somehow, I remembered my lines and we shot all the scenes in two hours, after which the cast and crew give me a standing ovation and Ross carried me back to my trailer.

Mercifully, the flu was mostly gone in twenty four hours, so I was able to keep shooting the whole time.

Next time, I thought, I might just have that heart attack.

❦   ❦   ❦

Six weeks before we wrapped shooting on Season One, I was doing a "what it's like to work on a TV show" report in order to get school credit for my work on the show. Ellie Simon was developing a class on "Acting in Hollywood," and using my success story as an example of the fact that even when you get really lucky and get your "big break," there is still a lot of hard work involved. I was supposed to answer a series of questions to help convince the students that the life of a Hollywood actress wasn't "all fun and games." During my hiatus, I was going back to Hudson to talk to the class. I had put off filling out the questionnaire for too long, and now it was overdue.

What's your typical day like?

I took out a pen, attempting to answer the questions as clearly as possible—I had gotten so used to Blackberrying everything in abbreviated form, I'd almost forgotten how to write with a pen.

I'm called to the set in the morning, usually 9 or 10. I go to my trailer, have coffee, and read any memos or letters from the studio or the network.

I wonder if I should put what I really did ... get to the set, mentally curse Juliet because she always called everyone in to set too early so she wouldn't get in trouble. Made serious effort to pass by the craft services table laden with delicious breakfast items. Smoked the first of many cigarettes, had coffee, and avoided phone calls from Attila until I could hear from the rumor mill of production assistants, cast members, and tech people whether it was a "red flag" or a "green flag" day. On a "red flag" day, I just turned off the phone, because I knew she was going to call and say something like "Star, we just got a letter from someone in Germany—they don't like the way you say the letter 'P'—can you work on that?" or even worse, call me into her office for a "one on one" meeting, where she could really get out her claws. And, let's face it, even on a green-flag day, she wasn't much nicer. So really, I tried to avoid calls from the network altogether.

I laughed out loud. That would definitely never do. I continued writing:

I integrate revised script pages into the script I received the night before, try on my costumes for the day, and call the wardrobe department if they need to be adjusted.

Actually, most of what I did was wait. First, I waited for a production assistant to come tell me that it was time for me to go into hair and makeup, where I got not only my hair and makeup done, but also got updated on any gossip that might have broken (in the industry in general or on set) by April, the head makeup woman, who had by that time completely digested the **Hollywood Reporter**, the **New York Post**, and several other publications.

Then I study my script to learn my lines for the day until it's time to shoot my scenes.

Then, I waited to be called to set. After the first six months of shooting, I didn't bother learning lines before scenes anymore, because with all the delays and hours it took to re-set after each scene, combined with all the times we had to re-shoot it because Greg Forster was always either hung over or actually drunk, we'd end up shooting the scene so many times that not only did I not need to memorize the lines, but by the end of the day, I usually wished I could forget them.

Do you have a close relationship with the other cast members? Are you friends outside the show?

I avoided scribbling "Michele McCann, who plays my friend and next door neighbor on the show, is a manipulative weasel who got her job through nepotism and can't act her way out of a paper bag" on the page, and wrote:

Autumn Leaves is a family show, and it's great because we're all so close, we're like a real family! When you spend fourteen to eighteen hours a day with people, you really get to know them well. I'm lucky to have such great people to work with every day!

I chuckled, commending myself on my perfection of marketing department rhetoric. Maybe a dysfunctional family show at best.

Almost on a daily basis, Vince came to the set (we were not allowed to leave, lest all the elements actually fell into place by the time on the call sheet). Once he got there, we had lunch and discussed the gossip of the day—I brought what I've learned from April in makeup, he brought news and updates from his other celebrity clients and straight from Perez, and we augmented that with what we'd pulled off the websites, including The Superficial, Defamer, Just Jared, DListed, and Pink is the New Blog, among others.

After he left, I'd email, watch movies, and listen to music for a few hours, then usually it would be time to go to the set and shoot some scenes, then shoot some more scenes because Greg had only a short window of booze consumption when he could remember his continuity. Then I went over to Ross' trailer to run lines (scenes between us were where we tried to make up for lost time, since we only had to do them once or twice). Made phone calls to friends back at home, to my mom, or to see who Vince was working for that day. Listened to music while I surfed the internet or read a book, and waited to be called back to set for more scenes. I wondered if they would care that I had 4,042 songs in my iTunes library.

At around 4:00 each day, I'd start trying not to think about the sumptuous array of desserts (and, deadliest of all, the giant bag of Famous Amos cookies) that adorned the craft services table, after which I'd take one of the black pills. I also spent a lot of time in the gym on set (a converted trailer); three days a week the network sent over a personal trainer to work on my "problem areas," and I sweated through 90 agonizing minutes of squat crunches, weight training, and trying to run on the treadmill while the trainer, a buff guy named Eddie, told me about how he was "working on a screenplay, and could I maybe get it through to one of my contacts in the industry?" Every time this happened, I tried to be cool, but I couldn't help but get annoyed. Wasn't everyone supposed to be responsible for their own career? Why did people always think I had all the answers?

What do you do to develop your craft?

I thought Sondra would probably kill me if I said "sit around with the other cast members, smoking cigarettes and gossiping," even in jest, so instead I wrote:

We have private acting coaches that come to the set, and occasionally if we're not on a heavy shooting schedule, we'll attend an acting class with one of the numerous fine acting teachers available in the Los Angeles area.

Not entirely untrue. We'd had an acting coach on the set a few times, just to get some of us through tough scenes. This man, Sid Stockwell, supposedly a famous acting teacher from the 1970's, reminded me a little of James Lipton from *Inside the Actor's Studio*. He'd given me a few pointers about eye contact and the subtly of hand gestures on camera, but mostly I'd just seen him chatting with the network executives and coaching the guest stars.

If you had to give a newcomer to the business one piece of advice, what would it be?

I laughed. I really had less than no idea what to tell people about how to get their big break. I wasn't really sure how I'd even gotten to where I was, and I suspected that if not for the divine hand of Fate, I'd probably be taking my finals at Hudson that very moment. I wrote:

Two words: hard work! Really, all parts of the process of becoming successful in show business require absolute dedication, patience, and a great work ethic.

This was actually true. Though I had lucked out in the "getting the part" portion of the process, I still worked hard at staying thin, doing well on the show, keeping myself in the magazines enough but not too much, and making sure Attila was happy. I knew I wouldn't be able to say all of this at the lecture, but I was the only twenty year old I knew with chronic insomnia and a family to support.

What's the one thing that is the most different about your life since you started working on the show?

This was a question I thought I could actually answer with some honesty and authority. When I first arrived in L.A., I noticed something really interesting—this was before the show become really popular, and I was still a "nobody." In L.A., people look you in the eye for just a moment too long—they're trying to see if you're "somebody" before moving on with their day, letting the moment pass by, whatever. Maybe to see if you're anybody worth getting excited over on spending any energy on. I still couldn't determine whether it was just the tourists, or everyone, but it's definitely a thing I hadn't observed in any other city. At first, I thought it was because everyone in L.A. looks like they might be someone famous. But, once the show got popular and I started being in the magazines and stuff, I could definitely see the difference—now I see the glint of recognition in people's eyes, as it goes from "isn't that …?" to "that is!" to "should I say something/should I ask for an autograph" It's weird how people think they know you.

This was happening all the time now, and I just tried to ignore it. Does it make you more valuable as a person if you pass the "recognition" test in L.A.? Once you have that glimmer of recognition from people, you start to expect it from everyone—to the point where if I went out and didn't get recognized, I felt a little bad about myself.

Also, since more and more people recognized me from the show, one of two things happened when I went out in public. For one, people came up and told me they liked my work. For some reason, this was always followed by the comment "oh my gosh … you look so much smaller in person!" or, they think I'm ugly or fat, and they hate the show or my character, and for some reason, they felt like they knew me, so they could be totally honest with me and tell me all of this in detail. Some, especially pre-teen girls, came up and told me really personal stuff, like how they hated themselves, had abusive boyfriends, or how they had eating disorders, and how I was so lucky to have such a fast metabolism. This just made me feel like a liar, and like I did not have all the answers. Even though I was on TV, I thought, I was still just a regular person.

But maybe I wasn't anymore.

❦   ❦   ❦

"Don't go. If I have to, I will physically prevent you from leaving!"

Carrie Ann made a face, continuing to pack too much stuff into an exhausted-looking suitcase. Either Vince or I had taken her shopping every day during breaks—she'd come to visit us in during a break from school, and we were determined to convince her to stay with us. I was lying on the bed in the hotel, watching her pack and encouraging her to take some of the sample stuff that got sent over practically every day. "Take the Chloe jeans, Car—they sent six pairs."

She made a face. "Yeah, right—those would seriously never fit me. You are way taller than me and besides, you're like a skeleton now."

I sighed. Somehow, you just can't understand it unless you're in it. I knew I was an impractically small size by her standards, but in according to Hollywood, I was just on the heavy side of "normal." I was tired of these comments, but it had been fun having the gang back together, and I was sorry to see her go. Vince had taken time off from being a fancy celebrity stylist to come over and regale us with scandalous tales of who had to be sewn into their dress, who was the biggest diva, and who was totally down to Earth and nice to work with—a category I made him promise to include me in when he talked about me. Our favorite story involved a certain singer and her refusal to perform unless she was provided with a bucket of chicken wings. Somehow, even though I was a celebrity, I still liked hearing these bizarre stories. The only difference was that after having the celebrity experience first hand, I could sort of sympathize with how you can become that way.

It starts with privilege—everything being handed to you on a silver platter. Anything you could ever want or need is available, immediately. Want a really specific latte? Done. Prefer only Swiss cheese in your sandwiches? No problem. People are overly accommodating to you when you're a celebrity—so much so that it makes you feel a little bad at first. Eventually, though, you come to expect it, and are actually surprised when you want something and can't have it. After all, you're surrounded by people who never say no, so when you can't get whatever you want, it feels wrong. This is how a person can start out a normal girl from Queens, and end up Mariah Carey. It could happen to anyone; in fact this might also be what happened to Michael Jackson's face.

She seemed annoyed. I poked her suitcase with my foot. "You're never going to get all that stuff in there, Car. Have the front desk pack up a box and ship it to you. Or … you could just not leave at all. That's always an option. Stay here! Vince has room in his place, or you can just live here with me. I have two beds, and I'm almost done shooting Season One—we can play for my whole hiatus!"

She stopped packing, looking up. "Yeah, that sounds really fun," she said flatly. "I'll stay here and be 'unidentified friend of Star Spencer' from now on." She sighs. "Amy, I've had fun seeing you guys, but honestly, I can't wait to get out of here and get on with my life."

I didn't know what to say. Carrie Ann and I had always been able to talk about anything, but now I could feel the distance between us growing. Besides, it kind of pissed me off that she was so blatantly rejecting my life in L.A. when she was the one who'd told me I had to be "willing to do anything" to make it. "It's not that bad," I said, trying to lighten the mood. "You get used to the fake people after awhile."

She looked up. "It's not even that—you totally don't even need to be talented to make it here. It's sick—it's all about who you know and how you look, and eventually the fakeness becomes reality. I wouldn't even respect myself if I made it out here." After she finished, she looked surprised. She covered her mouth, as if to keep any more words from coming out. There was a long silence, then she added weakly, "I wasn't talking about you."

Too late. I was mad. "You don't even know how hard I've had to work, Carrie Ann. You don't know the long nights, or the sacrifices, or the constantly watching every morsel I put in my mouth. Not to mention the talent it takes to learn a whole different kind of acting and carry a show. Are you kidding me with this?" She was packing faster, but I'd gotten up from the bed and was standing close to her face, yelling. We'd never had a fight before, and my heart was beating a mile a minute.

Her face turned red, and her eyes filled with tears. "Don't give me that crap—you fucking *fell* into your big break, and everybody knows it. I've been working every day since I was twelve years old to get my shot, and I'm going to New York, where they care about talent, to earn my success." She was yelling too, and I didn't think I'd ever seen her that mad. "Besides," she said through tears, "I signed you up for that audition—you didn't even want to go, remember? I was supposed to make it first. It's not fair!"

One silent moment passed, then another. "I'm going to miss my plane," she said. I wanted to tell her how fraudulent I felt when I first started, or how I'd just recently overcome feeling all the time like everything would go away in a heartbeat, and I was never really sure what I could do to make my good fortune keep going. I wanted to tell her how hard it was to have all this responsibility at such a young age, and to have people depending on you. Then I thought of my dad, and how it's important to not be mad when you say goodbye. I didn't want her to go with things like that, but I didn't know what to say. I started to be the bigger person, to apologize for whatever I'd done.

But I couldn't. She insulted me, and I was too tired, too hungry, and too stressed out to take it from her. Instead I just said "I'll call you a cab," and watched while she struggled to get her huge suitcase out the door. When she was gone, I tried to block out the voices in my head, took a whole Xanax, and tried to sleep.

CHAPTER 11

❀

The last week of shooting Season One, the network finally made the announcement that the show was getting a full pickup for Season Two. As soon as the news broke, every cast member was on the phone, presumably with their respective agents. Within the hour, everyone was renegotiating their contracts.

Since it was my first show, I didn't know whether to do this or not. First of all, I still thought the $500,000 I was already getting paid was a lot of money, so when my cast mates started talking about how they were "undervalued," it made me want to laugh. Still, I knew the network was making millions of dollars from the show, so I could sort of see their rationale. The mood on the set was alternately one of joy and righteous indignation, as the attitude of "they couldn't do it without me" spread throughout the cast.

Todd's office had been calling my cell phone every twenty minutes since the very moment the network announced the pickup. "Hi, this is Amber from Todd Whitley's office ... Please return at your convenience ... hi, this is Amber from Todd Whitely's office, I have him on the line for you...."

During the day's second break in shooting, I finally called him back. "Todd, what's up?" I said, not wanting to let him make me into one of those greedy actors who go for the jugular. Definitely not my image of myself.

"Star Spencer, my favorite client, how are you not calling me back after the big announcement? Do you not know what this means? This is big big big! You are getting a big raise, baby!"

"Todd, my contract is for five years, and it says 'non-negotiable' all over it. I thought I was only getting an "incremental" raise … how much can that be? Why are you so excited?" I said.

"Oh little Amy Spencer … so naïve. This is why you have me. I'm an animal, baby. I kill for you. Hello! *House* took off, and Hugh Laurie gets three hundred grand an episode! I'm in contract negotiations with your network since the announcement this morning, and I've already got them up to seventy thousand per. I can get them to go higher, but they have a few conditions they need met."

$70,000 an episode? I thought. This is insane. I did some quick math in my head. Over $1 million per year. That was before residuals, before bonuses, and before Todd the Animal told me the conditions. With $1 million, even for one year, I could make sure my family was taken care of forever, and make my own films. This was big. But … what were the conditions?

"What do they want, Todd? I'm already on the set every waking hour of the day, I never eat, and I have no life. Do they want to control my thoughts as well?"

No reaction. Sometimes I wondered why I wasted perfectly good humor on Todd. "What do they want?" I said.

"They are exercising the "appearance" clause in your contract that says they can request that you undergo certain 'procedures' to 'update or maintain your look.'" I knew he was making the quotation marks in the air with his fingers, even though we were on the phone. "It's no big deal, Star … they can do it over the hiatus, and the network is going to pick up the tab for everything."

"Todd, what are you talking about?" I said, but I thought I knew what was coming.

"They want you to get plastic surgery, and they're prepared to pay you to get it. You should definitely do it … it will be good for your career, you'll look like a team player, and you'll get a huge bonus. If you say no, they're just going to try to say you're violating your contract and you won't get as big a raise, and they might even find a way to fire you. So … I'm going to say yes … can I say yes to this?"

This information was at once repulsive and intriguing to me, and I paused for a long moment as I felt the blood rush to my cheeks. The concept of being forced to have plastic surgery was something out of a Ray Bradbury novel. Could they do that? Could I get fired for saying no to altering my body?

"What do they want me to have done?" I said finally.

"Just the basics … definitely lipo, some filler stuff in your face, a little off your nose. Trust me, I've seen them demand a lot worse," he said, chuckling.

My mind started to race. "Todd, I need to call you back," I said, snapping the phone shut. Get your head on straight, I thought.…

I sat down, trying to sort the feelings out. Revulsion, for sure. Requiring someone to get plastic surgery is so wrong! screamed the rational side of me. Then, a guilty twinge of excitement … I could finally be thinner than Michele! I sent Vince an emergency text message. *Come to the set right now … need to discuss something very important.*

I was sick to death of worrying about my weight, and had been considering a secret visit to a plastic surgeon just to see if anything could be done about some fat on my butt and thighs that wouldn't seem to go away no matter how thin I got. I'd always hated the way my butt looked in jeans, even before I became a big TV star. Now I was being offered the chance to fix something I didn't like about myself anyway, for free, and they were going to pay me to do it. Somehow, it was too good to be true and a little disgusting, all at once, like when your best friend makes a joke about your parents that you know is true, but you're too full of pride to laugh. Could I actually let them "fix" something on my body without feeling like they were somehow buying a piece of my soul? This was definitely not something I could run by my mother, as she was forever telling me that she thought I was too thin anyway.

What I needed was a rational opinion from someone who was actually in the industry. What I needed was Vince.

Millions of people get plastic surgery every year, right? I thought, pacing the floor of the trailer. Why not? I thought. Isn't being young, thin, and gorgeous one of the job requirements? Wouldn't this take the pressure off of me to always be dieting?

Vince burst into my trailer in record time. "Where's the fire?" he yelled, kissing me on the cheek. "Is this about the contract negotiation? How much did they offer you? I'm DYING! There's a rumor going around that Greg left the set with a migraine. Is it true?"

"Sit down … it is about that," I said. "You're never going to believe…." I trailed off. "They want me to have plastic surgery over the hiatus … they're going to pay for it and give me a bonus." I watched his face carefully for signs of revulsion. "Do you think if I do it, I've sold all the way out?" I said pleadingly. "Am I a media whore?"

More silence. I could tell he was carefully formulating his response, though for once I couldn't tell what that would be. Slowly, a smile crept on to his face. "Do you think they'll pay for me to get my back hair lasered?" he said, laughing.

I picked up a pillow from the couch and chucked it at his head. "I'm being serious!" I shouted. "Be serious! I guess I can fight them on it, not take the raise …"

"Oh my God," he said. "Why is this even a question? You have been complaining about that fat you can't lose since, like, the beginning of time. You hardly eat, and yet you're always stressed out about not being able to fit into the costumes. Now they want to pay probably the best plastic surgeon in Beverly Hills to HELP you with this problem, and you're worried about selling out? Are you kidding me with this? Who CARES if you feel like they're buying you? You probably would have done it anyway!"

I let out a long breath. "Are you sure?" I said quietly. "Will you respect me? Do you think it's insane? Will I lose my edge?"

"You're going to look so hot!" he laughed. "You know you want to get it … just let the network think it was their idea … what's the big deal? You know, on older actresses they call it the 40,000 mile tune up … one of my clients just had everything lifted … I mean, EVERYTHING, Aim." He threw the pillow back at me.

After swearing Vince to secrecy, I thought some more. I decided I felt better.

I called Todd back.

I said yes.

❦   ❦   ❦

Three days after the new contract was signed (with a $150,000 bonus and free plastic surgery), I was accompanied to the office of a prominent Beverly Hills plastic surgeon by none other than Attila herself, who wanted to "oversee my transformation." I assured myself that it was still my choice, and that I could always back out. Besides, with the bonus I could pay off the last of my dad's medical bills, AND I wasn't going to have to worry about everything I ate. What could be better?

The face of the girl at the front desk lit up as she recognized me. "Oh my gosh—hi!," she said, instantly realizing that she was supposed to be subtle. I prayed she wouldn't call the tabloids.

Immediately, she got up and rushed us back to an examination room. I changed into a paper gown, then there was a knock at the door, and the doctor entered, already chatting with Attila (with whom he'd already worked in this capacity, I gathered). I caught the tail end of their conversation, which I discerned was a summary of all the times I wasn't able to fit into a size zero since she'd known me. Charming.

"So anyway, she just needs a little off the butt, hips, and stomach, definitely some filler in the face, and her nose could use some shaping. We also think her lips could be a little fuller. Also, she's only got about six weeks for the whole thing beginning to end, so if you could do everything at once, that would be great."

The doctor had obviously heard this a million times before. "OK, let's take a look," he said, getting out a bright light and shining it at my face. "Your skin is sun damaged—how old are you?"

I looked at Attila. I was supposed to be sixteen on the show, and the marketing department had been telling the press I was eighteen. Even my IMDB listing had me as eighteen, though I really wasn't sure how it had gotten that way.

"She's twenty, Frank. That goes strictly under doctor-patient confidentiality, of course," she said, laughing.

"Well, for twenty you're wrinkling a little more than we might want. We'll take some of that lipo fat and use it to fill out your cheeks and lips, and some of those fine lines. That'll make a big difference." He said this all nonchalantly, while peering at me through a magnifying glass.

I wasn't sure, but I thought he was talking about taking fat from my ass and putting it in my face. Was I in the Twilight Zone? Was this an accepted practice? I made a mental note to tell this to Vince the very moment I got back, because this was something we thought was made up for *Sex and the City*.

I was considering the possible ramifications of having ass fat in my cheeks when he spoke again. "Now, as far as the lips go … the upper lip is a little thin, and we can definitely put some of the fat in there as a base, then follow up with regular injections of FineLine so that it looks the same for continuity. She shouldn't need a GoreTex lip implant yet. What size were you thinking?"

Before I could answer, I noticed that this question was addressed not to me, but to Attila.

"Not that big—we don't want her to be one of those hideous "before and after" comparisons that *US Weekly* is doing these days. Just plump the lips a little bit—add some fullness, but don't go overboard, you know?" she said, pointing a sausage-like finger at my top lip. I nodded, resisting the urge to bite her finger like a rabid dog.

I ignored the fact that they were talking about me like I was a) a Grade A steer, and b) not in the room. "I love Angelina Jolie," I said hopefully. "Can I have her lips?" Attila shot me the all-too-familiar "I wish I could put you on Mute" look, and the doctor shook his head.

"Those lips would overpower your whole face. She can pull them off because she has angular features and high cheekbones. You don't have that. With those lips, you'd end up looking like Ronald McDonald," he said, chuckling.

I started to add something else, then Attila interrupted me again. "We're also thinking a little refinement on the nose, Frank. Nothing too drastic. Just flatten out that bump a little bit—the makeup artist wastes a lot of time shading it, and they're tired of having to shoot around it. The real work is going to be on that butt."

I bit my tongue. This is a woman from whom I had personally heard the words "mmmmm … butter." The nerve.

"OK—let's take a look." The doctor nodded his head, indicating that it was time for me to disrobe. I looked again at Attila, mentally willing her to leave the room. "Can you … I mean, can we have some privacy?" I said sheepishly.

She snorted. "Honey, it's not like I haven't seen every "before" body in this business. Get over yourself." She did not budge.

I knew there would be hell to pay if I argued any more, so I gritted my teeth, dropped the paper gown, and waited through the agonizing silence as they surveyed my stomach, butt, and thighs, which were covered only by paper underwear. I could feel the last shreds of dignity slipping away as the minutes crawled by. To exacerbate this heinous situation, the room was lit fluorescently, ensuring that I would certainly die from sheer embarrassment before ever getting to collect my $150,000 plastic surgery blood money. I went to my happy place in my mind, where I took the TV money and turned it into quality independent films.

With a serious expression, the doctor poked at the fat that protruded at the place where my hip and thigh meet. I remembered for a moment that at 5'7" and 117 pounds, I was skinny everywhere else in the world. I was in the middle of giving myself a mental pep talk when he finally broke the silence.

"You have a lot of fat for skinny girl. I think you're going to get great results." He turned to Attila. "I think I can get six pounds out of her, easy. She's going to look amazing. We'll put her on the calendar for a month from now, get her in the hyperbaric chamber right after so she'll heal faster, and the show will go up at least 10 points in the Nielsens, guaranteed."

It took me a minute, but slowly I realized that a) they were still talking about me like I wasn't there, and b) they were actually equating the size of my ass with the Nielsen ratings of the show. Could there really be a direct correlation? Was this study based in science?

One week after shooting wrapped on Season One I was having a deja vu experience as I walked through the quad toward the drama department. Having delayed the mandatory plastic surgery until after my trip back to Hudson to be the guest lecturer at Ellie Simon's "Acting for Television" class, I walked through the campus with a weird sense of wonder. It had been a little more than a year since I'd left campus for the *Autumn Leaves* audition and never come back.

I looked around at all the students, who had been back from Spring Break for maybe a month. Most of them were scraggly with heavy backpacks, and I had a momentary pang of regret as I realized I would never be one of them again. I vaguely remembered the feeling of getting back into classes after a break, stressing over papers and finals, and staying up too late obsessing over a thousand mini dramas. It seemed like a lifetime ago.

I walked up the familiar creaky stairs to drama department office. Ellie Simon and I were supposed to have coffee and go over the schedule beforehand. I remembered the twinge I used to get in my stomach when I approached that office. I laughed when I thought of how afraid I'd been of Shannon, the mean MFA student who worked there. Attila could eat Shannon for breakfast, and still have room for bacon and eggs.

As I opened the door to the drama department, I drew in a sharp breath as I saw Shannon's familiar face, remembering how afraid I was of her when I was there. She looked up, and I saw a flash of recognition, then watched as she forced her face into a tense smile. "Hi … Star," she said slowly. "Nice to see you again. Ellie will be right out."

This was bizarre, I thought. I had sort of counted on the fact that I even though I was famous and everyone else wanted to be my friend, Shannon would still refuse to treat me with any respect. While I could see it was just the fame and success that were keeping her from being a bitch to me, I was a little surprised that she would even play that game. For some reason, it made me feel horrible that she was still in the same place, doing the exact same job while my life must seem to her like some Cinderella fantasy. I sort of wanted to help her—to see if I could get her a job on the show, or to offer to give her some money. I knew this would make it worse, though, so I just said "thanks," and took a seat in the ancient wooden chairs outside the office.

She looked like she wanted to cry, she was holding back so much vitriol. Ellie had probably told her to be nice to me, and she needed her job. I didn't want to hold this kind of power over her—I'd rather just let her yell at me if it would make her feel better. This just felt artificial and gross.

"How have you been?" I said slowly. "How are things in the department?"

She looked up slowly. "Great—things are great. I'm graduating in June, and I just found out I got a summer gig in the Oregon Shakespeare Festival."

"Congratulations!" I said, and I actually meant it. I wanted to tell her that while she was doing Shakespeare, I was going to be having plastic surgery to stay "competitive in my field," but even thinking of sharing that information with her would violate my contract, so instead I said "Wow, that's great!"

She snorted. "Yeah, I'm sure it seems big to you, after going to the Golden Globes and starring in a hit show," she said. I kept trying to see the old Shannon snark from the year before, but instead she just seemed sad.

I wanted to pull the curtain back on her impression of my life, just to make her feel better. In fact, I wanted to scream "I make a million dollars a season, mostly for waiting in my trailer! I have no idea how I even got here!" but instead I just I tried to smile, said "believe me, I wish I could be doing some good theater over the summer," then waited through the rest of the thick silence that hung in the air. Did she hate me more, now that I was successful? Did all the students feel this way?

Ellie came out of her office, rescuing me from this infernally awful exchange. "Amy—welcome back! How are you?" she said, giving me welcoming hug. Over her shoulder, I could see Shannon staring at her computer screen.

"I'm great," I said. "So glad to be back!"

Ellie laughed, squeezing my hand. She always had the power to make me feel better about things. "Let's go get some coffee."

Twenty minutes and three autographs later, we were sitting in the campus coffee shop and discussing the lecture. "Just give an overview of what you do, then let them ask questions. They all watch the show, and they're dying to know some insider dirt." She smiled. "Obviously, don't tell them anything that will get you in trouble, but you know, just tell them what it's like to work with Greg Forster and Ross Wong, let them ask you how you prepare for your dramatic scenes, that kind of thing." She smiled. I wanted to cry from the sheer relief of being able to just let my guard down and be myself again. I realized what it was—Ellie Simon was real, and she wasn't hiding anything. No one is really "what you see is what you get" in L.A.—everyone is sort of like Shannon, with the forced smiles and niceties. Once you get to a certain level of celebrity, you lose all chance of having someone want to know you for who you are.

I laughed. "Will you move to L.A. and work with me?" I said. "I need a real person on my side. Seriously—is there anything special you want me to tell the students? I have no idea how I even got to where I am."

She smiled. "Don't underestimate yourself, my dear," she said. "You got to where you are by being talented, Amy. Don't you know that E.B. White saying about being 'ready to be lucky?' You were in the right place at the right time with the right talent."

I sighed. "Sometimes it's so amazing, like a dream, and then sometimes I get scared that it could all go away in an instant," I said.

She winked at me. "That's why you have to be smart, hang on for dear life, and take all the opportunities you can while you're on top."

CHAPTER 12

❀

Even after taking an Ambien to sleep the night before the surgery, I was still haunted by dreams of going under anesthesia and never being able to wake up. Dr. Romano had assured me that it was completely safe to undergo multiple procedures at once, and I'd agreed, thinking I was probably only going to be brave enough to go under the knife one time. So, by the end of the day I'd have lipo, fat injections to my face and top lip, and a little off my nose. That's how they say it: "a little off the nose," like my face was turkey that you buy in a deli. I couldn't sleep, and I couldn't stop obsessing about a story I'd read where a woman had her legs amputated after a freak staph infection following a botched liposuction.

"Can that really happen?" I asked Vince in the car the next morning. I had a horror-movie type "death by liposuction" scene playing in my head, and I couldn't quite turn it off. The questions wouldn't stop—what's it going to feel like? Is it going to be horribly painful? What if I wake up in the middle of the surgery? What was Sondra going to tell the press if I died on the table? What if something went wrong? Don't only socialites over 50 actually die from plastic surgery procedures? Was I going to end up drooling in some nursing home because I pushed it too far?

I tried to make myself stop. I was young and healthy. I'd never had a medical problem. I wanted this stuff done anyway. It was going to be a piece of cake. But … what if it wasn't?

I'd already taken the big fat emergency Xanax that I saved for bumpy plane rides, and it started to hit me just as we got off on the Overland exit on the 10

Freeway. By the time we turned two corners and arrived at the surgery center in Beverly Hills, I felt the warm rush of the drugs taking over, and I started to care a little less about the latest irreversible step in my "transformation."

It was just like Dr. Romano said it would be … we entered through a back entrance so no one would see us and call the ***Enquirer***. I could just see it now: "Star Spencer's Surgery Nightmare!" The nurse took us right into the exam room. I changed into the dreaded Blue Paper Gown again and waited for the doctor.

"Are you nervous?" he said as he came in, his large frame filling the doorway. "Do you need a hug?" Like a big bear, he wrapped his arms around me, and suddenly I wanted him to be my dad—in fact, I wanted to be a little kid again, hugging my dad when he came home from work. Before Hollywood, before college, before high school, before the Big Dreams. Before the Plastic Surgery.

He took out a big purple marker, just like on those plastic surgery TV shows, and started circling my fat. After he was done drawing on my hips, thighs, and abdomen, he moved on to my face. My God, I thought … if *US Weekly* could see me now. "We'll inject the fat here, here … and here," he narrated as he drew little purple dots where the needles were going to go. I wanted to tell him that this was "too much information," but I found the sound of his voice soothing, like he was reading me a plastic surgery bedtime story. "Once upon a time there was a girl from Bay City, Michigan and a magic wizard with a tiny vacuum took the fat out of her behind and injected it into her face."

After he was done drawing on me, he left the room and then the nurse came in to take me to the OR which (surprise) was attached to the exam room. Last chance to bolt, I thought, and I almost did it. Then I pulled myself together, climbed up on the table, and the anesthesiologist immediately poked me in the arm. I thought they were going to do the "count backwards from 100" thing, like in the movies, but after, 30 seconds I felt sort of warm and funny, like I'd been in the Jacuzzi too long and fell over when I tried to get out. The room went kind of sideways, and literally the next thing I knew, they were trying to wake me up.

❈   ❈   ❈

"Star? Star … can you hear me?" It sounded like the nurse was yelling from somewhere very far away.

The whole "waking up from anesthesia' thing is completely unnerving … like you're going through a long tunnel in a dream, and you can never find the ending. Then your eyes are open, you're struggling to "snap out of it," you're freezing, then you're asleep again. After a few hours of this, I was lucid enough to be moved to the "recovery center," which was like a fancy hospital/hotel room combined. Of all the things I'd experienced since becoming a TV star, Secret Plastic Surgery was definitely the most surreal.

The first twelve hours after the surgery were a complete blur. While I was under, they'd somehow put me into a very tight "garment," which was black spandex, and extended from my ankles to right below my armpits and was held up by suspenders, with only a small hole designed to enable me to **never** take it off—not even to go to the bathroom. The purpose of the garment was to hold everything in place and compress the skin. I also had a splint covering my nose. By the time I really woke up enough to know what was going on, I looked and felt like I was a wrestler who'd lost a match.

"How long until I look normal?" I said to Dr. Romano a few days later. I was still afraid to look in the mirror.

He laughed. "Just relax—watch movies, and read magazines. You're not going to look normal, kid—you're going to look amazing. Trust me on this. I've been doing this for twenty five years." He checked my incisions and stitches, and poked at the splint on my nose. "Did you know we got seven pounds of fat out of you?" he said, as if he was sharing information about his golf game or where he'd had dinner the night before. "I told you you had a lot of fat for a skinny girl." He laughed. "Don't worry—you're going to look great," he said. "Call me if you're worried, or if you want me to come back."

❈   ❈   ❈

Ten days after the surgeries, I was well enough to start getting hyberbaric oxygen treatments, and I could already see the difference in my thighs and butt. I showed up at the first appointment moving slowly and wearing dark glasses, praying that no paparazzi had followed me.

"Just take a deep breath … if you feel faint or like you're gong to panic, let me know."

Mike, the nurse, was trying to tell me what to do while he locked me in a sealed chamber and pumped it full of oxygen. This was supposed to make my bruises go away faster, and the doctor wanted me to do it twice a day every day until Season Two shooting started, to insure the bruising and swelling from the surgeries would be gone by then. If I could take the claustrophobia, I'd be home free.

The initial "exam" had consisted of a doctor coming in and asking me a bunch of questions, while trying to pretend he didn't watch my show. I could tell he was tempted to say something about me or the show as he ticked off items on his clipboard. Since I knew he recognized me, I actually felt a little braver, like I had to maintain my composure not just for me, but for him.

"Any history of blood clots in your family?" he said nonchalantly.

"No."

"Stroke?"

"No."

"Clotting disorders?

Good Lord … what did the oxygen chamber *do*, anyway? I took a deep breath and thought of the big raise. I'd already let them operate on me. What was the big deal?

The chamber itself looked just like the one Michael Jackson supposedly used to sleep in. It was basically a big, see-through coffin. "Here's how it works," said Mike. "First, you get in and lay down, we lock and seal the chamber, and then we pump in pure oxygen for thirty minutes. Your ears might pop, and you might feel a little light headed. I'll be out here the whole time to talk to you, and you have a TV here that you can watch. Are you ready?"

I could not get up and run out of the office, mainly because if I moved too fast, my legs felt like they were going to fall off. How bad can it be? I thought. People do this every day, and you never hear about a "hyperbaric oxygen chamber death."

"This is going to really help with that bruising and swelling. Just lay back and try to relax, and if you get scared at all, just let me know and we'll bring you out of it. We have to take you "down" into it very slowly, because if we go too fast, you'll get the bends, like in scuba diving.

Yeah, that's not freaky at all, I thought. Seconds ticked by. My ears popped. "You're doing great!" said Mike, whose voice was now muffled by the hissing sound of oxygen filling the chamber. Was the tingling I was feeling in my toes a side effect of the "pure oxygen treatment," or all in my mind? Was this helping? Was I having a stroke?

Cynicism aside, after I relaxed about the whole "being locked in a sealed chamber" thing, the pure oxygen made me kind of sleepy, and I swear the bruises went away at twice their regular rate. After ten days of twice daily hyperbaric sessions, I felt ridiculously good.

Well, not good enough to tell anyone in Bay City that I'd been frequenting a Michael Jackson-like oxygen chamber, but pretty great nonetheless. After two more weeks, I could pull on my pants again without wincing and jog without feeling like the sides of my legs were going to fall off. My black eyes had gone away, my nose looked more sculpted, and my lips were returning to a normal-looking size, and when I looked in the mirror, I looked like myself again, only better.

In fact, I looked amazing. Hollywood amazing.

SEASON TWO

CHAPTER 13

✿

When we arrived on set in July to start shooting Season Two, it was like the first day back to school when you're a kid. Everyone was rested and relaxed, and even people who hadn't gotten along that well in Season One seemed happy to see each other. We also had new sets, a new cast member (Sharon Hikida, who had been hired to play the role of Ross' character's sister), and we were all basking in the glow of our newly-renegotiated contracts and raises.

For the first few hours, I was incredibly self-conscious about my new look. Would anyone notice my amazingly small ass? What about my new nose? I certainly noticed it when I got dressed every day—it was incredible! Would they say I looked like a freak? Since it was generally regarded as uncouth to say anything about people's work, I thought I could probably only count on Michele's reaction as a measure of how it really looked.

After the table read, she walked over to me slowly, like one of those gunslingers in the Old West. "Hi...." She said cagily, making no effort to disguise the fact that she was checking me out. "How was your break?"

"Great!" I said, trying to feel out the vibe. "I went back to Michigan to see my friends, gave a lecture at my old school, then came back here and just sat by the pool. It was awesome."

"Well, you look ... great." she said slowly, almost testily. "Really. What's your secret?"

I laughed. "Clean living, of course!" I said. There was no way I was telling her anything. I suspected she had the tabloids on speed dial as the **Autumn Leaves** inside source, trying to leak some information that would get me fired.

"Well, whatever you're doing is totally working," she said glumly. That's when it hit me. I actually looked **better** than her now, and it was killing her. Without meaning to, I had finally gotten the upper hand over Michele McCann.

"Nice to see you too," I said, smiling and turning to go back to my trailer.

This time, I really meant it. The victory was thrilling. Who knew crushing a person could feel so good?

❦   ❦   ❦

"Here's a good one. "Dear Star … I think you are so beautiful. I have a problem. I went to jail for drugs and lost my job, and I think if you wrote a letter to the warden, I could get out early. I just thought because I feel a real connection with you, you might be able to really help me."

My new assistant, Olivia Garcia, had created a file with all of the weirdest fan letters sent over from Todd at William Morris, and we'd started reading the highlights over lunch in my trailer every day. Even though I was Hollywood fabulous and had had the plastic surgery, I still objected to the whole concept of having an assistant. "No way," I'd said to Todd. "She's older than me, and I'm going to feel totally weird having someone clean up after me. That is wrong … I'm not the "hired help" type."

"Get over it, Star Spencer," said Todd. "I am tired of not being able to get you on the phone. I am sending Olivia over, and you will love her.

I'd kept insisting that I was fine to go get my own groceries and buy my own stamps, but with the show frequently shooting late into the night, I finally relented. Not only was Olivia funny and cool, like one of my friends from Michigan, but she had a really no-nonsense attitude about the whole assistant thing. Most of the time, she just picked up stuff for me while I was at work, and then on my days off we went shopping and went to lunch.

Olivia was almost done with law school and on her way to an internship at William Morris, and she'd been doing the assistant thing for three years. Olivia's stories over lunch were becoming the highlight of my week, ranging from weird celebrity shopping lists to mental breakdowns to three a.m. calls to "bring over a single slice of Yarlsberg Cheese," to everything in between. Immediately, I promised that I would never become that person, and made Olivia swear to let me know if I was doing anything that would cause her to tell a story about me later.

Because she had more experience with this sort of thing than I did, Olivia quickly took over the management of the "Celebrity Fan Mail" project. Mostly this just involved sorting, filing, and sending back signed photos of me (or the cast) to those who asked. Weird mail was separated into several piles: the "How Dare You" pile, where people ranted about everything from how much they hated my outfits to how I should be ashamed of myself for "fraternizing with the gays," to how I was too fat, or too thin, or too blonde, or my nose was too big (no longer a problem), or they don't like my elbows. After one week of trying to open it all myself, I was literally so traumatized, I had been letting the mail pile up in various offices (mostly Todd's and Sondra's). The "Funny But Not Dangerous" mail was separated out into a file and enjoyed over lunch, along with Olivia's famous Celebrity Nightmare Stories.

One Sunday, we drove with Vince out to Shutters in Santa Monica for brunch and stories.

As soon as we sat down, Olivia launched into a doozy involving a famous actress invited to be the guest speaker at a wedding. "To start, she'd just had a lip implant, and it hadn't "settled" yet, so the reading she was asked to give ended up sounding like she had a speech impediment. I had to go with her and drive her, because she was still taking the maximum dose of painkillers from the surgery, and couldn't even back out of her own driveway. No one said anything, but by the reception, everyone was talking about what must be wrong with her. She made me bring a change of clothes for her—I always kept a big box of "extra" clothes in her car in case she wanted to appear somewhere else or change her look in the middle of the day. For the wedding, she was wearing this really conservative, Jackie-O style pink Chanel suit, and for once her boobs were actually covered. However, by the reception, she was sick of this look, and we went to the hotel where the reception was being held so she could change. She was so high, she couldn't decide on an outfit, so she had me take the whole box of clothes into the women's lounge so she could pick for herself. Then she realized she'd left her makeup in the car, so she sent me outside for it. When I got back, there were clothes all over the lounge, and she was gone."

She took a sip of her coffee and paused for effect, leaving Vince and I on pins and needles. "What was she wearing?" said Vince. "A leather bikini?" These were Vince's own personal version of scary campfire stories.

"How much do I want her to just be naked at the reception when you find her?" I said. The best parts of Olivia's stories were the endings.

"Better," she said. *My* white spandex running pants that I'd put in her car for the gym. Black g-string, tie-on halter dress that barely covered her huge fake boobs, and knee high purple Ugg boots." She paused while we laughed, then finally: "The father of the bride actually came to ask me if I would "cover her up with a coat," because he didn't want her to appear in any of the pictures for the album."

Between Vince and Olivia, they could probably have made a million dollars, just from blackmail or stories sold to the tabloids. Thankfully, they were both too honorable to do it, so everyone's secrets were safe.

❧   ❧   ❧

I thought by Season Two I had seen everything, but every time I got that feeling, something happened that proved me totally wrong.

Jamie Powell had been cast to as a "bad girl who comes to town" for a five-episode run, and she started a couple of weeks into Season Two. Up close she looked at least thirty, but she was playing a bad seventeen year old on the show.

From the amount of food that Jamie consumed at the craft services table, I surmised that she had:

a) a fast metabolism
b) a raging case of bulimia
c) a drug habit.

After shooting scenes with her and chatting in between for a few days, I learned it was a combination of (b) and (c). "You should try it," she said with impunity. "People say throwing up bad for you, but it feels good, and if you keep it to once a day or so, it doesn't even hurt you." Aside from this skewed notion of reality in relation to food, she seemed like a pretty nice person, and I was eager for new people to talk to when Olivia and Vince weren't around. Also, everyone knew that Jamie Powell used to be the girlfriend of one of the Red Hot Chili Peppers, and I wanted some crazy "behind the scenes" stories about Anthony and Flea.

She came into my trailer at the end of the day, just as Olivia and I were discussing plans for the weekend. We were in the middle of planning a shopping excursion to the outlet stores in Cabazon when Jamie flung open the door and barged in. "I like you," she said, plunking herself down on my couch. "Let's go do something fun." As usual, she did not acknowledge Olivia, who rolled her eyes.

Jamie Powell was the kind of girl who never would have given me the time of day in high school, or even in the drama department, for that matter. With luminous blue eyes, shiny blonde hair, and a body so effortlessly perfect it hurt me to even look at her, she fit easily into the "Malibu World" of *Autumn Leaves*—so much so that she sometimes made me feel like an outsider on the show even though she was just a guest star. She looked like the kind of girl who would be your friend one minute, then talk an outrageous amount of shit about you when you turned your back. I actually sort of wanted to see Jamie and Michele together in a cage match, just to see who would be more vicious. I preferred the company of Vince and Olivia Garcia, super assistant. Perhaps because she was bound by a confidentiality agreement, I felt comfortable telling her stuff I would never have told anyone other than close friends and family. Certainly not Michele, and probably not Jamie Powell.

"I can't … I have to learn lines for tomorrow," I said, shooting Olivia a look. I was curious as to what a girl like Jamie did when she left work, but I also was a little scared of her. Where did she live? Who did she hang out with? Who did she know?

Jamie chimed in again. "Are you kidding me? You are NOT going home, Star Spencer. You are fabulous, and fabulous girls go out at night, to eat and dance and be with cool people. Let's go."

My curiosity got the best of me, and before I knew it, we were speeding up Melrose in Jamie's silver convertible BMW M3. Olivia had begged off for the night, claiming that she had to study, even though I know that she, too, was curious about Jamie. "Isn't my car great?" she said. "It goes totally fast. I get pulled over all the time, but I never get tickets," she said, giggling. "I love the LAPD."

I'd only known Jamie for three weeks, but she had already told me about the "totally harrowing" time she had when she got her boobs done, and scooped me on lots of other well-known people's plastic surgery. "Totally worth it, though—my career has improved so much since my procedure. What have you had done?"

"Oh, nothing … just diet a lot," I said. According to everyone on my team, celebrities were never supposed to share plastic surgery information. For all I knew, Jamie could call *US Weekly* and be "sources close to Star Spencer." I liked her, but I couldn't risk it. "What's it like to have fake boobs?" I said, diverting her attention. "I've been thinking of having that done. Does it feel weird forever, or do you get used to it?" *Considering* plastic surgery was much easier to deny, and I thought maybe it would get her off the subject of stuff I'd actually had done.

"You totally should … you would look hot!" she said, reaching over and pinching my leg. I couldn't tell if she was high or just weird. "I would be all over you!" she yelled, then commenced with a series of high-pitched barks, like she was a Pekinese in heat. Then, out of the blue, she leaned over and licked my cheek. Her tongue was warm, and the lick left a snail-like trail of saliva on my face. I wanted to wipe it off, but I didn't want to offend her, so I tried to subtly let it dry without thinking about just how weird that was.

"You are sexy!" she yelled, resuming the barking, which became a low howl. She managed to keep driving despite this apparent break from reality, and we pulled up to a stoplight. I put my head down to avoid 1) making embarrassing eye contact with the people in the car next to us, 2) being recognized driving down Melrose with a barking blonde girl, or 3) the very real possibility that I might be licked again.

I never knew what to do when people acted this kind of out of control weird. Like, did I just laugh, did I bark along with her, or did I just ignore it? Mercifully, she turned her attention back to driving, and soon we pulled up to a tall white apartment building. "You have to come in and see my place!" she squealed. "I'm going to change, and then we'll go out, ok?"

I looked at my watch. 7:42 pm. I really, really wished I had just gone back to the hotel to learn lines. I didn't want to go into Barking Girl's apartment, I didn't want to wait for her, and I didn't want to have dinner at 9:00 when I had to be on set at 8:00 the next morning.

"That's ok—I'm pretty tired actually. I'm just going to call a cab and go back," I said, but she was dragging me by the hand up the stairs to her apartment. "Just come up and wait … I'll be ready in like, two minutes and we'll go around the corner to the Spanish Kitchen for margaritas. Come on! Don't be a poop!" she yelled, and resumed barking.

I resisted the urge to break her grip and run down the stairs. "OK—ten minutes, and then I am leaving without you," I said, watching her pull out keys and open her front door. I was glad to see that even though she seemed to live on another planet in her mind, she had the wherewithal to manage practical, every day things like paying her rent and finding her keys. She had a driver's license and a guest-starring role on a hit television show, so she must have been doing something right. Something inside me wanted to know what made weird people tick, and how they functioned in the universe.

While she was changing in the other room, I checked out her apartment. Nice enough furniture—green Pottery Barn looking couch, geometric rug, black coffee table and entertainment center, plasma screen TV. Small desk area with normal-looking bills, headshots, and a bulletin board with some photos of friends tacked up on it. Maybe the barking was just for effect.

"What do you think?" she said, and I turned around that she came out of the bedroom wearing a tight black skirt and nothing else. Her large, tanned breasts stood straight out, and she was rubbing her nose and sniffing. "Aren't they great? Dr. T. did an amazing job. Touch them! I want you to." She walked slowly over to me, and all at once I felt like the stupidest person in the world. "I like you," she said softly, and leaned in to kiss me. Her lips were soft, and touched mine for the briefest second before I pulled away.

"Jamie … I can't … I don't … I'm not" I stammered. She looked unfazed. "Don't be silly," she said. "Everybody does it. Just touch them. Don't you think I'm pretty?"

"I … Jamie … let's just go eat," I said, sighing. I wanted no part of the barking, or the boobs, or whatever else was going on with her. I should have been used to crazy Hollywood people by then, but somehow, I always forgot where I was and expected people to act normal, then suddenly they went all barky and tried to get me to touch their fake boobs. "Come on … what's Anthony Kiedis like?" I said, trying to draw her out of her obvious funk. "Can't we just be friends?" I said.

Despite her obvious mental imbalance, barking Jamie's storyline was extended, and she was promoted to special guest star on the show. I never did find out the scoop on Anthony Kiedis.

❧   ❧   ❧

Time was flying. We were almost to the winter break of Season Two, the show was a huge hit, and Todd decided I needed my own publicist. "I'm setting up lunch with you and Arden Stone from RMG," he said one Friday. "You need more exposure—trust me. Best five thousand a month you'll ever spend. The offers are going to come rolling in. You're going to be huge! Bigger than Mischa Barton, out walking around in her pajamas. Arden is a force of nature. She'll get you *Vanity Fair*, *InStyle*, even Oprah if you need it."

The frugal Midwesterner in me balked at the sound of five thousand dollars a month, but I had really been wanting to get into *InStyle* magazine, and my loathing of Sondra was up there right underneath my hatred of her boss. Sondra was obsessed with getting us into TV Guide as a whole cast, handling the backlash from the show's themes, and making sure we didn't embarrass ourselves or the show in public. Since I knew I could use a better advocate, I decided to at least meet Arden to see what she had to offer.

Arden Stone was mid-forties, tall, beautiful, and forceful in a "Samantha from *Sex and the City*" kind of way. As soon as we sat down for our Todd-arranged lunch at Koi, I knew she was a whole different stratosphere from Sondra.

"Honey, you should be much bigger right now—it's about time we started working together. Where's your **Vanity Fair** cover? Who tips off the paparazzi for you when you travel, so the big executives know you're a busy girl? That network publicist—is it Sondra Smith? We worked together years ago—she's fine for the whole cast, but she's not going to grow your career. We need to strike while the iron is hot with you. You should be **everywhere** right now! My God, you can't even pass a newsstand without seeing Scarlett Johanssen on the cover of six magazines. Even Britney Spears is still on magazine covers, and she's not even promoting anything! She was pregnant for a hundred years, then BALD, Star. Come on!"

Arden knew everyone at Koi—in fact, Arden knew everyone, everywhere. "You are carrying a huge hit show with your character's name in the title. Honey, that is huge! **Ugly Betty** huge! We need to show your network that you're a hot commodity, and that if they don't treat you well, they're going to lose you. Now—first thing's first. We should start with the magazine placements right away. Do you know how to knit? I'll have some stuff sent over, and then we can start getting you mentioned in the publications when they do "stars who knit" stories. You know—Julia Roberts, Kate Hudson, Liv Tyler—they all do it. Knitting is the new yoga."

I laughed, thinking back to a few years before, when my mom bought me some knitting stuff and tried to teach me. "It will relax you," she'd said with a well-meaning smile. Four hours, a twisted knot of multi colored yarn, and some frustrated tears later, I had put the stuff in the closet, claiming that it made me more stressed out to learn knitting than I had been before.

"I can't knit," I said to Arden. "Apparently I am missing the knitting gene."

She laughed. "That's fine—we'll just say you do, and you can learn later if you want to. Or we'll think of something else for you. How do you feel about fashion shows?"

❧   ❧   ❧

Arden's aggressive strategies for getting me "seen" bordered on the absurd. At 8 am the next Saturday morning, I stood in an unknown person's living room as a fluffy white Persian made its way toward the couch, stepping nonchalantly over my feet. For the day, at least, this was my home. "Arden, do I have a cat?" I asked, half-jokingly. Soon the photographer would be there, and I was walking around, trying to get my bearings in a house where I had supposedly been living for a year, laughing to myself at the shameful artifice of it all.

Actually, I am deathly allergic to cats, and as soon as this one touched me, the journalist was going to know that this whole thing was fake, because my eyes were going to swell up, and I was not going to be able to breathe. Arden laughed, scooping up the cat with one hand while she pressed a perfectly manicured finger to her lips with the other, shushing me. She would have nothing ruin her perfectly orchestrated photo shoot. Here's a Claritin," she whispered. "Don't let the writer hear you say this isn't your place."

"Get this cat out of here!" she yelled to a PA. "Put it someplace where it can't get out. Or, better yet … take a shot of it in the guest room. That will make the place look more homey."

In an attempt to make me seem "more accessible and relatable" as a big TV star, Arden had booked me a shoot and interview for a magazine feature called Young Stars at Home. This was by far the most bizarre idea she'd had so far, considering the fact that I still lived at the hotel, and even then I was hardly home enough to sleep, much less decorate a whole place like that and hang out in the living room eating biscotti. But for that day at least, I lived in a three bedroom bungalow style home in Beverly Hills. She'd even gotten some "family and friends" type photos from me that she'd strategically placed around the house to make it look like mine. By noon, I was being photographed sitting on my plush suede couch, pretending to read a book.

The weirdest thing about this, to me, was that the purpose of a shoot like this to show you the private lives of stars, and yet even *that* was manufactured. Even the "interview" I gave after the photo shoot was just a series of talking points invented by Arden and her team. In fact, right before the actual interview began, I was once again in the bathroom, trying to learn more about myself. The journalist couldn't just read the bullet points and write the article about me … the words had to actually come out of my mouth. How I found the house, where I got all the stuff I decorated with (this one I got in Tahiti—I love vacationing there … so relaxing!). This is where I make enchiladas for my friends!

The only small victory for me of this photo shoot day was that originally, I was supposed to actually be *cooking* something in the kitchen when the writer got there, so I could serve her lunch. Apparently Arden had read a similar *InStyle* interview with Jessica Alba, and thought this would be a good way for me to go. I had actually laughed at this suggestion, then refused. "You have to cook," said Arden. "It will look so great!"

"You don't understand," I said. "I know less than nothing about how to cook … in fact, if I try to cook, I might actually injure myself, and that would make me look even worse. No way."

Arden had an advance copy of the article sent over to me as soon as it was ready. It looked great, but I just couldn't shake the feeling that the while the whole thing looked beautiful on the outside, that inside it was empty and hollow. That was sort of the way I was starting to feel.

❦   ❦   ❦

Right before the winter break in shooting for Season Two (before I got so famous I couldn't pee in a public restroom anymore), Vince and I were having brunch at Toast in West Hollywood. Actually, I was picking at a salad I hope didn't have too much cheese in it and trying not to think about the basket of bread sitting on the table, and Vince was eating a delicious chicken frittata-thing called "Power Protein." Toast on Saturday was our ritual, before we hit the Melrose Trading Post at Fairfax high school, then Buffalo Exchange. Vince had a bunch of celebrity clients now (besides me), and he was always trying to create new and exciting looks for them by mixing vintage stuff with the clothes the designers sent over. His apartment was filled to the brim with designer clothes—hanging up, spilling off of furniture, even in the kitchen. You never knew what you might find at Vince's place, or even in his car. Vince was like the Felix the Cat of L.A. celebrity fashion.

Sitting outside at Toast, we liked to play the "see and be seen" game, to watch who was out walking around, to see who was most popular in Hollywood that day (by watching to see who attracted the most paparazzi). On this particular day, I was beating Jessica Simpson for the number of photographers crowded around. A group of young-ish looking girls were frantically whispering and staring at us. Eventually, one of them broke away from the cute girl herd and came over to our table. I figure she was going to ask for an autograph, and I winked at Vince.

She walked up slowly. She was thin and blonde, and she was wearing tiny, low-waisted jeans. She looked like one of those "I can eat whatever I want and not gain weight" types. "Star Spencer!" she said. "You're on *Autumn Leaves*."

"Yes," I said. "Do you want an autograph?"

"No, I...." her voice trailed off. "I was the one who had the part of Autumn before you." She looked down. I studied her more closely. In fact, she did seem to be the exact size of the tiny costumes that had given me so much angst during the pilot.

"Wow ... I ... I'm so sorry," I said haltingly. But actually, I wasn't sorry. If something hadn't been wrong with this girl, if fate hadn't intervened to take away her big break, I would never have gotten mine. Now I just wanted her to go away. "What are you doing now?" I asked, just to make conversation. I was really not in the mood to hear this girl's sob story.

"Oh, I'm still in school, actually—I *was* really bummed about losing the part and I cursed you every time I saw you on a billboard for awhile, but I'm still auditioning all the time, and I just started my third year at UCLA. That's just the business. I've been doing this since I was ten, so I'm used to it. My friends and I love the show now ... you're really good." She smiled. She actually seemed cool, like someone I'd be friends with.

"That's great," I said, and stopped to take a good look at her. She was beautiful and young, and she was out to brunch with her friends. She looked well rested and happy. She didn't have the money, the fame, and everything that went with it. Then again, I thought, she was allowed to eat, and to have pimples, and to just be herself. Suddenly, I felt like telling her that she could have the part back, and that I wanted my old life back. But I didn't. I couldn't. Instead I just smiled.

"Why did they fire you?" blurted Vince before I could shush him. "I mean—did you not get along with Greg? Did you look bad on camera? Come on—tell us."

She looked around, like she was in the C.I.A. and on a covert operation. Then she leaned forward, and in a hushed voice said: "Don't tell anyone, but there was this insane producer, Mindy something, who got me fired because she didn't like my hairline. My hairline! She called a plastic surgeon, and when he told her the "hairline revision" surgery wouldn't heal in time to start shooting Season One, I was gone. My agent was furious and made them pay the contract anyway. I mean, that is just psycho."

She looked at me. "Good thing you don't have a widow's peak."

I sighed. A widow's peak would have been the least of my worries.

CHAPTER 14

My celebrity life was going along pretty normally when suddenly, almost without my having to do anything, I suddenly had a boyfriend. It started with lunch at the Ivy, arranged by Arden.

I pushed the grilled chicken salad around on my plate, praying I didn't already have spinach stuck in my teeth. I. Was on a date. With Brad Rockwell, star of the most famous action movie series of all time, ***Blood Vengeance***. Even in my former life as an indie film snob, I still knew who he was. I could hardly believe it myself—even with the show, the famous friends, and the money, I still never thought I would actually ***know*** someone as famous as Brad, much less be out on a pseudo-date with him. Sometimes, the stuff that happened in my life surprised even me.

Apparently, this kind of "fix up" is not uncommon in Hollywood. At first, Arden claimed that it was just for the photo op of the two of us out together, but then a couple of times she mentioned "you two would make such a great couple!" hopefully. I later found out that she was friends with his publicist, and that they'd been trying to construct a "power couple" for months. I found the whole thing a little weird, but I agreed to go to the lunch, mostly because my brothers would have killed me if I didn't at least meet the guy and get some good stories for them.

"So … how did you get started in the business?" I said, trying to make normal person conversation. The fact is, I had never considered that this guy might be a real person—what did he talk to people about? Did he read the newspaper? When the question came out, though, I realized I sounded like a magazine interviewer. Why didn't I know more about him? He was only the most famous movie star in the world. My brother Ian had actually dressed up as his **Blood Vengeance** character for Halloween a few years before. He's going to leave the lunch, I thought. He thinks I'm quirky. I was momentarily ashamed to realize that I really did care what he thought of me.

I tried to remind myself: "I'm on a hit show! I'm famous too … besides, I don't even like this guy's movies." Still, I kept having that feeling that I was floating outside my body, watching myself in a dream where I was a fabulous Hollywood actress, going on a date with a fabulous Hollywood Movie Star. To be honest, it was a little like going on a date with Santa Claus, or the Easter Bunny.

❧   ❧   ❧

Two days later, I got a call from Todd.

"Come in to the office," he said. "I've got a really interesting offer for you." Since I was already working eighteen hours a day on the show, I couldn't imagine what other offer I had time to consider, but if there was money involved, Todd would find out a way. I think if he could've cloned me and sent the clone out on appearances, he would definitely have done it.

Todd was dancing excitedly around his office holding a large manila envelope when I got there. "It's a standard work for hire contract from Brad Rockwell's office," said Todd, not even phased. "Basically, Brad's nominated for a Golden Globe, a SAG Award, and an Oscar this year, and his people want him to have a new romance to start right before the awards season. His company will hire you to play the role of Brad's girlfriend for no less than one year. It's got the standard benefits—use of his jets, rooms in his mansion, and an unlimited expense account, plus bonuses for awards shows and other public appearances." It also has you on a tiered payout schedule—one year is $250,000 cash, more for engagement, marriage, a baby, etc."

"Todd, is this a joke?" I said, incredulous. "Seriously … are you kidding? We had lunch. He was really hot. We talked about our cars. Now I'm his girlfriend?"

"This is not a joke, Star Spencer. This is going to make your career," he said in a loud whisper. I haven't seen an offer this good since … well, I can't say, but she's an Academy Award winner, she gets better looking every year, and **her** contract was the best career move she ever made."

Something Vince told me in my "Hollywood Crash Course" rang a bell. "Oh my God!" I shouted. I know this! Is it....?"

"Don't even say it," he said. "I couldn't tell you even if you were right, and I don't need her lawyers coming after me. I was an assistant at CAA when that deal came through, and I wasn't even supposed to know about it. I just photo-copied the original contract."

"Does Brad like me, even?" I said. This was by far the weirdest thing I had ever heard.

Todd looked up over the contract. "Not that it matters, but he thinks you're adorable. He loves your show. He had his manager Jon send over the contract right after your lunch. Listen … you're not even going to have to see him that much—between your shooting schedule and his, plus whatever film you're doing over this year's hiatus, you'd be lucky if you actually spend a weekend with him every couple of months. It's mostly just for awards shows, appear-ances, and candid photo ops to generate media. Plus, you can see other peo-ple—just make sure that no one sees you, especially not photographers. You should definitely take it … but Star … this is really important. You cannot tell anyone about this contract, ever. Not your best friend, not your mother, not your brothers, not your assistant. Nobody. Ever. I am totally serious."

But no pressure.

❦   ❦   ❦

You might be wondering why a (mostly sane) girl on a hit show would even consider getting involved in a crazy situation like this. One thing you have to understand is that the weirdness increases by degrees. Once you're in it, you get swept up in the whole thing and lose perspective. I had no time to date, I hardly went out, and I figured a few public appearances wouldn't kill me in exchange for $250,000. With that kind of money, I was well on my way to mak-ing sure my entire family was set for life.

Also, I hated to admit it, but I did get a secret thrill just considering the fact that I might get to make out with Brad Rockwell. He was so charismatic, I felt like I was being drawn into his orbit by tractor beam. How do you say no to dating a big movie star, no matter what the circumstances?

You don't. And so, two days later, I signed the contract and was touring one of Brad Rockwell's mansions.

"What do you do with all this space?" I said, calling out from a bathroom with a huge fountain in the middle. "This place is amazing!"

After his private chef made bone-in filet mignon and lobster for me, Brad took me on a tour. I was straining myself trying not to act overly impressed, but I really was. A few years before, I was a college student in Michigan, and now here I was, in the home of a man who made $50 million per film.

I had a million questions as the tour went on. This was bizarre. Did I live there now? Did I have to have sex with Brad? Or … did I *get* to have sex with him? Was that totally weird to ask? I'd been too chicken to ask Todd or any of the members of his Brad's team that I'd met. Now we were alone, and I was dying of curiosity.

For all his wealth and incredible success, Brad was quiet and shy in private, and he seemed distant, like he was putting a big smile on an ocean of sadness. I felt an odd kinship with him over this. Did everyone feel this way about their Hollywood life? He shrugged. "The house is mostly just an investment—I've got another one in the Hills where I never even go … I have to put the movie money somewhere, you know …" his voice trailed off, and I pictured him as a little boy. Was this what he'd wanted to be when he grew up?

"What kind of stuff do you do at night?" I said. This was the weirdest second date I had ever been on, for sure. Without cameras or other people around, Brad was the complete opposite of his exuberant public persona—like a withdrawn, depressed teenager. Had this man actually hired me to act like his girlfriend for a year? This was better than the weirdest David Lynch plot. I was sad that I couldn't tell anyone the details of the contract. Vince would have died.

He sighed. "Watch movies, in the screening room," or I learn lines if I'm shooting or looping something in town. Depending on what I'm shooting, when it's coming out, or what I'm promoting, I'm pretty much always traveling, so when I'm here, I try to just chill out. Sometimes I go out—we'll go out, you know? Anywhere you want. Mr. Chow, Dolce, Sky Bar, Morton's—whatever. Just let my office know, and they'll set it up."

I nodded. "What kinds of films do you like?" I said, hoping against hope that he was a secret indie film fan.

"I never tell anyone this," he said, "but … I love Westerns. And, of course, anything with fast cars and gadgets."

I smiled, making a mental note to tell my brother Adam that he and Brad Rockwell had the exact same taste in films. Then I remembered that I hadn't heard from Adam in at least three months, and got a little depressed. Maybe my new relationship would bring him around. I knew he was a huge Brad Rockwell fan.

I followed Brad down the hall, past an enclosed indoor atrium filled with what looked like a small rain forest. "This is all yours," he said, opening a dark wood door. "You can stay whenever you want … it probably says "twice a week" in the agreement. Just make sure your car is parked outside in the driveway, where the photographers can see it. The chef can cook anything, you have your own screening room, and the butler can get you whatever you need, like clothes or whatever. Just have your assistant give him a list." He waited for me to say something. I just nodded.

There was a distinct lack of chemistry between us. He stopped, turning around to face me. I could see his perfect muscles through his white cotton button down shirt. Even his feet were tan, and he looked so good in his Versace jeans, I thought I might pass out. This was the moment …

He reached down, and I waited for the movie star kiss. He pulled me close and I could feel his strong arms around me.

"Thanks," he said, giving me a positively parental kiss on the forehead. "You're a good friend. Don't worry—we'll have a great time this year. Have you ever been to Mexico?"

With that, he turned and walked away, going into one of the rooms at the end of the hall and closing the door. I thought I heard voices coming from inside, but it could have been the TV. He didn't invite me in. I was left standing at the end of the hall, baffled. What's going on here? I thought. It is me? Does he think I'm fat? Why the contract if he doesn't even find me attractive? I didn't want to **have** to have sex with him, but now I was a little offended.

❦   ❦   ❦

The next weekend, my confusion was compounded as Brad and I engaged in an epic makeout session at Morton's, after a steak dinner and a few martinis. "Is this ok?" he whispered. "I really like you." He seemed a little drunk and like a totally different person. I didn't even know where to start trying to figure him out.

Part of me was thrilled beyond belief. I knew how it looked to the rest of the world. "He does like me," I thought as I hugged him, running my fingers through his beautiful blonde streaked hair. His lips were full and soft, and he kept his arm around me the whole night, like he never wanted to let me go.

He held my hand on the way out of the restaurant, past the waiting line of photographers who had gathered outside in anticipation of our exit. As he helped me into the back of the waiting Land Rover, I felt like a princess.

As soon as we were in the car, though, he dropped my hand. "Good work," he said, smiling. "You're a really good actress."

And just like that, I turned back into a pumpkin.

❦   ❦   ❦

My second Golden Globe Awards was world away from my first. For one, my mom had the flu and could not come out. For the other, at this Golden Globes I was debuting in my new role as one half of the celebrity couple now known as "RockStar". Now, the regular award show craziness and chaos was compounded by the fact that I had new lines to remember—the "I'm With Brad" script.

This year, I arrived on the red carpet not with my cast, but on the arm of Brad Rockwell. I was nominated again for **Autumn Leaves**, and he was nominated for a serious role in a period piece. We were the Golden Couple of the Golden Globes.

Brad leaned forward, whispering softly in my ear. "Act like I said something funny," he said, and I laughed. He kissed me on the cheek, and the photographers went wild. We were momentarily blinded by flashbulbs and people yelling "Brad, Star … over here, over here!" I felt blinded and dizzy by the spectacle of it all, and I wanted to sit down, but Brad had his arm around my waist, anchoring me to reality. He was used to celebrity of this magnitude. He leaned in again to whisper what I'm sure looked like "sweet nothings" in my ear. "It's okay—you're doing great.—ten more minutes on the red carpet, and then we sit down." I wondered if he ever fantasized about walking the red carpet with someone he really loved. I wondered who he really loved. Truth is, I saw Brad so rarely, I knew almost nothing about him. Because we were photographed together every time we went out, though, it looked like we together all the time. I felt a little sad and alone, even though I was part of this amazing power couple.

A team consisting of Arden, Brad's publicist Liz, and several assistants from their respective offices shepherded us down the runway, stopping us to chat with interviewers from the major networks. "Stick to the script," Brad whispered in my ear. "I'll do most of the talking." I remembered the red carpet lecture from the year before, and how long ago that seemed.

When we got to the interviewer from E!, she asked what we did to get ready. "The usual," said Brad. "We slept late, ordered breakfast in bed, chilled out by the pool until it was time to go." I nodded and smiled, wondering if that's how he and his friends had spent the morning before his manager picked me up in his limo. "Are you nervous?" Juliana DePandi asked me. "No, not at all—not with Brad by my side. This is just a fantastic night, and he's an amazing person." We proceeded down the red carpet line, repeating the same sound bytes until it was time to go and pose for still photography. Brad leaned in again "Good job," he whispered.

Our outfits were color coordinated (gold Prada McCannth for me, Armani tux with gold cummerbund and tie for him), and by the next day, we'd been voted "Cutest Red Carpet Couple" by *People* magazine's website. Once again, I did not win the Golden Globe, though Greg Forster finally received his Best Actor award for the show, and Ross collected another Best Supporting Actor award.

Brad won Best Actor in a Drama. In his acceptance speech, he dedicated the award "to new love," and the camera panned over to me.

❧   ❧   ❧

Maybe because the rest of my life was so full of intrigue, waiting on the set to shoot my scenes was becoming unbearably boring. I needed Olivia around most of the time to entertain me, since I was tired of watching movies, listening to music, and trying not to answer any personal questions about my relationship with Brad. How do you keep your personal life a secret from the people you're closest to? I felt like a traitor every time my mom asked how things were going or wanted to know some details. I addressed this problem by hanging out with Olivia, who was very entertaining and didn't ask too many questions.

"Boob job." Olivia turned to a photo of a popular blonde actress. "There is no way you have tits that big when you have the body of a twelve year old Asian boy." She pointed to a photo. "And how does anyone not know her nose is fake? She looks like a different person now."

My new favorite thing to do with Olivia during downtime on the set was to look through *US Weekly* and speculate as to who'd had what plastic surgery. Our "speculation sessions" made the long hours of waiting on set very entertaining; Olivia was so good at this she could even identify which doctor had done which procedure. The fact that I'd had a little (though definitely not as much as some of the other girls) just made the speculation more fun; it was as if I was now in some secret club, the entrance price of which was to be surgically enhanced.

Technically, I was supposed to be learning my lines, but with a new writer on staff we'd been inundated with constant rewrites and script changes, so I was relying on my skills of fast memorization to get me through. Besides, I was 99% sure they wouldn't fire me. *Autumn Leaves* had finally cracked the Top Ten, and I was expecting a huge raise when Season Three negotiations got underway, otherwise I was considering the migraine trick.

She flipped to the next page. "Collagen lips, for sure. Botox, and a slight brow lift. Surprising for someone so young, but not unheard of. She's also had a lot of hair removal, like laser surgery—she looks so different from her first movie ten years ago! She had, like, baby fat and a mustache in her first movie, and now she's flawless. If you'd seen her ten years ago in the grocery store, you wouldn't have looked at her twice. All I'm saying is, some quality money and time went into creating that girl, and someone hasn't gotten their investment back yet. They just need to put her in a movie that grosses over $100 million, and they'll be able to recoup their initial outlay of cash."

She folded the magazine back, making a giant red circle around the face of an aging film star who I was always saying looked too amazing to be real.

"The key is—if you end up saying 'wow, she looks like she doesn't even age,' or if they still look like themselves, only a tiny bit older, then you know they have a good plastic surgeon. She, for instance, started early, and she just gets better looking every year. Did you know she's forty-eight years old? The bad ones all go to the same doctors, and they all look the same—huge lip implants, those hideous cat eyes, and the face that keeps growing vertically because of the chin implants, cheek implants, and face lifts. I once worked for a former superstar who couldn't even close her eyes, she'd had so much."

This was much more fun than learning lines.

❦   ❦   ❦

"What about this one? It's a *Scream* style fun teen horror feature that's being released in time for Thanksgiving break. You'd be great in that."

Todd was reading to me from a list of potential projects for the hiatus during our weekly check in meeting. Since I'd spent the first hiatus getting "made over," he and Arden both thought it was a good idea if I did a big budget film to raise my exposure and capitalize on my newfound "RockStar" fame. Todd had been receiving numerous scripts for projects people wanted to cast me in. Most of them fell into one of two categories: *Bring It On* type teen pop comedies, or summer blockbusters. All of them wanted to pay me obscene amounts of money, just for the huge box office numbers they were assured if I appeared at their premiere with Brad Rockwell on my arm. This time, I was sticking to my guns. After doing what had essentially become a nighttime soap for two seasons, I was tired of the show and looking forward to my indie film debut.

I sighed. "Todd, where's my *Sherrybaby*? I want to do something challenging, something indie. I'm sick of the soap and bubble gum," I said, putting my boot up on his desk. What about an Off-Broadway play?" I knew this would drive him nuts.

"Bite your tongue," he said. "Now is the time in your career when you should strike while the iron is hot. I can get one of these guys up to $500,000, for sure. You should definitely go with a big studio for your first film. It will establish you as a bankable star. Trust me on this. Your StarMeter rating went up from #476 to #35 OVERNIGHT after the Golden Globes and your new relationship. You are hot, baby! You need to cash in!"

"No way," I said. "I'm definitely doing an indie film. What about that script Josh Stein gave me?" I said. "Did you read it? It's really good, and it's shooting in New York."

I didn't know how to break it to him that I'd already pretty much decided to do the indie script I liked from Josh's production company, and that I actually had a meeting set up with the writer/director the next day to discuss logistics. Todd hated being out of the loop, since he thought he had his finger on the pulse of the whole industry.

The previous week, I'd been having coffee with Josh when he took a script out of his bag. "I think you should read this. My company is developing it, and the lead would be a great role for you." he said.

He slid a script across the table, and I picked it up.

Blue Gray by Daniel Roberts

"OK, I'll read it and get right back to you," I said. "Todd's going to be pissed, though—he wants me to do the *Scream* movie for the big money." I laughed. Josh looked at me seriously for a moment. "Amy, if there's one thing I've learned in this business, it's that you have to do things that fill your heart, whenever you can. I can't tell you what to do, but you definitely won't be sorry. Dan is great ... very creative. And I even have a place where you can stay in New York to help with the budget." I was glad we'd kept up our friendship after he left the show; I'd told him many times about my indie film aspirations, and I was thankful he was keeping me on track.

He was right, of course—*Blue Gray* was an amazing story. I'd read and loved it, and given it to Todd the next day, hoping that he'd stop bugging me about the summer blockbuster list.

"Don't need to read it," said Todd. "Art house crap. They have less than a million to make that film, so you're going to end up sleeping on your friend's couch the whole summer and shooting in some abandoned building. Also, they've never even called me with an offer, which means they are going to try to pay you scale. No way, Star Spencer. No way!"

He inched the stack of scripts toward me with his finger. "Just don't decide yet, okay? If you stick to marketing to the Disney "tween" market, you can easily do a whole series of straight to DVDs, like the Olsen Twins did, THEN you can do the indie film thing. You need to be thinking "money" right now. What does fucking *Josh Stein* know about building your name into a franchise? Nothing—that's what. He's the guy who *left Autumn Leaves*, okay? You need to read the other scripts before you make this decision."

It was already too late. The minute I read *Blue Gray*, I was going to New York. That is, if the director would have me.

❦   ❦   ❦

Even with my StarMeter rating at an all-time high, breaking into the indie film world was turning out to be harder than I thought. The day after my Todd meeting, I met Dan Roberts, writer and director of *Blue Gray*, at Le Dome for lunch. Apparently, it wasn't up to *me* to say I wanted to do the film—*he* wanted to suss *me* out to see whether I was too "teen pop" for his precious script.

I wanted to meet him, just to see if he was as arrogant as this request made him sound. Who did he think he was? Did he not know who *I* was? Did he not know I was turning down $500,000 and pissing off my agent, just because of my undying love for indie films? From what Josh had told me, Dan was desperate to do the project, but still wanted final say in casting. Who was this guy, anyway? I thought for sure he was going to be some mid-fifties granola type who'd just gotten lucky with a good script.

And so when he arrived at the meeting, I didn't expect him to be twenty six years old, and I didn't expect him to be from my neighboring Midwestern state of Wisconsin. Also, I didn't expect him to be disarmingly attractive.

With a plaid shirt, dark curly hair and piercing blue eyes, Dan was the exact kind of guy I would've had a huge crush on back in college. By the time I sat down, I was already a little in love with him before I remembered that I was, in fact, supposed to be Brad Rockwell's girlfriend, at least for seven more months.

Over lunch, Dan told me the story of how he wrote the screenplay during film school at NYU, then pushed it through the system—a sad tale of waiting tables, eating ramen, and almost giving up hope a few times while slogging his script to every agent and production company in L.A. and New York. As he told me the story, I secretly wondered if I would've had the staying power to withstand that kind of rejection. Dan had my respect from the very beginning—maybe his was going to be an even bigger "Cinderella" story than mine.

Finally, he'd gotten his screenplay to the right people at Josh's office, who came onboard to produce, on one condition—that I play the role of schizophrenic artist Marie Couret. Dan had almost walked away from the deal, but had finally agreed to meet me for lunch, to "see what I was about." I had to admire the nerve of a totally unknown writer and director to stand up for his project like that.

"So … did you really tell Josh you thought I was too 'teen pop' to play Marie Couret?" I said as we finished lunch. "That is cold. You don't even know me." I smiled.

He laughed. "What can I say … your show is huge, you're so famous, and I suppose it would be good box office just from people showing up just to see if you can really act, but this story means the world to me, and if I'm only going to get one chance to tell it, I have to do it right."

"Why is this story so important?" I asked, genuinely curious. "Couret's work isn't even in the mainstream." I'd done my homework, and I could tell Dan was impressed.

"I need an actress who can handle this role because this film could put her work into the mainstream. She died in an institution before her work could gain recognition." He paused, looking me straight in the eye.

"It's important because Marie Couret was my aunt," he said softly. Now I was impressed. We talked for three hours, and I learned that not only did we have the exact same taste in films, but that we had both gone to Hudson, both lived in the fine arts dorms, and both had grandparents who lived in Milwaukee. The next day, we signed the contract and announced that I was attached to **Blue Gray.**

Todd was madder than I'd ever seen him. Finally, I felt like my life had purpose, and like I was making decisions for myself.

CHAPTER 15

✤

"I guess you did the right thing, if you're going for the serious film career when the show ends … look at that girl who plays the nurse on ER … she did *Brokeback Mountain* for no money during her hiatus, and now she's poised for a really meaty lead in something. Though, I mean, you can't get any good recognition in the film industry unless you play a retard or a psycho, or get really ugly," Michele said, filing her nails. "I can respect that. I'm doing the *I Know What You Did Last Summer* prequel—I just couldn't pass up the big paycheck right now. I'm doing the 'one for me, one for them' thing, you know? Plus, I just don't know if I'm ready to get ugly for my career right now."

I nodded, taking a drag of my Camel Light, having come to regard Michele's philosophical musings on her career as white noise. Actually, if not for Josh and the good script, I might also be doing the typical teen horror flick fare. Instead, I seem to have lucked into an amazing project and a borrowed New York apartment. I was so sick of the show, I couldn't wait for the hiatus to start. I wondered—if *Blue Gray* was 'one for me,' then what was the 'one for them' I'd have to do next hiatus? I couldn't worry about that, though, because I was too excited about my summer in New York.

Two weeks before shooting wrapped on Season Two, the set had that "school's almost out" feeling, so much so that Olivia and I sat in my trailer most of the day, discussing new Hollywood theories and talking about our plans for the hiatus. There was no way I was learning lines, even though the Season Finale was a Special Double Episode which had me graduating from high school and my two dads adopting a baby from China.

During down time, and especially when she was supposed to be helping me run lines for upcoming scenes, we liked to look through endless gossip magazines, then form opinions and speculations on the other celebrities in them. Fat Girl/Skinny Girl was rapidly becoming one of our favorite new games.

Fat Girl/Skinny Girl consisted of us pointing at photos of celebrities and determining what "category" the girl fell into.

These categories were:

1. Fat Girl/Skinny Girls' body. This is someone like me, for whom every calorie is a challenge. Maybe because of a slow metabolism, maybe because of a penchant for junk food—these are the girls that blow up if they even look at a donut. Usually exercise obsessively, have muscles (so much the better to exercise their willpower!) and gain about 80 pounds if they get pregnant, because in Hollywood, pregnancy is the only time it's okay to eat. They don't want to fight it anymore. These girls are usually totally bitchy from hunger, and even when they get plastic surgery they still look chubby on magazine covers and have to be retouched. Also applies to girls who have babies and then become fat girls, almost daring you to challenge them even after the child is two years old.

2. Regular skinny girl—this category includes models and occasionally an actress who isn't totally full of shit about her fast metabolism (though most are—I'm serious). Put this girl on a diet, and in one week she's on the "skin and bones" covers. A rare exception, despite what they'd have you believe.

3. Skinny girl who got fat—Renee Zellweger in Bridget Jones, for instance. Look like themselves in a fat suit, like the extra weight is really uncomfortable. Applies to once skinny girls who never lost baby weight and aging actresses who married well and don't' have to impress anyone anymore.

4. "Normal" girl—really means 10 or 20 pounds below what you'd consider underweight by any normal (like Michigan) standards.

5. Skinny Fat girl—looks thin, but is strategically hiding fat, usually under fashionable clothes. No muscle tone due to lack of exercise. Doughy and soft to the touch.

Yes, some people read, some napped, and some of us came up with riveting social theories. We did find that every woman in Hollywood (those we knew and otherwise) fit into one of these categories, so this one actually had some validity. Maybe if the show ever got canceled, we could become sociologists.

Olivia held up a photo of a popular young actress. "Guess her weight, then her category," she said.

"105, tops," I said. "Skinny girl."

"No way! That girl has not eaten anything in two years. If she weighs 100 pounds, I am shocked. Normal girl with an eating disorder, for sure," she said, turning the page.

Since I started out weighing 135, at first I was considered "chubby," so when the paparazzi took my picture, the headlines always said something like "curvy" or "womanly," or they'd run some story about how I was upset and gaining weight. Then I lost twenty pounds, more photos came out, and they ran stories about my diet secrets (Arden leaked something about the Zone diet, but really it was just plain not eating that got me there, combined with plastic surgery, black pills, cigarettes, and coffee). The lipo had made a big differ-ence—at 107 pounds, I looked "amazing," according to the magazines. I was "in great shape," and "toned," and I was giving interviews where I claimed to have really "found my groove with diet and exercise."

Then like a week would go by and I'd lose another five pounds, and suddenly I was on the "skin and bones!" covers. It's a never-ending weight tight-rope—first they want you to be thin, then you're too thin, then once again you're too fat. Sondra said there was no such thing as bad publicity, but she also thought if I got the reputation as one of those horrible scary anorexic girls, ratings for the show might go down. Really, there was a window of three pounds that I had to live within, between being sick skinny and being horribly fat. The hardest part is making it seem like I wasn't starving myself while stay-ing within the three pound window.

❦   ❦   ❦

"Aim—not that outfit again! You have $100,000 worth of clothes in your closet, and yet this is the fourth day in a row you're insisting on this "black sweater and jeans" combo. What is going on with you?"

Vince was right. It wasn't like I was becoming some manic-depressive or a homeless person or something … in fact, quite the opposite. I was very aware that I should never go out in public wearing the same thing twice, so when I was hanging out inside or on the set, I wore the same thing every single day, just for the sake of familiarity and comfort (and perhaps to defy the system by being a slob in private).

I now had so much choice, I craved the routine of having some kind of uniform to put on every day, so I did. The more outrageously expensive clothing piled up in my suite at the hotel, in my trailer, and at Brad's, the more times I was compelled to wear roughly the same outfit—Chip & Pepper, Rock & Republic, or Seven jeans, white t-shirt, black Chanel wool cardigan, black Gucci boots, and black Fendi bag. There is just something about having to change clothes multiple times per day for work, then when you go out at night, to appearances or awards shows, that makes you frightfully unimaginative when it comes to dressing yourself. The actual amount of time I ended up wearing my favorite outfit always ended up being so small, I figured that over a month's time, it would just equal out to be a whole day in the life of a regular person.

"Actually, you're so wrong … this is like the ninth day in a row of the same outfit," I said, sighing. "But, it's just BCD, so I never wear it for long anyway. I just don't like having to think about what I'm going to wear when I'm not out, okay?"

"BCD," was a new term we'd made up to describe things that were "Behind Closed Doors." This applied to everything from clothes to hookups to drug habits, and it describes a world of Hollywood to which the general public has no access. For instance, if the majority of the world thinks a certain Hollywood actor is a macho action hero hunk type, but everybody in Hollywood knows that he's actually a screaming queen who enjoys getting blowjobs from young boys in gyms, that's BCD information. Hollywood insiders are really good at keeping BCD secrets. I even had a few of my own now—the thing with Brad being the biggest one, also my being a repeat offender with the same outfit, but also how I saw Jessica Alba in a Rite Aid, buying a few items you wouldn't think she would be buying. Did I call the *Enquirer* and tell them what she bought? Did I take a photo with my camera phone? No, I did not. Would I have done that two years ago? Yes, I would have. The difference was that now, I was bound by the "BCD Code of Honor," whereby celebrities never rat each other out. That means whether I saw a famous actress doing coke in the bathroom of Cipriani in New York, or a well-known movie star kissing his boyfriend at a Golden Globes after party, I kept it to myself.

"You have to be careful—if you go out carrying that Fendi once more, *US Weekly* is going to do one of those "I Love My Bag!" photo spreads of you carrying it at the airport, on Robertson, coming out of Crustacean, leaving the studio, etc. etc. Then you're never going to close that Coach deal." Vince grabbed my beloved bag and ran onto the balcony of the suite, threatening to throw it over.

He was, of course, speaking of the endorsement deal offered to me by Coach just the week before. Todd had called excitedly: "Star Spencer, guess who is trying to crack the youth market and wants you as their new face?"

"I don't know—Louis Vuitton?" I'd said. I hated it when Todd made me guess.

"No—they're doing the same thing, but they've got Scarlett Johanssen. Coach is trying to compete with them, so they're trying to sign you, my sweet little potato! This is going to totally make up for you betraying me with your crunchy granola hippie film."

I laughed. Todd had fallen into my TV deal in the first place and even made money off my "relationship" with Brad, so I didn't feel too bad. "Coach is sending over bags, shoes, and other stuff for you to use, to 'get the feel' for their products," he continued. "This deal is going to be huge. Seven figures huge!"

Todd had been sniffing around for an endorsement deal for weeks, since my StarMeter rating had been on the rise. "Mischa Barton has Keds … the *American Idol* girls have Candies … Cover Girl has the *America's Next Top Model* girls and Queen Latifah … we have to get you on this bandwagon, baby! Celebrity endorsements are the next big thing!"

I thought of an E! True Hollywood Story I'd seen recently about the "Death of the Supermodel," where they discussed how the celebrity endorsement was killing the world of modeling. Was I contributing to the extinction of the supermodel now? If I signed the Coach deal, would I be actually cheating some waifish model wannabe out of a day's wages? Sometimes it amazed me how much stuff I got for free. Not unlike the "craft services table" dilemma of too much free food and the inability to eat it, I found that the more money I made, the less I had to pay for. Since my rent and food were mostly covered by the network as part of my deal, I had only to pay for gas, cigarettes, sometimes a meal out here and there, if I wasn't at a business meeting type meal (usually paid for by the instigator) or recognized in a restaurant (usually paid by the restaurant for the free publicity of just having me there). I sometimes wondered if this was how Paris Hilton stayed so rich. A few years before, when I'd had no money and needed to get stuff for free, I couldn't. Now, I could pay, but I didn't have to. In fact, the more popular the show got, all I had to do is mention a product or an item of clothing, and the next day there was a box of them in my trailer.

I mentioned to Arden that I'd been re-gifting stuff I received at awards shows and other appearances, and she laughed. "Honey, everybody does that—my clients always give me stuff like those gift certificates for massages and facials that are in the gift bags at the Oscars. I haven't paid for a visit to Burke Williams in seven years. That practice is strictly Behind Closed Doors, though. The advertisers and sponsors hate it when they realize you gave your great aunt something that they hoped they'd see on you. Hate it! Nothing worse than some big star's never-photographed Great Aunt Hazel talking into a fabulous, Svarowski crystal encrusted Razor phone. The worst!"

I was glad to hear that my BCD term was catching on, at least Behind Closed Doors. I was less thrilled to learn that one of the stipulations of the proposed Coach deal was that I had to banish my beloved Fendi to permanent "BCD" status, never again to be carried in public. Apparently, being "the face" of a brand extends not only to advertisements, but to anytime you're in public and might be photographed. Since this was pretty much every time I went anywhere, anytime, for anything, I figured this meant I had to give the Fendi to my mom and forget about it. Sigh.

Note to self: Do <u>not</u> sign exclusive endorsement deal for clothing, lest I am forced to give up my BCD uniform of jeans and black sweater. I will not be told what underwear to wear!

❀   ❀   ❀

"Hello, can you ask 519 to stop stomping? I'm trying to sleep."

I rolled over and looked at the clock. The blocky numbers of the digital display flashed 2:00 am, which was exactly six hours until I had to be on set. I'd been awakened for the third time by loud stomping coming from the floor above me. While I was a big enough celebrity to live at the hotel, I wasn't Lindsay Lohan big, or they'd have moved me to the penthouse suite.

The phone rang in the room upstairs, then the stomping got even louder. My luck, it was probably Jake Gyllenhaal and some indie film starlet, or maybe the singer from Maroon 5 with one of his latest conquests. I laid back on my bed, readjusting my earplugs as random thoughts appeared in my head. Why did I keep living in this celebrity dorm? I could have my own wing of Brad's mansion. Oh—right—then I'd have zero chance of having sex ever again. At least this way I could hook up anonymously with cute boys in the hotel bar, take them back to my expensive hotel suite, and then swear them to secrecy. This was very Charlie Sheen of me, but it seemed to be working so far. I was more than halfway through my RockStar contract, and I hadn't been caught yet.

I pulled the pillow over my head, trying to go to my quiet place in my mind.

<pound pound pound>

What were they doing up there? My mind went back to my bad place, where I obsessed about who was making noise and why. Back in Bay City, it was our neighbor's dog Pom-Pom, who, when left outside unattended, would bark at random intervals that resembled POW sleep torture experiments. In the dorm, it was the people in the room below ours, slamming their door every day at exactly 8:42 am (what college kid has that kind of regular schedule?), and the guys in the room above ours, whose everyday activities included something that sounded like a lead pipe hitting the wall. Late at night, I would play "guess that noise," where I drew complex mental images of random sporting equipment, people roller skating at 3am, or anything at all that might make these sounds.

The insomnia problem sort of crept up on me after my dad died, and was nothing new. It wasn't like one minute I was one of those "I sleep like a log" types, then the next I was wide awake at 3am. More like, when I was a kid I couldn't go to sleep when something big was going to happen the next day, like the first day of school, a trip to Disney World, or a big test. Then it just grew from there, and before I knew it, I had a whole world of sleeplessness, complete with ear plugs and sleep mask that made me look a little like a sleep astronaut, sleeping pills of all varieties, and quiet activities that could be performed in the company of others without waking them up while I lay awake in the darkness.

It didn't take much to wake up the insomnia demon. Lately, one caffeinated beverage after 3pm, and I was pretty much guaranteed a bad night's sleep. I was dozing off again when I heard a peal of laughter coming from the hallway. "You guys, don't be rude … I was on Baywatch!" screamed a drunken voice. Exasperated, I got up and looked out the peephole to see a blonde head go by. Hotel rumors had her retiring from Baywatch, picking up a wealthy sugar daddy, and hanging out by the pool all day. My money was on her having a secret life as a porn star.

Finally, Baywatch Girl and her crew were gone, so I turned the light back off and got back into bed. Because of RockStar, no one was really supposed to know I was there, so I couldn't go up and tell them to be quiet. Arden would probably say it was bad for my image to not be at Brad's, and one of the party-goers was likely to call the *tabloids* the minute I left, or show up on some web-site with a "celebrity sighting" report. I was lonely at the hotel, but I was even lonelier at Brad's.

Maybe Hilary Swank was in the room next door, or Kirsten Dunst had an early call, because finally hotel security heard from someone who outranked me and sent someone to stop the insanity. The hotel was as reflective of the Hollywood food chain as the city itself; even when you're sleeping, it's all about who you know.

I was asleep for what seemed like four minutes when the phone rang with my wakeup call. As I was leaving, I picked up the phone, dialed *519, and let it ring until one of the stompers from the night before picked up. "Good morning," I said cheerfully, before slamming down the phone.

True, it was juvenile, but somehow it comforted me to know that none of us were sleeping.

❦   ❦   ❦

The following week, I'd been home from the set for ten minutes when the phone rang. "You have a package at the desk," said the concierge. "It's from your mother."

How did they know everything? "OK, bring it up," I said. It must be the photos I asked her to send. Maybe I should order a drink to prepare myself for this, I thought.

Since **Blue Gray** followed Marie Couret's life from when she was a kid to when she disappeared, as part of pre-production Dan and Josh had asked me to contribute real photographs of my childhood for the photo montage at the beginning of the film. I said I'd ask my mom to send some, then promptly put it in the back of my mind under "things I don't want to do" when it occurred to me that a) my dad is in most of my family photos, and b) that I hadn't looked at any of those photos since he died, and c) I didn't know if my mom had either, and I didn't want to upset her by making her go through a bunch of our family albums to pull them out. Thus, I had put off the "choosing of the family photos" until the very last day before the deadline. Now the box was here, and I was going to have to face it.

First, I called in emotional reinforcements. Vince arrived in record time, speeding over from his apartment. The box was still sitting on the bed when he arrived.

"I am pouring you a drink," he said, reaching into the fridge for the vodka and Red Bull. "Then we'll get down to business." I felt better already. There was no reason why he couldn't do this for me, right? He could just show me the ones he thought would be right for the film. I didn't even have to look. But, the minute he dumped out the box, one of the photos fluttered over and landed on my foot, catching my eye. It was a photo of me on my dad's shoulders when I was about five. Hot tears leapt to my eyes as I picked it up. For some reason, I remembered that day so well—the smell of the air, the feeling of my hand in my dad's. The pain of missing him made me feel like someone was stabbing me in the heart.

"UUgghhhh … I can't do this," I said. "Can't they just PhotoShop something?" I didn't want to think about it. Even with the serious subject matter of **Autumn Leaves**, I felt like I'd put my personal experience in a box in my mind, and I just didn't know if I wanted to get it out again. It just hurt too much. If I let myself go all the way over this cliff, I thought, I might never come back.

"It's OK … you're doing great," he said. "It's almost over." He pulled out a family photo from Thanksgiving when I was nine. I didn't know it then, but at that moment there were almost exactly eight years left in my dad's life. Would I have been less of a brat, eaten more of my turkey, enjoyed his company more if I'd known the clock was ticking?

"Not that one," I said. "They need some of me alone as a little kid, or at least something where they can cut out the other people. It's supposed to be a photo montage of the artist growing up."

Finally, we found one of me as an awkward eleven year old, smiling a gap toothed smile into the camera. My dad had taken that picture, and that right before he took it, he'd said "Smile, Bunny Luv!"

❖   ❖   ❖

"There's a rumor going around that Teddy's is closing … some scandal over mistreatment of civilians. Like, who cares if you mistreat a nobody anyway? We have to get you in there before they shut their doors altogether … what about the private Prince concert? Christina Aguilera is supposed to be there. It would look great for you if *US Weekly* saw you there and included you in the "Scene and Heard" column.

Arden and I were discussing my schedule of appearances (both casual and official) over dinner and Corzo Collins at Dominick's. I still loved ordering a big plate of spaghetti, even though I had almost no appetite and could only eat one or two bites before I felt full and totally sick. After six months of working with her I had to admit, Arden was a PR and marketing genius. Sure, she was ruthless and calculating and I would never have wanted to be on her bad side, but her brutal honesty about the Hollywood scene was amusing, and since I'd been working with her, I had been in so many magazines, I was a little sick of seeing my own face.

"Isn't that Friday night?" I said, taking a tentative bite of a crunchy breadstick. "We never get done shooting until, like, 3am on Fridays, but if I'm still awake, I'll try to go by."

She looked up from her bruschetta, which she had not touched. "Don't go if you're going to look tired in the pictures. We don't want to give them a reason to run a "Star Spencer is dying!" headline, which they will do if you appear somewhere looking thin and slightly less than perfect. Let us learn from Natasha Lyonne, shall we? Now … let's talk about New York."

Arden was also less than thrilled about my choice of film project over the hiatus. I was so excited about New York I could have cared less, though I did agree to keep my image in the press as much as possible while I was there. She was also not happy that I still hadn't hired a manager, despite her repeated suggestions and meeting fix-ups. It wasn't that I wasn't career motivated—it seemed like everything I did was career-focused from the time I woke up in the morning to the time I went to sleep at night. It was partially the money—I really did object to the concept of giving another fifteen to twenty percent of my earnings to another person. Mostly, it was the fact that with Attila, Sondra, Arden, and Brad's whole team, I just didn't want anyone else weighing in on every decision I made in my life. I knew I probably needed more career guidance, but I just didn't think I could take another "cook in the kitchen," so to speak.

She pulled out a piece of paper. "Here are some places you should be seen in New York, while you're on breaks from shooting. I'm not going to be there 24/7 to make you go out to do your 'see and be seen," so make sure you make an effort. You know how you get." She laughed.

She definitely had me figured out. Without her to force me into fashionable clothes and makeup, I was practically guaranteed to go back to my borrowed apartment and watch Tivo'd reruns of **Project Runway** on breaks from shooting the film. She'd threatened to assign me a "representative" from the New York office of RMG, but I'd declined, since I'd never shot a film before and didn't want someone pressuring me to go out and do things all the time. Besides, I *was* supposed to be on hiatus.

"At least you're not shooting in Arkansas," she said with a laugh. "Do you know how hard it is to get the paparazzi to travel? Those people from *Junebug* could have been lost out in the boonies, eaten by mosquitoes and never heard from again for the lack of press they got when they were shooting."

I was surprised she'd even heard of *Junebug*. Usually, that type of indie fare didn't even register on her radar. It might have been the fact that Amy Adams was nominated for an Oscar—though Arden had objected to her dress ("pockets at your first awards show—who is her stylist?"). Once someone was at the Oscars, Arden made it her business to know how they got there.

"OK," she said. "I had my assistant make this for you." She pulled out a typewritten list with NEW YORK in large block letters at the top. After each one, she paused to elaborate.

1. *SOHO.* "There are usually photographers waiting at the corner of Houston and Mercer, waiting for celebrities to come out of the Marc Jacobs store. Go in there on a Saturday and buy something, just so *People* can show you out and about."

2. *Butter.* "Do the see and be seen there, definitely." Ashley Olsen doesn't hang out there anymore since she and Scott Sartiano broke up, but they'll comp your whole evening just to keep the restaurant in the media. That place is huge now … did you know that guy is designing jeans with Ali Fatourechi? Dating the Olsen twins was the smartest thing those two ever did. You don't get a clothing line without a ton of money and celebrity connections."

3. *Elaine's.* "George Clooney goes there when he's in New York, but if you see him there, I do not want to read a Page Six rumor that you were "at his table for half an hour canoodling," or that you two were "getting very cozy." That will not fly with Brad's people. Just go there, get the steak and the martini, and get out. Wave at George if you must, and say hi to the bartender for me. His name is Charlie."

4. *Premieres.* "There is some good stuff premiering during the summer, but whatever you do, don't go with a man, even if it's a male friend. Even if he's gay. Show up alone, or you will end up with a call from the Brad Rockwell camp."

5. *Magnolia Bakery.* "This one is on the list because I know how much you love your sweets," said Arden, smiling. "Don't go nuts, but I swear they put crack in their cupcakes. They are like nothing else you've ever experienced, and there's always someone like Gwyneth Paltrow or Jennifer Connelly down there."

6. *The Mercer Hotel.* Uma Thurman's sometime-boyfriend owns it ... I'll set up an interview for you to do when you're there, just so you can be seen leaving. It'll be great."

She took a sip of red wine, leaning forward. "There are just a few things you must avoid while you're there—off the record, of course. Listen, I do not want to see a photograph of you waiting in line to see the Empire State Building," she said earnestly. "That is something that civilians do. If you feel that you cannot live without seeing the view (which is spectacular, I must say), let me know and I'll set it up for after hours viewing. This includes the Statue of Liberty, Coney Island, or one of those red double-decker buses. And Star—seriously, I know you're obsessed, but even if they're still doing the "Sex and the City" tour, don't take it. I will tell you where everything is, if you're curious, and you can go there in a cab."

I stifled a laugh. I *so* would have taken that tour.

"Please do not hang out with your less than attractive co-stars," she said, her expression growing serious. I mean, I don't know what the film is about, and good for you if there's a 500 pound blind guy in it or something, but don't lead him through the West Village, eating ice cream from a Mr. Softee truck. That will make you look bad." I pulled out a napkin and a pen. There was no way I was going to remember everything.

"If you want to go see a Broadway show, let me know—we have to be careful, though, because we don't want the press to pick up the story that you're thinking of doing a play. That will piss off your network and make them think you want to leave (though you might be able to work that to your advantage when it's time to renegotiate your deal). Also, don't go to anything Ben Brantley gave a bad review to—you don't want to be Rosie O'Donnell, flogging that tragic Boy George musical. Know what I mean? Since you're doing the indie thing anyway, stick to off-Broadway stuff that's got good buzz. You'll probably see Ethan Hawke in the audience, but don't let him hit on you."

Food. "If you're getting a little too thin and you notice the press is running a lot of "scary skinny" stories about you, New York is a great place for street food photo ops. Just go to Central Park, buy a hot dog or a pretzel, make sure the photographer gets a photo of you taking a bite, then toss it. This throws them off the scent and makes the public think you're eating. Avoid the shwarma guy at the corner of 33rd and 3rd, though. A friend of mine got sick there once."

I folded up the list and put it in my purse.

"OK, now that we've done New York, let's talk about Mercedes-Benz Fashion Week, which is coming up before you leave. We need to get you in the front row in a few good shows, so you can appear in the "Fashion Wrap Up" in the magazines." She pulled another sheet of paper out of her leather portfolio. "Did you hear about that request for you to model black underwear for Frederick's of Hollywood? I heard Sondra Smith was *livid.*" She laughed. "Coach probably wouldn't want you to sully your image either. I just thought it was funny. Why would anyone want a girl who plays a seventeen year old on TV to do a lingerie show? It just doesn't seem like a good fit to me. Sondra probably ripped them a new one." She paused to order another drink.

"Anyway," she said. "I have your estimated shooting schedule from the show for next week, and I've got you appearing in the front row of all the shows that correspond with your breaks."

"Can I bring Vince?" I said. "He's my fashion brain."

"Has Vince been cleared by Brad's people?" she said. "They're not going to want you to appear with a guy unless the press knows he's gay."

I laughed a little inside at the fact that I was having a conversation that made me sound suspiciously like I was in the C.I.A.

"Yes," I said. "He's been cleared."

❦   ❦   ❦

Brad and I had been "dating" for four months at the beginning of my Season Two hiatus. We both had a few weeks off at the same time before I was leaving for New York to start shooting, so his people suggested we go away to Mexico for ten days to stay at Villa de los Amigos, a famous beach resort.

Part of me was excited. I had to admit it sounded amazing to be able to sleep in, lay by a beach all day, and drink umbrella drinks.

Another part of me was terrified. What was I going to talk to Brad Rockwell about, all alone for ten days? I had a hard time getting a whole sentence out of him when we hung out at his place or had dinner just the two of us. I always felt stupid, like I was trying too hard, or like he thought everything I said was weird. Even though Brad was older than me, he and his friends spent most of their free time getting stoned, playing video games, or watching Jackie Chan movies. I never felt like I fit in, and I never, ever knew the right thing to say.

Sure enough, I felt like I'd used up all of my conversation starters by the second night of the trip. My face ached from smiling for the multiple paparazzi that had followed us down there and were capturing our every moment of our "love fest," which had consisted mostly of us lying on the beach connected to the $15,000/night villa, We did spend a few moments cuddling and frolicking in the water, but once we were inside, it was business as usual, and I'd run out of ideas. In fact, it seemed the only thing we had to talk about was our respective crazy work schedules—the thing that usually kept us apart.

I was drinking an umbrella drink and watching *Say Anything* in my room when I heard Brad call out from the screening room. "Star, come in here—you have to see this!" My heart soared, and I instantly kicked myself. Why did I care if he liked me? He didn't even know who Hal Hartley was. He wasn't my type, and he didn't have to love me. Still, being around him made me feel so lonely sometimes, I wanted to crawl out of my skin. When he actually initiated conversation, I felt like crying from relief. Something to break the silence! I walked into the screening room to find him drinking a beer and watching the latest cut of the about to be released *Blood Revenge 4*.

"This is awesome … you have to see this," he said, beckoning me into a seat. "I actually jumped down the side of this mountain, and fell 500 feet. These Swedish guy who is famous for skiing these crazy sheer drops plays the villain. This guy is insane!"

He paused the film on a particularly scary-looking shot of him chasing the movie's criminal down a mountain, both of them on snowboards. "The snow is so powdery there—it feels like falling into baby powder," he said, and I nodded. I'd never been skiing, but I was grateful for the conversation. We watched the rest of the cut and I offered my comments on the story, which Brad actually seemed to find helpful. "You're good at this stuff," he said, smiling. "You should write, or be a producer or something—then you'd have a say over the storyline, and you get a share of the profit. You have to start thinking big!"

I smiled. Maybe Brad was deeper than I thought. Somehow, in the midst of our crazy fake relationship, it felt like we were becoming friends. I almost asked him if he wanted to watch *Say Anything* with me, but then I changed my mind, deciding to quit while I was ahead.

I wished him goodnight, went up the stairs to my room, and turned the movie back on, dozing off right around the "100 songs about Joe" scene. I woke up again to turn it off right at my favorite part, where John Cusack is standing outside of Ione Skye's house with the boombox. I don't know whether it was the umbrella drinks, or finally having a good conversation with Brad, but before I knew it I was sitting on the floor crying. How had I gotten so far away from what I'd wanted only a short time before? Why had I let myself be carried away by money, and success, and fame? If my dad could see me, what did he think? I wanted so badly to do something I cared about, to have someone feel that way about me—how come Brad didn't feel that way? I thought of calling my mom, or Vince, Ian, or Carrie Ann, but it was late and I didn't want them to worry. Besides, what would I tell them? As far as they were concerned, I was in love with Brad Rockwell. Why would I be upset? I couldn't wake up Brad—what would I say, "I want you to be a better fake boyfriend?" It seemed absurd.

My soft, choking sobs seemed to echo throughout the cavernous halls of the villa. Why was I so upset? Why did I always have to cry? I thought I could do the "just friends" thing with him, but the loneliness was crushing whenever we were together. This wasn't worth $250,000, but now there was no way out.

I got up, wandering down the stairs of the villa to the private beach. The night was black, and it was dead quiet except for the sound of the crashing waves. I sat down on the sand, staring out at the ocean. Maybe I was overreacting. Technically, I could date whoever I wanted—I just couldn't go out in public with them, explain why not, or tell them anything about Brad and me.

Maybe I wasn't overreacting.

Somehow, this had made starting a relationship seem kind of pointless, so most of this was my own fault. I listened to the waves, watching the tide go in and out and thinking about my dad, wondering what he would say.

After wearing myself out, I laid down in one of the cabanas, finally falling asleep to the crashing sound of the waves, counting the minutes until **Blue Gray** started shooting. It's almost over, I told myself.

❦   ❦   ❦

After we got back from Mexico, I got an email from Todd on my Blackberry. "Come to my office," it said. "Re: Brad Rockwell promotion."

"Brad's camp thinks you're doing a great job," he said. "They want you to think about getting engaged before you leave for New York for the summer." He took a sip of coffee. He did not laugh. Todd never laughed when we talked about money.

"Engaged at twenty?" I said, incredulous. "Doesn't that seem … young?" "Young" seemed like a better word than "fake" at that point. In an attempt to avoid the obvious fact that my pretend boyfriend was never in town and didn't even seem to like me that much when he was, I offered the "I'm too young" defense when Todd informed me that Brad's camp had offered me a "promotion." This thing was fun while it lasted, I thought, but enough was enough, especially after my meltdown in Mexico. I wasn't marrying this guy just for money and publicity. My mom had only one daughter, and if I ran off and got married without telling her, she'd be heartbroken, especially since I could never explain that it wasn't real.

"You don't have to really go through with it," he said. "I think it's a good idea. Look—Jessica Alba was engaged at twenty, and Jessica Simpson at twenty-one. You have no idea how much press you can get out of a broken engagement, especially if it's nasty. I mean, first there's the rumors, then the actual event, then the fallout, then who you're dating on the rebound. I'm telling you, that's six months' worth of *Life & Style* and *US Weekly* covers, guaranteed. Nick and Jessica are still milking their breakup, and they were a real couple, Star Spencer.

Come ON! They're even offering to let you pick your own ring!" He pounded his desk vehemently.

"Stop pushing me!" I snapped. I stared out the window at the city of Los Angeles sprawling below. I thought of all the little girls in the world, dying to come to Hollywood, become famous, and marry a movie star, and I got even sadder. I gathered myself up to give Todd a piece of my mind. I started to tell him he was crazy, that arranged dating was one thing but engagement quite another, and that my mother would kill me she read in the *Enquirer* that her only daughter was engaged. I started to tell him about the lonely nights at the mansion, the awkward lack of conversation, and the sexual ambiguity of America's favorite action hero. I started to tell him that I wanted someone to want to marry me for real, and that acting like part of an in-love couple was just about the loneliest thing I'd ever done in my life.

Then Todd did something unprecedented even for him. He took his headset off, walked over to the window, and put his arm around me. Then he started talking to me like I was a real person. He started slowly, treading lightly on sensitive subjects.

It was more shocking, even, than the prospect of a fake engagement.

Todd was being sensitive.

"Listen," he said quietly. "I know that things aren't how you thought, and that it's not all fun and games being in a relationship that's just for the benefit of the public … but think of it this way … it's a lot more money and exposure, and you're basically in the same contract anyway. Nothing will change at all—just ride out your contract, buy your mom a bigger house, and keep the ring when it's all over. No one will be the wiser. Besides, I checked Brad's schedule, and he's going to be in Montreal shooting *"Avenger"* for most of the summer anyway—you'll probably only have to see him once or twice. This is free money and publicity—you'd be crazy to turn it down. I know what you want is to have a good career in independent films after you're done with the show, and I think this is really the way to do it. The more exposure we get you now, the more the world is going to be open for you once you're done with *Autumn Leaves*. You're never going to have to worry about money, or auditions, or anything like that. After this, no one in your family will ever have to work again. After this, you can write your own ticket. You could start your own production company. Amy—I'm being serious. This is the chance of a lifetime."

I started to object, but he was actually making sense. If what I wanted was a career that didn't depend on the show, I needed enough money and power on my own to be able to call my own shots. And, I thought, if I had the ability to take care of my family for life, I should take it.

"OK," I said, wiping my eyes. "I'll do it." I tried to put the creepiness of the situation out of my mind.

After the engagement was announced, my IMDB Star Meter ranking went up to 19.

CHAPTER 16

❀

The day before I was supposed to leave for New York, I got an email from Vince marked URGENT. He'd been busy working eighteen hours a day with clients and going out with Perez, and I'd just been busy, so we hadn't seen each other in a week or so.

I'm leaving for Carrie Ann's graduation the day after tomorrow. What flight are you taking? We should go together.

I read the email twice, and then it started to come back to me in a rush of details. Graduation? Graduation! How had I completely forgotten my friend's imminent graduation from the college that I had attended, with her, just two years before? Was my life really so hectic that I had lost track of an entire year?

I flipped open my calendar. Tickets, reservations … crap crap crap! If I booked everything right then, stayed up all night packing, and left the next day, I could still make it to the graduation ceremony, then to New York by the time shooting started on **Blue Gray**. Why didn't I remember this? What was wrong with me? This was only going to be the most important day of her life … Vince remembered, why didn't I? Was I becoming a terrible person? Carrie Ann and I were still in touch, though not as often as I would've liked. I should have remembered.

I dialed Vince's number.

"Hey, it's me," I said into his voicemail. "I … I'm going to the graduation—we should talk before we go, so we're not late for Carrie Ann's big day." I didn't have the guts to say I'd almost forgotten, and if not for his email, I would have gone straight to New York. He didn't know, but that message had probably saved my friendship with Carrie Ann, since if I'd forgotten her graduation, I was pretty sure she never would have talked to me again.

The next morning, Vince and I were on a flight to Detroit. We had just enough time to get a rental car, change, and get flowers before the graduation ceremony started. Aside from a few autograph-seeking freshmen, the people at Hudson were surprisingly cool about my being there. I knew the paparazzi wouldn't follow me all the way to Ann Arbor, but the crowds of people were sometimes a problem. What I was most concerned about was stealing Carrie Ann's thunder. She was receiving the Outstanding Senior Award and was graduating Summa Cum Laude.

As it turned out, her news was even bigger than me that day. Carrie Ann had already started living her Broadway dream, keeping in touch with everyone she'd met during the previous two summers. During spring break that year, she'd been to New York to finalize her apartment, and had gone on two auditions for Broadway shows. As Dr. Simon called her name, he also announced that the next day Carrie Ann would be leaving for New York to join the cast of **Phantom.** A cheer went up through the crowd, and Carrie Ann took a little bow as she accepted her diploma. Vince and I wiped away tears. "Now we're all living our dreams," he said, squeezing my hand.

I had to agree.

"So … why didn't you tell us?" Vince said to Carrie Ann as we sipped champagne at the drama department reception. "It all happened so fast … it just didn't seem real," she said, looking over at me sheepishly. "I still feel a little like it could all go away at any minute."

I hugged her. "I totally understand," I said. "Don't worry—it's not going to go away. You earned your success through being talented and dedicated, and no one can take that from you. Remember that, okay?" For a minute, I thought of Ross. That was definitely something he'd said to me when I first started. I was a show biz veteran at twenty.

She laughed, wiping away tears. "I guess I just had to see for myself, right?" she said. "I'm really sorry, Aim. I didn't get it."

It's okay, I said. "I'm just glad we're back. Now … what flight are you on to New York? Did you know we're going to be neighbors for a few months?"

Dr. Simon came over. "Girls, let me get a picture of our two biggest successes," she said, pulling out her camera.

"This is definitely going in my *Biography* story," whispered Carrie Ann as we posed for the photo. "Did you know that Danny DeVito and Michael Douglas were roommates in New York before they got famous?"

I laughed. "I did not know that," I said.

❦   ❦   ❦

The next day, a cab dropped me off in front of Josh's friend's apartment at 31st and Madison.

As soon as I said "Apartment 5H," the doorman raised his eyebrows. An older, handsome Latino man with bushy eyebrows and a freshly pressed suit with "Borrero" embroidered on the coat, he looked like he'd turned a lot of people away from this apartment. "You sure?" he said. "Nobody's up there.…"

"I know," I said. "It's … a friend of a friend's place. I'm using it for eight weeks while I shoot a film here. The producer … Josh Stein's office faxed over the paperwork, and the super confirmed that there would be a key waiting for me when I got here."

He riffled through several pieces of paper behind the front desk. Was he the only person in America that didn't watch my show? How did he not know me? Had he never heard of RockStar? "Oh, okay … Amy Spencer? Right … here you go" he said, handing me two keys attached to a round silver keychain. "Take the elevator to 5, and make the left. I'm Miguel … call down on the intercom if you need anything. We don't let anybody into that apartment without authorization."

"Whose apartment is this, anyway, Madonna's?" I said, joking. Most likely it was just some investment banker/producer friend of Josh's. Miguel winked. "You don't know? It's your friend's friend!" He laughed. "You'll see."

I shrugged, took the keys, and lugged my Louis Vuitton duffel bag over to the elevator. "I'll get the rest," called Miguel down the hall, loading my stuff into a rolling silver cart. I pressed "5" on the elevator panel and made the left, putting the key in the door.

So, having seen lots of movies where the heroine lives in a shoebox size apartment in New York City, and having looked at the online photo albums of the tiny places where Carrie Ann had stayed during the last two summers, I was in no way prepared for either the size or the opulence of Josh's friend's apartment. A spiral staircase cut through the ceiling of the first floor, leading to God only knew where. The kitchen, to the left, was spotless, outfitted with brand new, expensive looking brushed steel appliances and granite countertops. "Oh my God," I said out loud to no one in particular. I walked into the living room, which contained immaculate furniture upholstered in burgundy and white stripes. Did no one live in this apartment? Above a huge fireplace, one soft light was turned on—the light beneath a lovely painting that I thought I recognized as a Picasso from a freshman year Art History class. Good Lord. I thought about my suite at the hotel, strewn with clothes, makeup, scripts, and DVDs. Someday, when I have a break and can pull myself together, I thought, perhaps I will be able to decorate an apartment like this.

"This is crazy," I said, walking through the cavernous apartment. The living room had an enormous Baby Grand Piano with a single black and white photo in a frame. Maybe this was the mysterious "Owner of 5H." Now I was dying of curiosity. I tried to turn on the light on the piano without smudging it with my fingers. When I did, I found that this black and white photo was a family-type photo of a man holding a little girl on a merry-go-round. At closer inspection, I determined that the man in the photograph was not just a man. The man in the photograph, in fact, was rockstar Pete Wilde. Then it hit me. I. Was standing. In Pete Wilde's apartment.

My first impulse was to run upstairs to what seemed to be the master bedroom, to look for the leather pants and eyeliner. Did that make me a geek? I thought back to the vintage Destroyers album that Vince found for me on eBay the Christmas before, and let out a silent scream. Pete Wilde's apartment!

Pete Wilde's gigantic outdoor patio had an up-close view of the Empire State Building, where I promptly went out, lit a cigarette, called Vince, and screamed out loud about Pete Wilde's apartment. When that was done, I dialed Josh's number. "Amy!" he said, picking up on the first ring. "Did you get there? When do you start shooting? Do you like the apartment?" He sounded very amused with himself.

"How do you not tell me that your "friend" is Pete Wilde?" I said, incredulous. "I'm staying at Pete Wilde's apartment? Where is Pete Wilde?" I think I knew that Pete Wilde and his latest wife, a Russian supermodel, lived in New York City—but there? Were they going to come home and find me there?

He laughed. "I know him through friends. I think he's on tour. Actually, it's a place he never uses, but he's owned it for a long time, and he keeps his art collection there. More of a real estate investment … I use it when I'm in New York too. Don't worry about it. You'll be fine."

"Josh, oh my God—this place is too nice. I can't eat Peanut M & M's on Pete Wilde's Mies van der Rohe furniture! There is a Picasso on the wall, and a signed photograph of Muhammed Ali hanging in the hallway. "Dear Pete, we're the greatest.…""

He laughed. "Have fun," he said. "See you in June. If you see Pete, tell him I said hi."

Was this my life?

*   *   *

After two weeks of shooting in New York, I was finally getting comfortable in the city. From Pete Wilde's apartment, I could find east, west, the subway, and the Magnolia Bakery. I was in love.

"Amy, I can't believe you haven't spent more time here," said Allen, my **Blue Gray** costar. I had refrained from telling him how much I loved him on **Law & Order** the moment I met him, so as not to break the "I'm a Big Celebrity" mystique, but finally the veneer had caved, I fessed up, and he'd started calling me Amy like all my friends. During days off, Allen was my unofficial New York tour guide. Since the press knew we were shooting **Blue Gray** and had already taken plenty of shots of us, they seemed to be uninterested in creating scandal for the moment, so we could roam without fear of cheating reports getting back to Brad's camp.

Since shooting had been limited mostly to SOHO, I felt like I had that area covered. Allen had taken me to Chinatown for dim sum, to the top of the Empire State Building (after hours of course), and to some of the great museums on the Upper East Side. "You're not at all what I thought," he'd said on the second day of shooting. "They make you out to be this famous diva princess, like ..."

"I know, don't say it," I interrupted. "You have no idea how much of my life is made up by other people." Finally, a person who actually understood my pain, who had his own network problems and was unlikely to rat me out. Allen confided that he was contractually obligated to wear a hair replacement system whenever he was out in public. "They glue it on once a month with silicone," he laughed, leaning forward to I could examine the top of his head. "As if there are no photos of me from ten years ago, when I was bald. I went along with it for the salary bump, but I have to admit—during the summer, I wish I could take it off. It kind of itches."

I studied his head, trying to detect the place where the mesh netting stopped and his scalp started. "Impressive," I said. "Want to see my fake teeth?" My liposuction scars had faded, or I would have shown him those too. "Sometimes my hair breaks off from being dyed so much—I wonder what would happen if *I* went bald?" I laughed.

Shooting the film had already been one of the greatest experiences of my life. Every day, I wished that *this*, instead of the show, were my real job. Sadly, my scenes with Allen were almost over, and he was moving on to Mississippi to shoot another indie film. "You think your head is hot here," I said on his last day. Already I felt like a New Yorker. I never wanted to leave.

"You should guest on my show," said Allen, munching a slice of pizza. "You could be the guest star who has a breakdown—did you ever notice that if you see a famous person's name in the *Law & Order* credits, they always have a breakdown by the end of the show?" He laughed. "Star Spencer did it."

In fact, I had noticed, though I didn't want to say anything for fear of looking like a dork.

❦   ❦   ❦

"OK, that's a wrap for the day. Thanks everyone."

After the third fifteen-hour shoot day in a row, I felt like wilted lettuce, but more satisfied and happy than in the past two and a half years combined. I didn't even mind the fatigue, the heat exhaustion, or the lack of trailers and craft services. It was possible that Dan's whole budget for **Blue Gray** was equal to the budget for one episode of **Autumn Leaves**, so I had learned to drastically scale back my needs—all the way back to not complaining about using an abandoned building as our primary set.

Four days into shooting, in fact, I felt something brush against my leg, and looked down to see a rat scurry by, then down into a hole in the floor. Unintentionally, I let out a scream so loud, when I was done everyone was laughing. "It's okay," said Dan. "I think you scared him off." If not for his easygoing nature, we might have all complained by then. But Dan's commitment to the film was so deep, he had us all pulling for his success, and nothing could quell our enthusiasm—not even rats, garbage, and fifteen hour days in the New York heat.

Somehow, possibly because of Dan's determination, this film was coming together despite the odds.

❦   ❦   ❦

It was dark when the car picked me up at 4:30 am, but it had already begun to get hot on the streets of New York. We were shooting the big "Marie goes crazy and disappears" scene that morning, and Dan's vision was to have me walking aimlessly up Fifth Avenue, just as the sun was rising over the Empire State Building. Apparently, that was the last time Marie was ever seen before she was discovered ten years later in a Rhode Island mental institution. This was the final time the character would be seen in the film. While researching the screenplay, Dan had interviewed a witness who saw her turn toward the west at the Empire State and walk down 34th street. That morning, he was going to try to capture that moment.

It was dark in the car, but I could see that Dan was upset. It couldn't be easy for him to be shooting these scenes about his aunt's life. I knew I would've had a hard time shooting anything to do with my dad's death without becoming horribly depressed. I leaned over and put my hand on his. "Are you okay?" I said, and he smiled. He took my hand in the dark, and I felt a pang in my heart.

Were hands supposed to fit together that perfectly? Why didn't I feel this way about Brad?

I'd told Dan about my dad almost immediately after meeting him. It wasn't like this was a fact I shared openly with everyone—half the cast of my show still didn't know, and both Sondra and Arden had done a good job of keeping it out of the press. Maybe it was the fact that he obviously felt the loss of his aunt the way I did that of my dad. Maybe it was his warmth, and how close he was to the script. Maybe I just felt like I could be myself. At any rate, in two weeks Dan knew more about me than I'd told Brad the whole time we'd been "dating," or most of my cast mates in two whole seasons of shooting the show. I was sort of glad we were almost done with the film, because I was really starting to have feelings for Dan, and I knew "feelings for another guy" was definitely not part of my RockStar contract.

❧   ❧   ❧

The day after *Blue Gray* wrapped, I was sleeping in for the first time in what seemed like forever when there was a knock on the door of my apartment. Crap! Would I never sleep again? I opened the door to find Dan standing in the hallway, looking impossibly awake and cute for 9:00am. He had a Dunkin' Donuts bag under his arm, and was smiling his amazing smile.

"Um … can I help you? How did you get past Miguel?" I said playfully. I couldn't believe he was actually on my doorstep.

"Yes, I thought that since you'd be leaving tomorrow and we are no longer working together, I would take this opportunity to hang out with you."

My heart skipped a beat. "At 9am?" I said. "Wow, you are ambitious. Besides, what about my fiancé?" I wondered how much trouble I would get in with Brad's camp if someone saw me in public with Dan. He's the director of my movie, I rationalized. The press doesn't know the exact day we wrapped. What can it hurt? I thought. I'll probably never see him again anyway. We're going for a walk, I thought. What's the big deal?

He grinned. "Well yes, since you've talked about Brad Rockwell and how much you love him so much in the past eight weeks, I'm sure you'll be heartbroken to spend one more day without him. Listen, it's our last day in New York, and I wanted to hang out with you as long as possible, and I figured 6 am was out of the question, so I waited until 9. Get dressed! I have many surprises in store."

I wondered if he'd figured out the "arrangement" I had with Brad. Dan seemed to really like me for me, and didn't care at all how famous I was, how the show was doing, or who I knew. When I was around him I could just be my self—my real self, like when I hung out with Vince and Carrie Ann back in Michigan. I was really going to miss him when I went back to L.A.

There was no time for a shower, makeup, or anything resembling fashion, so I brushed my teeth, put on sunglasses, and we were off. Right in front of the deli where I got coffee every day, Dan took my hand in his. I was walking on a cloud as we passed the barking dogs in Madison Square Park, turned, and walked west on 23rd.

"Where are you taking me? What if someone sees us? Do you want to be "Mr. Unidentified" in *US Weekly* next week? You are going to get me in trouble." I said.

He squeezed my hand and laughed. "That is three questions in one, Miss Amy—the answers are: 1) It's a surprise, 2) No one cares, and 3) I don't care."

Somehow, I didn't either.

We made our way down into the subway station. After an impossibly long ride on the F Train (patience—not my strong suit), we got out and walked along a creaky boardwalk. It was like we'd taken the subway to 1950. The place smelled beachy mixed with the scent of suntan lotion and hotdogs, and the air was filled with the sounds of delighted kids on summer break.

"Welcome to Coney Island," he said, smiling. "Surprise!"

It looked like an amusement park that was frozen in time—there was even a really old roller coaster, a freak show, and shooting gallery with real shotguns. "Feeling brave?" he asked as we approached the Cyclone. "In 1927, this was the tallest roller coaster in the United States. It's probably still got all the original equipment," he said. "Amy Spencer, are you man enough for the Cyclone?" he said, laughing.

I was amused to note that we had to wait in line for the Cyclone, even though it had been more than two years since I'd had to wait in line anywhere, for anything. Coney Island, apparently, hadn't gotten word that I was a big big star! It felt kind of good.

My heart leapt to my throat. My dad and I loved roller coasters. In fact, I had always prided myself on my tolerance for scary roller coaster rides. My dad and I had ridden every roller coaster in Disney World, Mall of America, and Six Flags. I looked up at the very tall and creaky-looking Cyclone. This was my big chance to show Dan I wasn't one of those Breakable Hollywood Types.

"I'm game if you are," I said.

Up close, it was even more imposing. If the Cyclone really **was** one of the first roller coasters built in the U.S., it's possible that the same freaky fat guy was still running it that day. In fact, when the wind blew, I swore I could see the whole monstrous structure swaying and creaking in the breeze. My mind briefly shifted into "Attila paranoia" mode ... how mad would she be if she knew I was there? Was there some clause in my show contract that prevented me from doing dangerous things? I was, after all, not even allowed to cut my hair or eat a cracker without getting permission from the powers that be. "**Autumn Leaves** actress Maimed in Freak Roller Coaster Accident," screamed the headline in my mind, and I had visions of Attila threatening to sue me for getting hurt. I was supposed to be packing to go home, and instead I was on a pseudo-date with a guy who wasn't my fiancée, riding a dangerous looking roller coaster. How irresponsible of me! But, I reminded myself, I just turned twenty-one. Sometimes you get to be stupid when you're twenty-one years old.

With great effort, I pushed Attila out of my mind. "Let's go!" I said, pulling Dan into the seats. The man running the ride, a 300 pound man with a stained plaid shirt and a nametag that said "Stevie" laughed as he pulled the handle. When he smiled at us, I notice he was missing most of his teeth. I was not at all confident in his ability to handle emergency situations. What if he died of heart failure while we were up there? Who would stop the ride? Most of all, when did I get so serious?

This roller coaster exceeded anything else I'd ever been on in my life, including the stand-up roller coaster that leaves you dangling upside down, and the one where they put you in a big chair, take you up to the top of a tower, and just drop you. In fact, at the top of The Cyclone, I looked down and couldn't even see any tracks below us. Oh my God, I thought, I am going to die on this ride with a man I hardly know.

Maybe it was the fact that I was very thin and over caffeinated. All I knew is that The Cyclone was, by far, the scariest roller coaster I had ever encountered, in the history of my life. I hung on to Dan for dear life, screaming bloody murder into his shoulder. It was at once fun, terrifying, and other worldly, just like the rest of the day. Totally unshaken, Dan was my rock, my beacon of calm. He laughed and screamed right along with me, and never took his arm away.

Somehow, Dan had found the one place in New York with no photographers, no Attila, and no pressure. With no one watching, I found it was okay to be hungry without getting nervous, and Dan encouraged me to eat whatever I wanted. We had hot dogs at Nathan's, shared cotton candy, and drank cold beer from plastic cups. With the setting sun pink in the sky, we sat on the pier, our legs dangling over the side and barely touching the water.

I didn't want the day to be over … in fact, I wanted to cry like a three year old at the prospect of going home, back to my life, back to work. "This was amazing," I said, resting my head on his shoulder. "This was a great day. Thank you."

He leaned in, and suddenly we were kissing. This was it! This was my perfect moment. Nothing in my life had ever compared to this feeling. This was real, and solid, and amazing, and I never wanted to let it go.

We were just coming up for air when I heard a clicking noise behind us. We turned around just in time to see a lone photographer, who had captured the whole thing.

Right then, I got the feeling that the real roller coaster ride was just about to begin.

SEASON THREE

CHAPTER 17

✵

Almost immediately upon my return to L.A., I was brought in for a sit down with Attila to discuss the "Coney Island Problem." I'd barely shut the door and sat down before she started yelling and pounding the desk with her flabby fist.

"There is no way, no possible way you are going out with a civilian at this point in your career!" she yelled. "Are you fucking kidding me with this? You have Brad Rockwell and the lead in an award-winning TV show, and this is what you do? You really must be an idiot!"

She was so mad, I could see a tiny blue vein starting to protrude from the side of her head, and it reminded me of a chapter I read in Bio class once on over-weight people, high blood pressure, and strokes. I supposed there was no chance she would succumb to one of those at that moment, but a girl could dream. Somehow she'd heard about the photos of Dan and I, and she'd been plotting my death for the entire time it taken me to fly back from New York.

She continued, her voice rising to a pitch I was pretty sure only dogs could hear. "Your team has created one of the greatest Hollywood power couples of all time, and you are throwing it all away on a guy with a hot dog stand? She gasped for breath. You … are … such an idiot!"

"Actually, his name is Dan Roberts, he's the director of my movie, and he took me to Coney Island for hot dogs …" I said. "Don't worry about it … Jon called me and told me they paid off the photographer. He was pissed, but it's already taken care of." I tried to sound nonchalant. In fact, I'd gotten the bitching out of a lifetime from Jon, who had even threatened to sue me if I ever saw Dan again, but I didn't want her to know that.

"Why are you still talking?" she said. "I don't care who he is, or what he does. You are never seeing that nobody ever again. Is that clear?"

I took a deep breath. "It's really okay," I said. "I've got it covered." She didn't know about the contract, and I wasn't allowed to tell her.

"Mindy … Brad and I…." my voice trailed off as I remembered the meetings, the contract, and Todd's warning about lawsuits about confidentiality. This thing was bigger than all of us, and extended further than she could ever realize. It killed me to not be able to take Dan's phone calls or emails or even to tell him why I couldn't see him again. I'd found the perfect guy, and now I had to act like I didn't like him. I wasn't even going to be allowed to do press for Blue Gray when it came out, and I knew this meant the film wouldn't get distribution.

Sweat dripped from the top of her pudgy upper lip. "You and Brad what?" she sneered. "Are getting married next year if you don't screw things up? Are a golden Hollywood couple? Are beyond your wildest dreams for yourself?" I visualized the blood clot making its way up into her brain, but no luck, she was still standing.

She slammed her hand down on the desk. "Listen to me, little girl. You will keep being the girlfriend of Brad Rockwell for as long as is humanly possible, or I'll send you back to Podunk, Michigan to work in some fucking fried chicken house, then I'll call the *Enquirer* and give them the address so they can do a "Where are they now?" cover on you. You will never be able to show your face anywhere, ever again. You won't even be able to get a job on that fucking *Flavor of Love*. Is that clear?

I laughed. For some reason, her rampages were having less of an effect on me. Finally she dismissed me, and I figured this wouldn't be the last I heard of this issue. Now there was just the matter of getting Dan out of my mind for the next few months.

✤   ✤   ✤

There was still a week to go before we started shooting Season Three, so Attila sent me back to Dr. Romano again for some more "routine maintenance." This time, he suggested a chemical peel to get rid of the sun damage from New York. "It's going to hurt a lot," he said, "but this is the best way to get a good result in the shortest period of time. You'll really need to stay out of the sun, and of course out of the public until the peeling stops. Then your skin is going to be as smooth as a baby's bottom on camera. Trust me."

When a doctor says "it's going to hurt a lot," you know it can't be good. I accepted the "light IV sedation" he offered.

A physician's assistant named Melissa came in, putting a headband over my hair. She was a short Asian girl with flawless skin, sparkling brown eyes, and absolutely no wrinkles. "This is the best!" she squeaked. "I had it a month ago, and it made a HUGE difference!" The IV sedation was starting to kick in, so even though I was thinking "your skin looks great," I couldn't quite form the words, so I just nodded. "OK, have fun!" said Melissa. "The doctor will be right back."

I was dozing off when Dr. Romano came in. "Are you ready?" he said. Again, I could only nod. He started to wipe some liquid from a bottle onto my face with gauze pads. When the burning started, I felt a little like my face was on fire, but I managed to say "you're burning my face." Even though I wasn't stressed out about it, my face was KILLING me.

"It's OK, said he said. "You're doing great. It's almost over."

I could feel my face burning and sizzling as the acid ate off the top layer of skin. How the hell was this going to heal in only a week? Surprisingly, when I look in the mirror it just looked a tiny bit pink, like I've been in a windstorm or out in the cold for too long.

"Wow, I thought it would look worse," I said.

He laughed. "Just wait. In two days your face is going to look like a leather handbag. Then it's going to peel off."

I could not wait.

❈   ❈   ❈

Three days later I looked like Freddy Kruger and was hiding out in my suite. Luckily, that was the day I got the advance copy of the cover I shot in New York showed up, so Vince was on hand to read and celebrate with me, even though he insisted on shrieking like a little girl every time he looked me full in the face.

He read it aloud while we smoked Camel Lights and drank vodka and Red Bulls. Even I had to admit, Arden had outdone herself this time, setting me up with the reporter she knew had the biggest crush on me and would write the most flattering article.

Star Spencer saunters into the lobby of the Mercer Hotel like she's living in another era. Her alabaster skin glows as she slides into the leather banquette in the back, her sparkling green eyes revealing a hint of something left unsaid. If this were the Enlightenment, she would certainly be Georges Sand in a salon in Paris.

Vince looks up. "Amy—my God. What did you do to this man? You mesmerized him!" He fell back into his chair, laughing. "Good God—this is better fiction than Tori Spelling's E! True Hollywood Story."

"Oh, that's just the beginning, baby." I said, mixing another drink. "What till you get to the part with the cheeseburger."

Vince flipped frantically through the glossy pages, skipping over four shots of me in all my airbrushed glory. Arden thought it would be good not only for my career in general, but for the show as a whole for me to do a cover while I was in New York. "To expand your market share to women age 28–35." she'd explained.

With the grace of a dancer, Star folds her impossibly lithesome legs up under her delicate chin, resting it for a moment on her red-nailed hand. Defying logic, she orders a cheeseburger, fries, and a Coke. "Extra cheese," she says with a smile.

"WHO IS THIS REPORTER?" said Vince. "Did you drug him to get him to print these outrageous lies???"

"Notice how I never actually **consume** the cheeseburger during the course of the interview," I said testily. Actually, the waiter had brought it and set it down in front of me, but since we were going to start shooting Season Three soon, I was back on food restriction. I did keep wondering, though, what the reporter would have written if I'd just grabbed the cheeseburger and started eating like my life depended on it. Which, I guess you might say, it did. "Read more." I said, poking at my scabby face with my fingernail.

Vince looked up at me, shrieked again, then continued to scan. "That's actually a really good picture of you—they shaved like, half an inch off your chin," he said, tearing it out. "This one's going in the "Airbrush Wall of Fame. You look a little like Hillary Duff here." I scowled at him, and he started again.

Since being plucked from her dreary Midwestern existence and catapulting to fame as "Autumn" on **Autumn Leaves,** *Star Spencer has quickly captured America's heart and assumed her rightful place on the throne of America's Sweetheart previously held by such luminaries as Julia Roberts, Sandra Bullock, and Reese Witherspoon.*

Vince wiped away a pseudo-tear. "Our little Star is all grow'd up," he said. "We so proud of her back on the farm." He lit another cigarette. "By the way, I just wanted to take this moment to say that Ryan Phillippe is freaking HOT, and if Reese ever gets tired of him, I am available."

I looked over his shoulder at the magazine. "Damn … they cut the part about my Uncle Jerry's emus," I said, flipping to the next page. "I thought that story was funny."

❦   ❦   ❦

The next day, my cell phone buzzed in my pocket. I took it out, and saw Ross' number.

"Ross!" I said excitedly. "How are you? My trip to New York was so great … the movie was amazing … I can't wait to see you! How are you?"

"Amy, did you have your Season Three meeting yet?" he said, sounding uncharacteristically downbeat.

"No … why? Is everything all right? What's going on?"

Ross sighed. "I just had my meeting. Let's just keep this between us … They gave my character cancer, and he dies in the middle of this season."

My heart started to pound.

"What are you talking about?" I said. "What does that even mean? They can't do that … you've been in the cast since the pilot. We're a family! They wouldn't … what? Why?"

"They didn't say … they're killing off Peter, and I'm off the show after the first five episodes, except in occasional dream flashback scenes with you and Michael."

My head was spinning. Ross was one of my only links to sanity on the set, and without him, I might just go over the edge. Besides, I'd come to love him like a father or big brother, and I didn't even want to think about doing the show without him.

"They can't do this!" I shouted. "We can't do this show without you. This is totally wrong. Do you want me to do something? What can I do? I can threaten to quit if you want!" I was serious.

While I was trying to think of favors I could call in or RockStar clout that I could use, Ross laughed softly. "That's just the business, darlin'. I'm sad that it's over, but there will be another show. I've already got my agent looking around for pilots, since I'll be done in December."

We hadn't even started shooting Season Three yet, and already I was dreading going back to work. I felt like I was losing yet another member of my family, and once again, I didn't know who to blame. The thought of being on the set without Ross was heartbreaking. How could they just kill off a major character who had been in every episode since the pilot and won two Golden Globes and an Emmy for the role?

It just didn't seem right.

❧   ❧   ❧

"Find your mental staircase," said the man in my trailer. I stifled a laugh.

Two weeks into shooting Season Three, the stress of the plotline was already getting to me. I was going days without sleeping, and it was starting to show. I shut my eyes, determined that hypnosis was going to be the key to solving the insomnia situation.

"Jesus Christ," said Attila the last time she'd seen me. "It looks like someone hit you in the face. What is wrong with you? Can't the makeup department cover up those eye bags?"

"I know," I'd said. "I can't sleep … insomnia. It just takes one thing.…"

"Well, now we're getting letters about it … why does Autumn look so tired all the time? What's wrong with Autumn?" You've got to do something about this. Get some sleep, or figure out a way to look like you got some. I'll send over a hypnotist.

And so I sat in my trailer in between scenes with a white guy named Saresh who wore a flowing white skirt, trying to visualize myself climbing down a beautiful white staircase, one step at a time.

"OK, just try to relax. I'm going to count back from ten."

I wanted it to work. In fact, I would have given anything to completely give over to sleep, blissfully unencumbered by the constant hunger and stress that had been keeping me awake. More than anything, I would've loved to just take a deep breath, fall back into my bed, and succumb to the pressing fatigue and exhaustion that had made me a walking zombie for weeks. I reminded myself—this was the job that 99.9% of the world would die for, and all I wanted to do was sleep it away. I felt my heart skip a beat and tried to push the heavy thoughts out of my mind.

I tried to picture how this was going to work when I was lying in my bed at the hotel or at Brad's place, haunted by the fact that I had to shoot yet another day of scenes in a hospital. The show was getting to me, I couldn't stop thinking about Dan, and all I wanted was a good night's sleep and a banana split.

Needless to say, I could not picture the staircase.

❦   ❦   ❦

Three days (and still no sleep) later, I sat on a lounge chair on the roof of the hotel, smoking cigarettes and shivering in my favorite sweater. The Santa Ana winds blew in circles around the city, and I could almost feel the seasons changing from winter to spring. I'd watched so many episodes of *Law & Order*, I could tell by the first commercial break what the whole plot was about and who did it.

With Brad shooting an action adventure movie in Japan, I was off of "Rock-Star" duty temporarily, though Jon had been calling me frequently to see if I was minding my manners in his absence. "Are you okay? Do you need anything? Let us know if you're going out with anyone, just so we know, okay?" Jon did not sleep, had a Rolodex in his brain, and had 3,000 numbers programmed in his cell phone. "Really, it's no trouble … I'll send the driver right over," he said.

"That's okay … I just need to sleep. I'm going to hang out at the hotel," I said. "When does Brad get back?"

Silence. So unlike him. What was going on?

"Um … Brad's shooting schedule got held up—he'll be back next week. Is there something you want to talk to me about instead? Are you okay?" Jon was sweet, but he was business, and I never get the "warm fuzzy" vibe from him.

Vince had been off with a new guy lately, and I hadn't seen him in weeks. I'd pretty much been going to the studio to shoot my (very depressing) scenes for the show, going back to the hotel, and trying unsuccessfully to sleep. On days when I was not called, I took one of Brad's assistants and his Black American Express to Lisa Kline or Barney's, though they'd been sending over so much stuff I was hardly hurting for clothes. Mostly, I just felt lonely. Since Season Three started, I'd had this gnawing homesick feeling growing in my stomach, like I was going to disappear into nothingness. Despite the outward appearance that my life was perfect, I felt more and more out of place.

I got out my cell phone, scrolled down, dialing Carrie Ann's new number in New York. Voicemail. Of course—she got home from the show at 2am, probably went right to sleep. Next, Vince. Voicemail, as usual. I was on the verge of leaving a tearful "I need you message," and was seriously considering waking up my mom in Bay City, just to hear a friendly voice. I'd promised Olivia I would never call her in the middle of the night. I wondered what Dan was doing. I lit another cigarette, and the fought the urge to jump off roof of the hotel. That would be a great headline. Would it even matter? Really, I wanted to run outside into the street, to see a familiar person—anything that would reconnect me with the world.

What do you do when you have everything, but still feel like nothing?

That's it, I thought. No matter what he was doing, Vince wouldn't care that it was late. He would hug me and make Jabba the Hut jokes about Attila. He would make me hot chocolate and play my favorite Miles Davis CDs. We would watch *Say Anything* for the millionth time. Maybe at Vince's, I would be able to sleep. This was a good plan.

I quickly went back to my room, grabbed my stuff, and ran downstairs, already cheered. Vince was the answer to my loneliness.

There was hardly any traffic on the surface streets, so I cruised right down Laurel, past the Coffee Bean where I always saw Perez, and parked on the corner, relieved to finally be going someplace that felt like home. I marched triumphantly up the stairs and down the familiar corridor to Vince's place, # 2F. No lights … that's okay. This was still a good plan.

After some persistent knocking, both at the door and the window, I figured I'd just use my key to let myself in, like I had in the past. Since moving to West Hollywood and hooking up with Perez, Vince had been quite the party boy—sometimes he came home from the clubs and would regale me with his exploits. He never brought guys home, though, because the apartment was so packed with clothes. Just as I found the key and put it in the lock, I heard voices from inside the apartment.

"Darling!" I whispered playfully. "Didn't you hear me knocking? Let me in … I can't sleep, and I miss you."

The door didn't budge. "Vince, are you holding the door closed? Is something wrong with you?" Now I was worried. "Seriously—I'm standing in the dark, it's late, and I'm worried. Let me in or I'm calling 911." I leaned on the door even harder, trying to force it open. Was he passed out against the door? Was someone in there killing him? What was going on? I started to panic.

Suddenly the door opened, and I fell into the apartment, spilling the entire contents of my bag all over the hardwood floor. As I picked up my stuff, I look up to see Vince with a strange look on his face. "My God—is something wrong?" I said, picking up my stuff. "I just wanted to see you … you never called me back …"

Just then I had a strange realization. From where Vince was standing, it couldn't have been him holding the door closed. All at once I was thinking "Vince never has guys over," "I'd better go," and "I wonder who it is."

Vince was speechless, like a dog that's been caught on your Thanksgiving table eating the turkey. His mouth kept making this little "O," like he was obviously trying to think of something to say, but was frozen. "Aim … I" he trailed off, looking plaintively behind the door. Slowly, the door closes, and I turned around to see a half naked Brad Rockwell emerge from the shadows.

"Brad … what are you…." I started, but I couldn't finish. My mind was racing. Jon said Brad was still in Japan, but instead, he was in my best friend's apartment with no shirt on. Brad had never tried to make a move on me in private, and we were supposed to be engaged. Brad only wanted to kiss me when we were in public.

Brad was Vince's new boyfriend.

"This is covered under our Confidentiality Agreement," Brad muttered, buttoning his shirt. "I don't want to ever hear about this again, or you'll be hearing from my lawyer." He pushed past me and walked quickly out of the apartment. "See you later," he said to Vince over his shoulder. Vince looked crushed.

❦   ❦   ❦

I didn't even know where to put this new information in my mind. Of course, I didn't think Brad was really in love with me … but Vince? I sank back to the floor in the middle of my stuff and cried for a good twenty minutes as I thought of all the awkward conversation I'd tried to make, all the times I'd felt deathly alone with Brad. Was there something about Vince that suddenly made Brad into a warm and compassionate person? It seemed so unfair ... it was as if I'd been jilted twice. My only solace in this world—Vince. "Why would you do this to me?" I wailed. "I need you."

"Aim ... I'm so sorry. It didn't start out this way—I didn't mean for this to happen. He made the first move—I can't believe I'm saying this ... Amy, I love him."

Now I was mad. "Vince—he's my fiancé, and further more, he's Brad Rockwell ... a big straight movie star. You're not in love, and even if you are, you're not going to be a couple. This is insane. You have to stop this, or you're going to get hurt. Besides, you're *mine*." Vince didn't know about the contract, and he obviously didn't fully understand the power of the Brad Rockwell machine.

"Aim ... he loves me," he said over and over, crying. "I kept trying to tell him it was crazy, but he said he doesn't care. He comes over here all the time, without his entourage, and we just sit and talk for hours."

Part of me really wanted to ask him what on earth they talked about, but I was still reeling. "Vince ... he's supposed to be marrying *me*. He's sneaking around behind your back and mine. Who knows who else he's dating? He doesn't bring anyone here because no one knows he's gay. Can you imagine what would happen if his fans found out? The studios? Oh my God, Vince ... his career would be over. *Blood Revenge 4* starring an out gay man? No way. The studio would pull out for sure. Look—I'm his fiancé, and I don't even know about this part of his life ... don't you find this strange?"

"Aim, he said he had a plan, and I trust him—that's good enough for me. Are you mad because he's not in love with you? I thought you had an open relationship ..."

I wondered how much Brad had told him, but I was afraid to fill in the blanks. Suddenly, I wanted to be far away from him. My only connection to home, my homesickness cure, my angel Vince had been pulled into my drama, and I couldn't even tell him everything.

I gathered up my stuff. "I should go back … I have a 9 am call, and they're already pissed about my eye bags. I need to get some sleep." I rushed past him, out the door, and started down the stairs.

"Amy … don't leave like this." Vince ran down the stairs after me, following me all the way to my car. The combination of shock and exhaustion had combined to make me feel like I was going to pass out, and my heart was racing. I longed to be back in my bed at the hotel.

"I just need to get my head around this," I said, speeding off. "I'll call you later."

I had never felt more alone.

❧   ❧   ❧

"OK, one more sun salutation."

Desperate for human companionship after the Brad/Vince situation exploded, I did the unthinkable.

I let Olivia take me to yoga class.

And so, instead of being at brunch on Sunday like a sane person, I was lying on a mat at Santa Monica Yoga, gathering my strength before I attempted the yoga Sun Salutation that would surely kill me while secretly plotting the death of my assistant, whom I had joined for what turned out to be 90 minutes of pure torturous hell.

"Just try it," Olivia said. "It's relaxing, and it will help your insomnia. Besides, paparazzi love to photograph celebrities coming out of yoga class. They'll put the photo on the "Stars—They're Just Like Us!" page!, she'd said jokingly.

Finally I'd relented. Olivia was one of my best friends now, and she'd been trying to get me to go to yoga with her since we met, claiming that it would "make me more centered." Now, with the "Peter has cancer" plotline heating up and many emotional days on the set, I found that I often felt like one big raw nerve. I sort of just wanted his character to die already, just so I don't have to shoot anymore scenes in hospitals or where I was crying. But, then there would be the funeral scene which, frankly, I was not looking forward to either. Even with another big raise and a new trailer, season three was already turning out to be more challenging than any of the others, and many of us had started showing up late to set. Olivia suggested yoga as a way to get my mind off the depressing vibe.

Now, with my upper arms burning and my head spinning, I was seriously regretting that decision. A girl in front of me was twisting herself into a pretzel, looking back at me occasionally as if issuing some kind of yoga challenge. "Take that!" her perfectly arched back seemed to say.

I extended my legs as far apart as I thought they would go, and the yoga teacher came over and repositioned them to go even farther, after which I fell over.

"Olivia, I want to go," I whispered frantically. "Everyone is better than me." She smiled. "Find your center," she whispered back, giggling. "Be the tree."

Pretzel girl looked back at us and scowled. "Shhhh," she hissed. So not yogi.

I collapsed onto the mat. If there were photographers outside, they were going to love the sight of me with rubbery legs, covered in sweat and unable to stand up straight. After 90 minutes of yoga that was supposed to be "introductory," I was longing for a nice game of tennis or the long walks around campus that Carrie Ann and I used to count as cardio. Whatever the case, I liked yoga, but not enough to go all Gwyneth Paltrow or Christy Turlington.

In Hollywood, even stuff that's supposed to be relaxing is stressful.

❧   ❧   ❧

"I'm telling you, she's too fat to fly on a commercial airline. That is why we fly on the private jets."

Autumn Leaves had been syndicated in Germany, Austria, and Switzerland, so we were flying over to Europe for some promotional press. Matt Pierce, who played my love interest Zach in Season One (before his character got caught shoplifting and sent to fictional jail) was sitting next to me on the plane. We were entertaining ourselves by counting how many times Attila had to get up to "stretch her legs" during the flight.

"It's because her ass is too wide to fit in an airplane seat," he whispered. "That, or she's secretly had a hip replacement and is trying to stretch it out right now." We laughed. I was sad that Matt left the show—he was a really nice guy, from Illinois (so, sort of Midwest), and he and I had first bonded over California and its bad drivers.

She walked by again. "You know, that hip thing could be for real," I whispered, as we watch her attempt to contort herself into several yoga-like poses, then do a little dance. "I saw a guy on Oprah last week who was so fat, he broke his own knees."

This comment caused Matt to shoot his airplane vodka tonic out his nose, and Attila looked over at us and smiled. She was careful not to be vicious when no one was watching. In fact, we'd had some positively civil conversations with other people around. "Did Oprah buy the guy some new knees?" he said, acting serious.

Attila went back to her seat. "No," I said. "The whole thing was about tragic fat people, and the guy was in a little film where he was trying to walk on his broken knees. Can you believe I actually saw this on TV while I was at the gym? I swear, I think the studio programs the TV with this kind of stuff to make us work out longer.

The German press junket took place in the Steigenberger Hotel in Berlin, where we'd also been to promote the show the year before. It was your typical junket—enter large hotel conference room divided into many small, room-like sections for the different media affiliates, go from little room to little room, tell amusing anecdotes about the show, say how excited you are to be here, lather, rinse, repeat. I successfully resisted the urge to tell the "fat guy who broke his own knees" story, because I knew that Attila was watching, headphones cutting into the sides of her face. I also found the restraint not to badmouth the new plotline, even though I thought it sucked and was longing to get out of my contract.

On the plane on the way back, Matt and I guessed that she waddled by us a total of thirty seven times.

❧   ❧   ❧

My phone had been showing "three voicemail messages" for two days, and finally I had stopped being mad at Vince long enough to pick them up. I knew it was probably him leaving the messages, but I just didn't have the energy to sort the whole thing out. Shooting Season Three was wearing me down to a nub, and I had made a tentative plan to avoid everyone in my Bizarre Gay Love Triangle for at least two months. It all seemed so unbelievable—did I really just find out that my best friend was having an affair with my fake fiancé? Wasn't this the stuff of daytime talk shows? Not even the **Weekly World News** would believe this one.

My voicemail clicked in—

Hey Amy, it's mom—I don't know if you're coming here next week, and I was trying to make some plans.

Note to self: call mom back.

Star, it's Jo with your call time for tomorrow—I'll send you a text message.

Delete.

Aim, it's Vince … I have some stuff I want to say.

I sighed, dialing Vince's number. He picked up on the second ring, sounding paranoid.

"Hello?" He whispered. In spite of myself, I laughed. What was he hyperbolizing now?"

Long pause. Was he being coy?

"Vince? Are you still there?"

"Yes—Aim, I need to come over there. I'm a little freaked out right now."

Twenty minutes later, he met me by the pool at the hotel, insisting that we had to be outside. "Oh my God," I said, annoyed already. "Are you in the C.I.A. now?"

"I know, I'm sorry—it's just … after that night when you saw Brad and me together, I haven't heard from him or you, and I keep getting these hang up phone calls from "Unknown Number.""

"Well," I said, trying to be the voice of reason. "Brad left for Toronto a few days ago, so maybe he's just busy. It's not me calling … you know my number."

"Aim, I know—but it's weird for me not to talk him for this long. We are usually on the phone, like, every two hours."

Was he trying to rub in the fact that my fake fiancé liked him more than me? Herabbed my arm, pulling me close to him. "There's something else," he said. "Two days after you saw us, I found a dead pigeon on my car—its neck was broken." A cold chill ran down my spine. "There was a note tied around the bird's neck—it said "squawk and die.""

"Are you making this up?" I said, but I could see that he wasn't. "Who would do that?" Vince was pale and trembling. "I don't know," he said. "Do you think they mean about Brad? I can't get him on his cell phone, I'm totally panicked, and I can't sleep. Aim—his people must know where I live. There's been a black car parked outside my house practically since you left. Why would he do this? Everything is really opening up for gay actors now. I thought he was going to come out. I mean … I really did."

I wanted to tell him about the contract, about how Brad and I had never even slept in the same bed, how Brad's "team" would never let him come out in a million years, how he wouldn't be a bankable movie star if he was openly gay. Then I thought of the dead bird, and figured that was the least of my worries if I told Vince the truth. According to Todd, no one broke the "movie star confidentiality agreement." "Basically," he'd said, "you play out your contract's time, then you're still bound by the terms for the rest of your life. Like, you can't go writing a book in ten years about your life with Brad, and you can never give an interview about what really happened while you were dating."

I shuddered. Vince didn't have a contract, and he actually had feelings for Brad. Should I warn him? I decided against it, figuring the more he knew, the more trouble he could get himself in. "Listen," I said. "Just drop it. Maybe he decided he wasn't ready, or he needs some time, you know? Maybe he'll call when he's done shooting. Don't wait around for him, though." I tried not to make it sound too urgent, because I didn't want to scare him, but I hoped he'd somehow get the message and drop the whole thing. "You can stay here until everything blows over," I said, and he looked relieved. "I'm thinking of moving to Santa Monica," he said. "Away from all the Hollywood drama."

We'd never covered the whole "you stole my fiancé" topic, but I thought he'd probably figured out that Brad and I were "just friends," and was scared enough to not go to the press.

I knew Brad would never talk to him again.

❦   ❦   ❦

I made it through one more week of long shooting days shooting Season Three before I began to seriously explore ways to get out of my *Autumn Leaves* contract. With my unhappiness at a peak, I hired Barry Schoenfeld, a private attorney, to advise me on the possibility of leaving the show.

"No, no … I just don't think it's possible," said Barry, sliding the contract across the table back to me. "Why would you want to leave a hit show, anyway? You've only been in the business a few years. Why would you want out already?"

I laid my head on his desk exhaustedly. The glass top felt cool against my cheek, and for a moment I thought I might just be able to go to sleep. "Barry, I've played the exact same character for two and half seasons. Every week, it's the same plot. I can't work on movie or other shows because I'm working eighteen hours a day here, and my producer doesn't want me to wreck my "image." I just want to know how soon I can get away from it … get on with my career. Plus, this plot line we're shooting is seriously driving me to the brink of a nervous breakdown." I knew it sounded weird to be complaining, but I didn't care anymore. "What can I do?" I said. "Do you think a *Playboy* shoot would work? Somehow, I knew this was a moot point too, as nudity would probably violate my RockStar contract.

Barry ran his hand over his greasy bald head. "Yeah, cry me a river. You're young, beautiful, and rich, and you're trapped in everyone's dream job."

I could feel my frustration growing. Why did I think he was going to under-stand this problem? "Barry, I need you to tell me my options. I don't want to do the next two seasons. I want out of this contract. I am totally serious here."

He looked me in the eye. "I'm, being serious too, Star. They've got you for at least the next two and a half years. Short of killing someone or robbing a bank, there is nothing you could do to make them let you out of this contract."

CHAPTER 18

❀

"Oh my God ... Amy, speed up ... that guy is following too close."

At 7:30pm on a Thursday night, Vince and I were in my convertible Mercedes (an engagement gift from Brad), speeding along the winding curves of Sunset Boulevard in an attempt avoid traffic on the way to Gladstone's in Malibu. I hadn't slept in so long, I felt like I might black out, I was freezing even though it was 75 degrees, and I was struck by the overwhelming urge to just lay somewhere and be quiet. Now I regretted having committed to the long drive—I wanted to pull over and let him take the wheel, but there was nowhere to stop—it was actually a toss up between what might be more dangerous—driving down the precariously divided road, or pulling over to switch. Sunset has no shoulder, it was dark, and he was right—there was a car driving so close, I was being blinded by its headlights in my rearview mirror. To further add to my anxiety, Vince kept getting up and turning around in his seat, yelling "GET OFF OUR ASS! ARE YOU CRAZY?" I was really afraid he might fall out of the car.

I needed to get some sleep soon, or I was going to go over the edge, and I was intermittently feeling dizzy, hot, and cold. The air whipping by felt like knives cutting my face. Can you go through menopause at twenty-one? I thought. That's the thing with sleep—you only get a certain number of good days without it, and then you're just a walking zombie. Still, when Vince called to say he wanted to go to Gladstone's for some oysters, I went to go pick him up after work instead of going back to the hotel to lie down. Work had been stressful—many script changes, retakes, and twelve long hours of shooting. The cancer plotline was still dragging on, and Attila had visited the set that day.

Whenever I tried to eat in front of her, I caught her staring at me disapprovingly, my throat started to close up, and I couldn't swallow. Also, the numerous pills I took every day were starting to make me a little shaky all the time, like I was vibrating on a higher level.

We got past a really curvy area, almost over the 405 freeway into Brentwood. I looked to the left, thinking maybe I could get on the freeway to at least make the guy stop following me. No luck—even the onramp was bumper to bumper, and I was in the wrong lane to merge.

We were almost to Bel Air when Close Follower pulled up beside us. I breathed a momentary sigh of relief which turned immediately back into panic as I realized that not only did the car contain two paparazzi, but that one of them actually had a video camera. We were all still going 50 on a winding road at night, the wind was whipping my hair around my face, and it was starting to rain.

"SLOW DOWN," screamed Vince, maybe at me and maybe at the photographers. "ARE YOU INSANE?!!." The driver, a fat, balding white guy with a stained brown shirt, laughed and threw his cigarette out the window. His friend with the video camera, a smaller, filthy-looking guy in a plaid shirt, never took the camera off of us. "Hey—smile for the camera!" he yelled, punching his friend in the arm. "Get closer to them," he shouted, hanging out of the side of his car.

Fat Guy veered even closer to our lane, and my heart was pounding as I sped up to get away from them. "Who's your friend?" screamed Little Guy as Fat Guy hit the gas and pulled ahead of us, slamming on his brakes. The dizziness was increasing, and I felt like I was falling over. The faster we drove, the harder my heart beat, and I was having trouble catching my breath. I needed to get off the road, right away.

"Vince, call 911," I screamed. "Tell them we need help." He grabbed the phone and dialed as I tried to speed up even more to lose the photographers. The more adrenaline went through my system, the more I felt like I was going to lose control, making me crash the car. "Keep it together," I said to myself, over and over again. "Concentrate on the road." The middle divider was going faster and faster, until it was the only thing keeping me conscious. Vince hunkered down in the bottom of the seat so he could hear the phone.

"Hello … we're being chased by photographers, and we need help," said Vince frantically. "It's Star Spencer in the car, and her friend … we're on Sunset near the Palisades … the photographers are swerving, and have almost hit us twice.…"

Fat Guy's car veered precariously close to ours, and I swerved to avoid them. Vince looked up at me in feat, then went back to the call.

"What do you mean, what do I want you to do?" He yelled. "Send someone to arrest them. They're putting our lives in danger." He threw the phone down in disgust. He turned to me. "Just pull over … the side of the road is better than this. I'll drive."

But I couldn't pull over. Fat Guy was driving like he was in the Formula One, matching me turn for turn. When I slowed down, he slowed down, and when I sped up to try to lose them, he was right on my tail. Since he was in the right lane, it was impossible for me to get past him to pull off to the shoulder. I felt like I was driving fast and leaning to the right at the same time. Everything started to spin.

Finally, we approached the top of the hill, the left turn on Temescal right before it starts down the hill toward PCH. If I could just keep myself conscious until we got through the light, everything would be fine. This was my chance to pull over and wait for the police to arrive, and I knew for a fact there was a gas station just after the light and a little ways down the hill. The light was green at the intersection, and I gunned it, trying to get us through the light and down the hill. Surely the photographers' beat up Toyota was no match for the Mercedes 500 series in this capacity.

We were almost to the light when Fat Guy decided he was going for it—he was going to try to make the left, only it wasn't a double left turn lane—it was a single. In what seemed like slow motion, I saw him speed toward our lane, trying to catch up with us. I was still looking at his face when the sedan crashed into the back of my car, turning us the wrong way toward traffic and landing us in the intersection. Next, we were hit from the other side by a car that had pushed through the yellow light and just made it.

The next five seconds felt like three hours. First, I very clearly saw the words "I am having a car accident" in my mind, and for a moment everything became perfectly clear, like the surface of a lake. I observed that I finally didn't feel exhausted anymore, everything had stopped spinning, and in fact, I was kind of relieved. Then the questions started. How did I get here? What was happening? Was I dead? Was that me screaming? Was this a dream?

And just as quickly, the sound of crunching glass and metal, screeching tires, and screams filled the air. Then silence.

❧   ❧   ❧

It took a moment or so for all of us to realize we were okay. Fat Guy and Little Guy's car was undriveable, and all of my airbags had deployed. Vince had a gash over his eye, and blood had begun to pour down the side of his head. No broken bones, and, from what I could see, no concussions.

Little Guy got out of the car, still holding the camera. "Hey Eddie—check it out! We're the first on the scene for the Star Spencer car crash! This footage is going to be worth a million bucks."

Suddenly, my mind was flooded. The pressure, the lack of sleep, the cancer plotline, the hunger. I looked up at the face of Fat Photographer, who had gotten out of his car and come over to ours. He was unhurt, and was leaning in close to my face. He smelled like stale beer and too many cigarettes. "Anything to say, girlie?" he laughed. "You're not a very good driver. Where's your fiancé?"

And that was it. I didn't care anymore. I didn't care about the money, or the fame, or the show. All I wanted was to kill this guy, who embodied every frustration I'd had in the past three years. He was Sondra, and Attila, and jealous people, and all the food I couldn't eat. He was lack of sleep and bad press. He was Brad Rockwell, and Todd Whitley, who wouldn't even look twice at me if I wasn't a somebody. He was everything, and I wanted to kill him.

I jumped out of the car, forgetting we were still in the middle of the intersection, ran up to Fat Guy, and punched him in the face as hard as I could. "Is this what you want?" I screamed, sobbing so hard I could hardly get the words out. "What do you want, some fucking scandal? I hope you die. I hope everyone you love dies. You prey on people, you filthy parasite. You animal. You created me, and now you're destroying me. Is this all a game to you?"

I didn't hear the sound of the police sirens in the background. Rage had filled my mind and my body, and I just wanted to tear this guy limb from limb. I kept hitting him in the face and arms, and he kept laughing. "Are you getting this, Jim? Little fancy girl has lost her shit, and she's trying to kick my ass! This is fucking great! Don't stop rolling!"

Over his shoulder, I saw his camera sitting in the front seat of his car, telephoto lens sticking out. If I couldn't kill him, I thought, maybe I could destroy his livelihood. Still screaming, I ran over to the car, picked it up, and smashed it to the ground. "Is this what you love?" I screamed. "Were you going to kill me to get your story? Fuck you, you worthless piece of shit. I hope you die!" I stomped the camera with my boot. "Is this what you want? Crawl on the ground and get it! You'll do anything for a picture, right?"

He knocked me out of the way to get to his camera, and I tried hitting him again. Just then, the police arrived and restrained both of us. "What's going on here?" said one of the officers.

"I got the whole thing on film," said the Little Guy. "She assaulted my partner, and destroyed his property. We were just involved in a regular car accident, and then she went nuts. Maybe you should test her Blood Alcohol Level, officers."

"They were chasing us all the way from Hollywood," said Vince. "We called 911, and no one came. These guys wouldn't let us off to the side, and then they crashed into us." The police officer was still holding on to my arm as I tried to swing at the photographer. "They tried to kill us," I said.

Then I felt it. It started out as a hot black feeling around my eyes, and then it seemed like I was melting. I was passing out. Just before I hit the ground, I heard myself saying "Don't call my mom … she'll worry."

❦   ❦   ❦

Two minutes later, I woke up, as if from a nightmare. I was already in the ambulance, and it felt like we were going downhill. I tried to reassure myself that I was alive, that everything was fine, but for some reason, I couldn't calm down. Finally losing control like that opened the floodgates, and now I couldn't pull myself back together. I felt hot, then broke out into a cold sweat, started gasping for air, and wanted to run away, or to crawl out of my skin. My heart was beating too fast. It felt like every system in my body was shutting down at once, and I was trying to get away from the failure. I started to scream, then to cry, then to scream again. I was twitching uncontrollably. And, over and over again, I was thinking "Get a hold of yourself … you've lost control, but you can get it back … come on … you can do it …" But I couldn't. I tried to focus, and the next wave of adrenaline transported me back over the edge into nightmareland.

I screamed again, but it was like a scream inside a dream, where your mouth is open and you can hear someone far away making the noise. The scream lasted for what seemed like a long time. I tried to lie back, tried to take deep breaths to slow my heart down. I was freezing, and so uncomfortable I couldn't even lie back without writhing around. Every time I closed my eyes, I could see the inside of my skull. This in turn was so scary that it made me freak out even more. The paramedic kept trying to tell me to calm down, only he didn't understand—I couldn't calm down, I was just observing what was happening from the outside, like him. If I could stop it I would, I thought, but I'm just along for the ride. The scariest part of this episode was that intermittently, I felt totally normal, like I'd just woken up from some bad dream where something was wrong with me. That lasted for a moment or two, and then I was slammed back into the worst terror of my life, times ten. Slowly, I realized that I felt a crushing pain in my chest. What was happening? Was I having a heart attack? I looked up into the face of the paramedic. "This isn't me," I whispered. "Something's wrong."

"You're okay … just calm down. You were in an accident," he said. "You probably broke some ribs. Keep the oxygen mask on."

Now time was coming in segments. I was lying in the Emergency Room, and someone was yelling, "Star, what did you take?" It actually was a little like the show *ER*. I kept wanting to snap out of it, only I was still in it. I wanted to say "I didn't overdose … some fat photographer crashed into my car," but I couldn't. In fact, I couldn't breathe at all.

That's the last thing I remember, then I passed out again.

❦   ❦   ❦

"Oh my God … what day is it? I have to be on set!"

The first thing I noticed when I finally woke up was that the room was filled with people, and that I felt like I was in a drug-induced haze. I could tell I was in the hospital, but from the amount of people present, the timing didn't make sense. Carrie Ann had to come from New York—that would take at least six hours. My mom—how did she get a flight from Detroit? How did all these people get here so fast? I thought, then I went back to sleep again.

"You're awake!" My mom's face unfurled itself from desperate worry to relief. "We were worried."

"I told them not to call you." I said weakly. Slowly I begin to notice that my whole body hurt. "What's going on?"

"You were dehydrated, and you had a fever, and you had a car accident," she said softly. "And, Amy," she said with tears in her eyes. "You weighed 99 pounds. Why did you do this to yourself? Are you on drugs? Do you have an eating disorder?"

"I wanted to take care of you guys," I gulped. "It was so much money, and we had the bills, and dad would've wanted me to take care of you, but I was so hungry, and stressed out, and I couldn't take it anymore." I looked up at her. "I'm sorry … I just did what I thought was best for us."

She leaned over, taking me into her arms and hugging me like she was afraid she'd break me. She stroked my hair. "I had no idea you were under so much pressure."

At all once, I felt like I was seven years old, when I'd have a bad dream, go into my parents' room, and they'd hug me until I felt better. I felt one tear slowly make its way down my face, then another. "I missed you," I whispered. "I miss dad." Then I was crying for real. "I tried to be strong, but I'm so scared—everything could just go away, just like that, with no warning." The tears washed over me, like a warm river. I just didn't care anymore. Finally, I let it go.

My mom cried too, and hugged me. "You're going to be okay," she said. "Everything's going to be fine."

❦   ❦   ❦

When there were no more tears left, I slept for real, for twelve hours. It wasn't just sleep, either—it was the little kid sleep, where it takes you away, and nothing can get to you. When I woke up, my mom and Vince explained more about what happened to me. The combination of stress, lack of food, lack of sleep, and diet pills had resulted in fever, dehydration, and tachycardia. In other words, while my idle always ran a little high, I had redlined my engine and burned it out. My body was so overworked, I needed 36 hours to sleep it off.

Just hearing all this made me tired.

I went back to sleep again for another four hours. When I woke up, I was antsy. "Can I have the remote?" I said groggily.

Vince shot my mom a look. "I don't think you want to watch TV right now, Aim."

I went back to sleep again. This time, I dreamt about a car chase, a fat photographer, and me screaming. Then I woke up, realizing that it wasn't a dream. "How long have I been here? Did we crash?" I said to Vince. He hadn't shaved or changed clothes. That must mean I'm really sick, I thought.

"Sweetie, you have a concussion," he said softly. "We can talk about this when you're better."

A few hours later, I could finally keep my eyes open for more than two minutes at a time when my mom came in. Standing behind her was a handsome Indian man. They both smiled. "Amy, this is Dr. Shah from Cardiology, and he wants to talk to you. Do you feel up to it?"

Great. First I crashed, then I hit a guy, then I freaked out, and now a cardiologist wanted to talk to me. Did I also have a heart defect? "Did I have a heart attack?" I said, bracing myself.

"No," said the doctor, and I exhaled. He was holding a manila folder, which I assumed was my chart. "Have you ever heard of clenbuterol?"

"No," I said. This was not Behind Closed Doors. I really didn't know what he's talking about.

"It's a steroid that's commonly used to treat asthma in horses, and some people in the industry have been using it as a tool for weight loss. We found high levels of it in your blood."

My mom chimed in. "Amy, you need to be honest with the doctor so he knows how to help you. Why have you been taking this drug, honey? What's going on?"

For several long moments, I thought back to everything I'd consumed over the past few weeks. Water, Diet Coke, cigarettes, salad, tuna in cans … "I haven't had much of an appetite, I guess," I said. Had someone been drugging me? Was it possible that I'd been getting steroid injections in my sleep? This made no sense. Wouldn't I have had side effects?

Then for a second my mind cleared, and I blurted out "the black pills!" stopping myself before I also said "given to me by Mindy Steinman, Executive Producer of **Autumn Leaves**."

"Black pills?" said Dr. Shah. "Do you have any more? Can I see them? Where did you get them?"

"In my purse," I said weakly. I didn't know what was going to happen, but I knew that no good could come from ratting out Attila. I had visions of a horse's head in my bed. "Someone on the set gave them to me," I said. "I don't remember who—they said they were appetite suppressants, and that they were totally safe." There was no way I was turning state's evidence in the war on drugs in Hollywood.

"You're not in trouble … we just want to know what kind of "clen" it is, so we know if it's caused permanent damage to your heart. You're actually lucky you didn't have a heart attack or a stroke taking that stuff. We need to do some more tests and to test the pills you have, to see what we're dealing with."

Now I was listening. "What?" I squeaked. Did Attila really give me a potentially lethal drug to make me thin enough for her Nielsen ratings go up when she knew heart problems ran in my family? What the hell?

Luckily, the clenbuterol I'd been taking was "clean" (though still illegal and banned by the FDA). After a battery of frightening tests and about a gallon of blood drawn, I was informed that the drug had not caused permanent damage, but that I needed to rest, in bed, for at least two months in order to allow my heart time to repair itself. "No working," said Dr. Shah, and offered to write me a doctor's note. Pieces of Attila's phone call flash through my head "Martin Sheen … *Apocalypse Now* … heart attack … back on the set the next day." If she hadn't had me written off the show by now, this would probably do it. Through the fear and weakness, I felt a glimmer of happiness.

After a few more nights of IV fluids, food, and sleep, they released me, on the condition that I not exert myself in any way, and never take clenbuterol again. "Just sleep a lot, and let your body heal," said Dr. Shah. I was so relieved, I would have done anything he said.

There was a crowd of photographers waiting outside the hospital. Sondra and Jon, Brad's manager, were waiting for us at the hotel.

❦   ❦   ❦

It didn't take long for them to fill me in. The footage of me beating up the photographer had been running non-stop the whole time I'd been in the hospital. The tabloids had been having a field day. No one wanted to hear my side of the story. People love to see celebrities go nuts, even when they don't know the circumstances. I never believed it until it happened to me. Footage of me unraveling was now the most downloaded clip of all time, flying back and forth in cyberspace. A techno song had been made, the back beat thumping over the lyrics of me screaming "I hope you die! I hope you fucking die!" Spoofs had been made, Saturday Night Live was developing a sketch, and the incident had been mentioned on late night talk shows around the world. There was no escaping it. The only thing to do was wait it out.

The official line from Sondra and the show was "exhaustion," which is what they always say when a celebrity goes into the hospital for anything drug related. Shooting was on hold until the studio and the network decided what to do about my "health problems." Todd was in emergency phonecall mode, and had basically set up camp in my hospital room. The police were investigating Vince and I, and Fat Guy and Little Guy were not only pressing charges for assault and for destruction of property, but were also filing a civil suit against me. I felt a little like I should be resting and enjoying the peace and quiet, but I had a strong sense of dread, like this was something from which I could not come back.

After another nine hour "nap," I awoke to find my room crowded with people. Mindy Steinman, two assistants, several other serious-looking people in suits were there, as well as Todd, Arden, my mom, Vince, Dr. Shah, and two nurses.

"Wha …" I said weakly. Had something else happened? I looked at my mom. "Can you … I mean, can you get them out of here?" I watched as everyone but Todd and my mom filed out.

Todd spoke first. "Amy, the network has to make a decision on what to do. They're willing to work with us to spin the incident, as long as you take full responsibility for your drug problem and the accident, and agree to go into rehab for the next two months." He leaned forward. "You don't really have to go to rehab, of course … we can get you a condo or something where you can just rest. But they have to issue a statement ASAP."

I rubbed my eyes and looked over at my mom. "Todd, Mindy gave me the pills. I'm not a drug addict—I have a heart problem caused by a drug that she gave me." The unfairness of it all gripped me like a vice. She could give me poisonous drugs, then blame it on me when I got sick? There was a special place in hell for her.

Maybe it was the newfound clarity from sleeping so much, but the answer seemed crystal clear to me. Doing what other people thought I should do had almost gotten me killed.

"Tell them I'm not going to rehab. They did this, and people should know."

Todd rubbed his hand over his face. "Amy, they're going to fire you from the show. If you go into rehab, we can file a disability claim. It's going to work better for everyone. Besides, what's the difference? I'm going to say yes to this. Can I say yes to this?"

"Todd, you're fired." I blurted out. I was surprised at how good actually saying the words felt. "Get out."

Todd's eyes widened, and then he packed his briefcase up and left. "No one is going to touch you after this," he said casually as he packed up his briefcase and started to walk out the door.

"Hey Todd," I called after him. "My name is Amy. AMY!"

I heard him laughing as he walked down the hall. "OK—Amy, you are fucked," he called out.

I'd been out of the hospital for exactly two days when I got a letter messengered to the hotel. Inside it was a single sheet of paper from the law firm representing the network.

September 15th

Dear Ms. Spencer,

Please be advised that, as of today, your contract with the network has been terminated, on grounds of violation of statute 76.011. If you have further questions, please feel free to have your attorney contact us.

Very truly yours,

Martin Franklin
Attorney at Law

It turned out that "statute 76.011" was the often cited but almost never invoked "morality clause," where the network contends that the actor can no longer fulfill the function of playing the role because they haven't held up sufficient morals in their personal life. In other words, because of the "incident," viewers would not be able to picture me as wholesome, naïve Autumn anymore. The show would go on without me.

Because I could no longer do any public appearances or events with Brad, the terms of my RockStar contract were also null and void.

The next day, the headlines read "RockStar Splits, Star Cracks Up!"

CHAPTER 19

⚜

Around 10am, I was awakened by the soft sound of my mom knocking at my bedroom door. "Amy, are you awake?" she whispered. "Someone is here to see you."

I'd probably slept more in the seven weeks since leaving Hollywood than in all of my previous twenty-one years combined. Something about the darkened windows of my childhood home, the silence, or maybe the mandatory bed rest had immediately taken the pressure off, and I felt like I could finally just relax drift off. With Carrie Ann in New York, Vince still in LA, and my high school friends off doing their respective careers, I couldn't imagine who would be dropping by for a visit on a Tuesday morning at 10. The show would be in the middle of a marathon session of shooting in order to get new episodes in the can that explained Autumn's decision to go back to the Midwest for college, and to refocus the show on her little sister Jessie. Besides, Attila had probably issued a decree that they weren't allowed to talk to me anyway. "I'll be right down," I said, slowly pulling the covers off and stepping out of bed.

I pulled on my jeans and black Chanel cardigan. After I got fired from the show, the network took my hotel suite back as part of my cancelled contract. My mom had packed up everything I'd accumulated, and shipped it back to our house (along with me, of course). Even after almost two months of unpacking and sorting, trying to make sense of the last few years of my life, my room was still two feet deep in expensive designer clothes, purses, and shoes, as well as old books, scripts, and my DVD collection. For once, my mom had not been giving me a hard time about cleaning my room.

I surveyed myself in the full-length mirror in the wall. Eye bags = gone. In fact, daily walks had left me looking positively healthy. Though still a size two, I looked a little less like a skeleton, and my collarbone no longer stuck out at the alarming angle it did before. My golden blonde hair was showing an inch of sandy-brown roots (must do something about that!), and sat in a scraggly bun piled on top of my head. Surprisingly, I just didn't care. Eight weeks of bed rest and watching DVDs had healed my heart, and I passed my last cardiologist checkup with flying colors. Soon, I would have a clean bill of health, and I'd have to figure out what to do with the rest of my life. Go back to college? Try Hollywood again? Move to Fiji? I had been sitting up in my room, writing in a journal and pondering these questions for weeks. Did I even have any "leverage" in Hollywood that I could use, or had I blown it all? I almost didn't want to know.

At first, the press was relentless. I stopped reading the magazines almost immediately, especially avoiding them when I saw the incredibly stupid headlines and theories. "Star Breakdown!" they screamed, in the largest font possible. "Broken Engagement Pushes Her Over the Edge!" "Little Girl Lost"! I remembered when Vince used to sit in my dorm room at Hudson, devouring the weekly magazines and speculating on the real stories behind the tabloid headlines.

I brushed my teeth and put on a little bit of makeup. Maybe my high school boyfriend was back from being on tour with his punk band, and had decided we belonged together. If I'd learned anything, it's that you just never know what (or who) is around the next corner, and it's always good to be prepared.

As I walked down the familiar stairs, I constructed numerous scenarios in my mind. I was still trying to guess as I turned the corner to the living room. "Mom … who is it….?"

I stopped, frozen in my tracks as I saw Dan Roberts sitting on my living room couch.

First of all, it must be said that if Dan Roberts could have gotten better looking since Coney Island, that had happened. Flecks of snow were caught in his curly brown hair, and his green eyes lit up when he saw me. He swept me up into his arms for a hug.

He started talking fast. Was he nervous? "I'm so glad you're okay … I'm sorry to just show up, but your voicemail was full, so I called Vince a thousand times, and finally he relented and gave me your mom's address. I had to see you, to see if you were ok, and to tell you the good news. Are you ok?"

I laughed out loud. "What's the good news … the network didn't put a hit out on me?" I said. "What could you possibly say that would cheer me up right now?"

Dan was dead serious. "Amy—**Blue Gray** got into Sundance, and there's good critical buzz. We actually might win."

That would do it.

❧   ❧   ❧

The moment we stepped off the plane in Park City, I felt everyone's eyes on me. Park City is packed with Hollywood types that whole week, but there's always one person that gets photographed more than the rest, like when Jennifer Aniston showed up to promote **The Good Girl**. Right then, that person was me. People really wanted to see if all the rumors were true, if I'd really gone nuts, if I was on drugs, and if I could really act. One drop of insecurity here, one ill-timed Mariah Carey inspired striptease, and I was doomed. Luckily, I felt healthier and saner than I had in years.

"You look amazing," whispered Vince, squeezing my arm. He had always been able to read my mind, to know exactly what I needed to hear. Dan took my hand. "It's going to be great," he said. "My aunt and your dad are watching over us." He smiled.

Carrie Ann had taken a 3-day weekend from her show (the first time ever) and was flying in from New York to meet us. We headed back to the airport later in the afternoon to pick her up in time for the screening. We were all trying to act as normal as possible despite the thousands of questioning eyes staring at me everywhere we went. I wanted to get a big intercom, stand on a mountain, and yell "Hey, I'm not crazy—I got squashed by the Hollywood machine, but now I'm back!" Instead I went snowboarding, saw films, and waited for the screenings of **Blue Gray**. With no agent and no publicist, I could say whatever I wanted, and yet I was surprisingly silent. Besides, who would believe me?

The first screening of **Blue Gray** was packed with people, presumably wanting to get a glimpse of how crazy I was. Dan led a "Q & A" session with the cast first, and I could tell the press was dying to ask about the accident. Like the dedicated director and gentleman that he was, Dan deftly avoided all questions that didn't relate to the film. Ted Casablancas looked pissed as Dan ignored him for the whole Q & A, then signaled for the film to begin.

Dan held my hand through the whole screening. It felt so good to see a record of my time in New York, our hard work, and the great summer before every-thing went so crazy. I was more certain than ever that this was what I really wanted to do with my life.

As soon as the lights went up, the audience gave us a five minute long standing ovation. Ted came up afterwards and hugged me. "Welcome back!" he said with a smile.

After the screening, Vince, Dan, Carrie Ann and I were on Main Street coming out of Morning Ray when I spotted her.

Attila had come to Sundance.

Flanked by two new interns with fresh faces and hope in their eyes on her right and a low-level producer looking guy on her left, she was barking instructions in her usual militaristic style—head down, not looking at them. "Do you think you can manage that, Samantha?" she snarled to one of the assistants. She looked up as she almost ran into us. I watched for a second as she gathered up her game face, with Vince poking me in the side the whole time. None of us moved, so they either had to step off the curb to get by, or talk to us. Her eyes seemed even beadier than usual, and even though it was twenty-four degrees outside, she was sweating.

"Star! Oh my God!" she fairly shouted, drawing attention from some of the onlookers and photographers. This was the performance of a lifetime. She probably thought she would never see me again after she'd had me fired from the show. If anybody found out she was the cause of my downfall, she would probably be fired herself.

"Star, I was just telling John here how great I thought your film was. Great! You were just … fantastic." She put a chubby hand to her mouth in a gesture of fake emotion. "I felt like my little girl was all grown up!"

For a moment, I didn't know what to say. I'd played this reunion a million times over in my head, and somehow it always involved a good head stomping or karate chopping her in half like a giant melon. Watching her have to kiss my ass in public, though, was just about as good. Now I just wanted to see her squirm.

"Thanks, Mindy." I gushed sarcastically in return. "What was your favorite part?" I knew she hadn't seen it. I definitely would have sensed her evil aura in the audience.

She was quick with the duck and cover. "I just … you are so great!" Star, I need to have you come into the office so we can talk to you about this show we're developing just for you. It's going to be so amazing!"

I stared blankly at her. After the accident, I couldn't even get any of her assistants to put me through, and I'd had no chance of even getting back on the network lot. Two months before, I was persona non grata, and now she wanted to do a new show with me? I wanted to tear off her head and spit in her neck. She was the embodiment of everything I hated about the business—as if every fake smile and disloyal word were boiled down to form her pale, puffy, squinty eyed face. I took a deep breath.

"Thanks, Mindy … actually, I just ran into Bob, and I'm having lunch with him next week. I'm pitching a series about an insane network executive who tortures everyone around her, including giving them illegal drugs. It's going to be really big."

She squinted, trying to read my face to see if I was serious. I saw her assistants trying not to smile. Robert Washer, who'd been in the audience of **Blue Gray** and had led the standing ovation, was the president of the network and Mindy's boss. I actually *was* having lunch with him the following week. I had been bluffing about the pitch, but it was just enough for Mindy to know that the balance of power had shifted, and that she could never push me around again.

Vince, Dan, Carrie Ann and I quickly turned and walked away, leaving Mindy, her assistants, and her producer friend in our wake.

I felt free.

❈   ❈   ❈

After Sundance, Dan and I were having lunch with Vince at Polly's Pies in Silverlake. Since the success of **Blue Gray**, we had been in meetings non-stop. Everyone in Hollywood seemed to have forgotten about the accident, the video, the supposed breakdown, the whole thing.

I'd been staying with Dan since returning to L.A. With him, I never felt like I had to pretend to be something I wasn't. This was maybe the only thing that had allowed me to come back.

Brad Rockwell never spoke to me again. Right after the accident, Jon leaked the Coney Island photos to the press, and the breakup was the scandal of the year. Brad referred to me publicly as "the one who broke his heart," though I liked to think of him as "the one who broke my contract." Of course, I could never tell this to another living soul, or risk something worse than a dead bird in my car. Unfortunately for Vince, Brad never spoke to him either, stayed in the closet, and got a new blonde fiancé. I kept the money, the ring, and the Mercedes, which I got fixed.

Since I was a "viable commodity" again due to the success of **Blue Gray**, every agency in town was now looking for me. I'd been attempting to assemble a team of people to help with my "relaunch." Problem was, I was having a hard time finding anyone who didn't make my skin crawl. Arden, who promised to be on best behavior and not give me grief about my weight, was allowed back on the team. I still had no agent, though; I kept avoiding Todd because—well, because he was Todd. Finally, everything was up to me. I even got to choose my own charity to work with, so I started volunteering with P.S. Arts, an organization that promotes arts education in public schools.

I had never been happier.

Dan, Vince and I were in the back of Polly's finishing lunch when I heard a familiar voice. "Amy? Oh my God!" Olivia Garcia walked up to stand next to our table. "How are you? You look really great."

"Sit down," said Dan, and Vince moved our stuff over to give Olivia room. Dan felt like he knew her already from all of my stories, and he knew I still regarded her as one of the only people I could trust.

While I was gone, Olivia had finished law school, completed her William Morris internship, and had become an agent in the same office as Todd. "I was going to call you for a meeting," she said, "But I didn't want it to be weird. I wanted to respect your privacy, and give you your space." She paused, tears coming to her eyes. "I'm so glad to see you. It was awful what happened. I want you to know that I never told anyone any stories about you."

I looked at Dan. "Olivia, I want you to represent me."

She broke into a huge smile. "I would love that!" she said. 'You are officially my first big celebrity client. Todd's going to be so pissed!" We both laughed.

We sat and talked strategy for the rest of the afternoon. After awhile, the waitress came over to see if we wanted anything else. Olivia looked at me quizzically, and I remembered that the last time I saw her, I was on the "500 Calorie a day Hollywood Starvation Diet."

I winked at her, then looked up at the waitress.

"I'll have the key lime pie."

978-0-595-44116-7
0-595-44116-5

Printed in the United States
74862LV00003B/70-87

9 780595 441167